ARMADILLOS

P.K. LYNCH

Legend Press Ltd, 175-185 Gray's Inn Road, London, WC1X 8UE
info@legend-paperbooks.co.uk | www.legendpress.co.uk

Contents © P.K. Lynch 2016
The right of the above author to be identified as the author of this work has
been asserted in accordance with the Copyright, Designs and Patents Act
1988. British Library Cataloguing in Publication Data available.

Print ISBN 978-1-7850795-9-7
Ebook ISBN 978-1-7850796-0-3
Set in Times. Printed in the United Kingdom by Clays Ltd.
Cover design by Simon Levy www.simonlevyassociates.co.uk

P.K. Lynch trained as an actor and her first professional job was playing Lizzie in the film of Irvine Welsh's novel, *Trainspotting*.

After having a baby, she completed her first stage play, *Promise*. Her second play, *King of the Gypsies*, played at the Edinburgh Fringe, and then toured.

She then enrolled on the MLitt Creative Writing programme at the University of Glasgow where *Armadillos* was awarded the Sceptre Prize for Fiction.

Armadillos is P.K's debut novel.

Visit P.K at
lynchpinpauline.wordpress.com

Or on Twitter
@lynchpinpauline

For hope, for love, for all the odds and ends.

You are obliged to tell our story in a truthful way. To tell it, as Oliver Cromwell said about his portrait, 'Paint us with all our blemishes and warts, all those things about us that may not be so immediately attractive.'

JFK
Displayed in the Sixth Floor Museum,
Dealey Plaza, Dallas, Texas

|

She said the world is divided. She said there are tribes in the world, and countries, and countries at war, and factions within factions within those countries, and basically there's a whole load of fucked up shit going on. But the biggest difference, she said, the biggest basic difference was between people. That's what she said.

She said, basically, not all people are people. That is to say, not all people are human. They walk human, they talk human, and in every conceivable way to the untrained eye they are human, but that don't mean shit.

I didn't believe her.

She said you basically got human people and you got sub people. And we were part of that category. We're the subs.

We were sitting in the bedroom and I asked her why it was we were sub. She said it was time I knew and went downstairs. When she came back, she brought company. Seemed I was a woman now, she said, and we kept it in the family. Had done for years. She said.

What goes on inside four walls stays behind four walls, and sometimes what goes on behind four walls isn't even talked about there. There was three of them but only two did it. I never liked it none.

You knew it was coming. It would start on a Wednesday before Pop came home early for supper. Jojo turned up the volume real loud and we'd bounce to Destiny's Child, one sharp eye trained on the window so we'd know he was coming. Only reason Pop allowed that album in the house was the 'Gospel Medley' slipped in at the end. He didn't know we always skipped that one. Jojo was obsessed with that band: *Them's Texas girls, Aggie, and look at 'em now,* she told me. *Them's God-fearing girls,* she told him, *good God-fearing girls.* She shook that tush like she could dance her way out of our crappy kitchen all the way to a Broadway stage. In reality, she couldn't even dance away from Pop's pinching fingers.

He knew how to fill a room, did Pop. We'd all three of us be in the kitchen, Jojo working, quietly humming whichever tune we'd got to before we had to turn it off, and me suddenly with my nose in a book. I did like to read, so it was a convincing lie. Pop would lean back in his chair at the head of the table and stretch his arms out over the wood, stroking it with his big old knobbled hands. You were born on that table, he told me, conceived on it too, and he'd start to laugh. Same every week. I couldn't figure what was so funny. Sometimes he pointed to a stain on the wooden floor beneath it, and told me it was my blood. No laughing then.

I'd stare at that big dirty patch for hours on end, trying to figure what it really was. Jojo was in the kitchen all the while, moving between cupboards, getting it all together for him. No matter how prepared she was, he always managed to surprise her and the food was never just ready to go.

Day after that was Thursday and instead of taking sandwiches out, Cy would come in from the fields for lunch. Somehow he'd always manage to get in Jojo's way while she sliced his bread. I used to worry where that bread knife would land when she was trying to dodge him.

For years it was as if Cy had never even noticed me but it got to the point where, on Thursdays, he would ruffle my hair and pinch my cheeks. Jojo would bang the knife off the countertop and tell him off but he just laughed and said it didn't hurt me none. It did hurt a little but I was just real happy to have him smile at me.

On Thursday nights, both men came in for supper. Before it started on me I never noticed the little things. When Jojo put his plate in front of him, Pop would give her hair a little tug. If she dropped something, he'd smack her backside but he'd be laughing the whole time and winking at me. I practiced real hard just so I could wink back. For years, I didn't see it as anything other than fun. Don't remember Jojo complaining much about it, not even when he threatened to cut that mole off her face. She said later he would never have done it. They left her alone once they started on me.

Pop went first. He didn't take long. Four Sinner's Prayers, usually. But Cy took longer. Pop would laugh and it made Cy go rougher and I'd lose count of the prayers in my head.

Ash never did it. They'd tried to make him once but he couldn't. After that, they just made him watch. Once Pop and Cy were finished and gone, he'd hand me a handkerchief to wipe myself with and then leave, not looking at me, not saying nothing about it. I'd wash it and slip it in with his clean laundry afterward. Same every week, until the day Ash left. I asked Jojo about him and she just shrugged and said, *I guess he's different*, and that was the end of that.

That was my people. Pop, Cy, Ash, Jojo.

The Jones family.

They called me Aggie.

We lived on a sheep farm but we had a couple of bulls too. Cy bought them without Pop's say-so after getting lucky in a card game. Pop was set to blow. *What we want bulls for in the middle of cattle country, when every damn farmer already had all the bulls he wanted?* Cy was to take them back but he never did, even when Pop cocked his gun. Cy just banged both his fists down on the table and screamed *Do it!* His face was red and spit flew out. Before that, I never knew men could scream. That was the only time I saw Cy stand his ground with Pop.

Cy wanted to be a cow man. Said sheep were for women. It's true we were the only sheep farm around, that I knew of at any rate. Anyway, guess Cy knew what he was doing, because there was something about those bulls. People used to come hire them and they'd get taken off to do their business with the lady-bulls, as Jojo called them. She used to be good at getting me to laugh.

The bulls were kept indoors over winter and looked after real well. They got the best food Cy could find, and when I grew tall enough I was allowed to comb them. As long as you stayed calm and kept sharp, you'd be alright. It paid to keep an eye out for Pop as well, because the bulls got nervous around him. Everybody got nervous around him.

Me and Jojo never had much to do with the farm until lambing season. Then we'd go from five hundred sheep to five hundred sheep plus a thousand lambs. It got real busy around then. I'd finally got to an age where I could help at night. I was tired from March till June but I liked it alright. Jojo showed me how to feed them from a bottle if their momma refused them. But the rest of the year it was just Pop, Cy and Ash doing the work. Jojo fed us and looked after the house while I was kicked off to school in the town.

The town was dead. One little main street with a few stores selling random stuff, one dusty antique place that I never in all my life saw open, and a filling station in front of old Huck Rawlings' place. The only thing the town had going for it was the school. It was big and modern. Looked out of place sitting beside the rickety town but someone somewhere had decided we were the best spot for it and kids were bussed in from all over. I cycled the four miles there and back until the snow came, and then Jojo put the chains on the truck and drove me.

School was deadly dull apart from the times you got pulled into a scrap. I respected the teachers, even though most of them were dimmer than glow-worms in fog, but some of those kids needed a bashing. They'd get smart with me and say things about my family, leaving me no choice but to straighten them out. Jojo used to argue about me with the principal, Mr Ginn, until eventually everyone decided it would be best if Jojo taught me at home.

Our momma made our house look like a library. Books took over the whole place until one day, Pop got the devil in him. The devil always arrived with the whisky. He built a bonfire and threw dozens of Momma's books on, before passing out on the porch.

One we saved was a prize given to Momma when she was a girl. Inside the front cover it said *Awarded to Marilyn Coombe for General Excellence.* Jojo kept that one separate from all the others. There was a story called Jack King the Pirate Kid. John King was a bad boy who deserted his momma and ran away to sea with a bunch of pirates. I used to make Jojo act it out with me in the old fishing boat my momma had brought with her from the coast when she married my pop.

I'd whittled the name Jack King into the wood, even though Jojo had told me boats had to be girls and it was weird to make it a boy boat. I said it wasn't any weirder than having a boat moored on a sheep farm, miles away from any water, and Jojo said Momma was a stubborn kind of gal. After Momma walked out, Ash worked on it, said one day Jack King would be back on the sea, but that old boat sat there for years, rotting its way through every season. Me and Jojo sailed it a thousand times. If a person's got the mind for it, they can travel anywhere they like without moving an inch.

At the time, I had no real recollection of our momma. No one said anything much about her, except Pop, who got the conniptions every now and then and started shouting the part about her being a whore. He used to tell me she'd run off with pirates, and for a long time I believed him.

Don't you girls go getting any of your momma's hifalutin ideas, you hear? You're good girls. Not like that pirate whore I was damned to call a wife. Aint that right, Cy?

Cy nodded, his teeth exposed by his tight smile, his tongue darting between dry lips.

That's the truth, sir. That sure is the truth.

Jojo basically raised me herself. I learned all about everything from her and Momma's books. Being farm folks, I liked to know about the country. I learned about how the land had always been here but the people constantly changed. First we had the French folks, then the Spanish and Germans too, and then we had to fight to get away from Mexico that one time. Guess everyone's fighting to get away from someone. Unless they're Jojo. Unless they've got no fight left at all.

The day my story starts happened by accident, which I guess is how a lot of stories start, because who in the world gets up in the morning knowing for sure how their day's going to end? It had been a long, slow burn of a summer. Time was I used to love the summer. Must have been pretty boring for Jojo having to look after such a little sister but she never let it show. She was so much older, she should have been going to parties and meeting boys instead of building dens and baking cookies with me, but to her credit, I never felt she wanted to be any place other than where I was. Not that Pop would have let her go anyway. But this was the summer after it started and things with me and Jojo were different now. She hardly ever spent any time with me, and when she did, she'd just get annoyed and snap when I tried to talk about what was going on. After a while, I learned not to ask. I fell in with her silence. Guess it was the silence eventually that allowed me to go.

I was coming down the stairs carrying laundry. The front door was wide open and the thought slipped in and planted itself. I could just leave right now. It was that simple. Momma had done it. Ash had done it. Why not me?

I put down the basket and looked out. We had six hundred acres of land. We were small fry but it was big enough to get lost in. I guessed the men must have been on the far side of the farm. I stood in the doorway, half in, half out, waiting for any of them to appear. Funny how just a thought can make you feel guilty.

The summer had been a gusty one with more dust devils than normal blowing through, but everything that day was so straight and calm. Above me, a single wisp of cloud stayed still and quiet, abandoned in the big blue.

I started to walk. Just casual, not going anywhere really. I ran my fingers over the bow of the patched-up fishing boat as I passed it. Insects hummed and scratched in the long grass beside me. Every step I took on the graveled track sounded like thunder. As I got further from the house and my plans were gradually making themselves real, I began to pray I wouldn't meet Pop or Cy coming the other way in the tractor.

Halfway along the track, right where the ground rises a little bit, I stopped and looked back. Still see it in my mind's eye, clear as that day itself. Our house, painted white with burnt orange shutters, trusted keeper of secrets, and her alone, upstairs at my bedroom window, staring down at me. I'd never looked at her from this far away before. I didn't realize she could be so small. How long did we stand there holding each other's gaze, reading each other's thoughts? I willing her to join me, she willing me to come back.

The spell broke. Pop appeared from round the back of the house, bellowing something, I couldn't say what, and he charged in through the open door, fierce as one of Cy's bulls. When I looked back at the window, Jojo was gone.

I ran hard. Every time my feet hit the ground, little bits of dust and stone blew up and filled my shoes. Flew in my mouth too, but I didn't notice till later. Kept my back straight and didn't look back once.

I reached the end of the track and for a minute I was stuck. A person could only choose left or right from our gate. The right road led to town where people knew me. I chose left. That way was the rest of the world. No saying how long it would take before I got to any place worth being. No saying

I'd even manage that.

Pretty soon I had no run left. I slowed to a walk but kept looking over my shoulder. I couldn't guess if Jojo had covered for me. Every time I saw a car coming I dived down the bar ditch, knowing all the time that if Pop came after me in the tractor, he'd be sitting so high that no ditch short of a canyon would be deep enough to hide me.

Seemed I walked a good long way before coming across a patch of snakeweed, all rude and yellow, and I almost laughed out loud. Pop hated that plant, as did just about every farmer because it's poisonous to animals, and here it was, thick enough to hide a person. I hunkered down behind it and waited for nightfall, and all I could hear was Pop's mocking voice: *Look at yourself, girl. Nervous as a long-tailed cat in a room full of rocking chairs.*

Hard sitting still so long. My heart beat like a drum for the crickets to sing to. Mouth so dry, I scraped my tongue along my back teeth to try and make saliva. There was nothing to distract me from the thoughts rolling round my head. What would happen to Jojo when Pop realized I was gone? If I went back now, maybe it wouldn't be so bad. But then his hands, his thick bristles. My fingers sank into dust, scrabbling for something to cling to, something to keep me there, anchored, as though I'd ever find courage to move. My throat ached with the effort of not crying out her name. I should have asked her one more time. Begged her. Her voice came to me then, more real than the stones that scratched my fingers, saying the same thing I'd heard a thousand times before.

But what if Momma comes back, Aggie? How will she find us?

Pop needs us, Aggie. He aint no good without a woman to look after him.

His hands. Those bristles.

It aint right, Jojo. It just aint.

A buzzard circled above me. I must have seemed pretty small to him, sitting all crunched up behind that bush. I flapped

16

my arms to scare him off but he just came lower, like he was sizing me up. I searched the ground for something to throw but then he swooped and landed a little further down the road where some creature had come to a sticky end. There was nothing to do but watch as the sharp beak pecked and forced its way in, tugging at the insides like a rope. The bird fed a while and was joined by two more. Their heads hammered up and down, in and out of the deadness, and when a car or truck came by they scattered, returning seconds later to feast some more.

At last the sun sank and the moon sailed high. I forced my head to tell my body to stretch out, stand up, start walking. I passed what was left of the road kill. Turned out to be a luckless armadillo lying on its back, two front claws pointing skyward in pointless defense.

The road was almost dead in the night, save for those snakes that seeped from the grass and lay down on the tarmac to draw the day's heat. I paid them no mind, more wary of approaching headlamps than the coon tail rattlers. Whenever they gleamed in the distance, I lay flat in the ditch until they passed by. One time I heard a rattle real close in the grass beside me but I didn't move an inch, preferring my chances with a snake than with Pop.

The moon was fat and made a good light to walk by. I willed the rain to come, and when it did I tipped my head back and caught a drink. Lucky I didn't catch a chill as well. As I told myself over and over, there's always a silver lining.

Knew I'd have to rustle up supplies from somewhere once the sun came up, though. My belly growled. I thought about the pumpkin pie Jojo had made that afternoon. I thought about my slice, all orange and good and creamy, sitting uneaten on a plate in the refrigerator. How hard would it have been to pack some food? If I'd really thought about it, I could have hidden out in Cy's car when he was headed on one of his trips south. Could have jumped out at any point. Could have checked a map and picked a destination. All kinds of things I could have done to make my life a little easier, and the further I got, the wilder my inventions came. Could have got Cy to teach me to drive and then stole his car. Could have caught a horse from the livery and rode off on it. Could have taken Jojo with me. But how do you get someone to run away with you if they won't even see there's a problem? If there's no problem, they don't need help. Don't need to face up to anything. It got so I despised the tears she cried into our food. I could taste her misery in every bite. And still she wouldn't leave.

With every step, I put more and more distance between me and them. If she'd known I was leaving, would she have let me go? She'd have made me pack a bag, at least. She'd have put in my favorite shirt, the blue plaid one that used to be hers, and maybe some thick socks for hiking. I sure would have found them useful around about now. She would have made me a picnic, and slipped in something delicious like her peanut butter brownies, but told me not to eat them until I'd finished all of my sandwich. And I'd have nodded, even though we both knew those brownies would be gone in under a minute. She'd have walked me down the track to the gate so she could wave me off. As I walked away, I would have called over my shoulder – *Come with me, Jojo* – but there would have been no reply. And if I stopped to look back, she'd be gone.

I should have known she'd never be gone.

I'd been walking for hours. My feet were on fire, my legs heavy as lead. Behind me was all road and sky; in front of me was the same. Seemed like I'd been walking on the same damn spot all night. Tiredness pressed down hard, and my spirit was fair broken. I looked down at my feet, willing them on, and realized I was about to step on a bashed-up car bumper. I kicked it to the side and carried on, walking through a spattering of broken glass and shredded car tires. Just ahead was the dark shape of a car parked half on, half off the road.

It was a wreck. Every window lay shattered on the ground,

or spread out over the back seat. The sides were crumpled up like an old accordion. A keychain of pink crystals dangled from the ignition. Pretty. I reached in and turned it, but it gave out nothing. Not that I could drive it even if it did.

I tried the driver's door once, twice, then realized all I had to do was lift the button on the inside. 'Dumb Aggie,' I said to no one, but it felt good to break the silence. Through the darkness, I almost heard Jojo: *Tired Aggie,* she'd say. That's about right, I thought to myself, as I yawned almost big enough to turn me inside out.

I sat inside and the seat was comfortable. I opened the glove compartment and found an old map. I gave thanks and took it. Whoever heard of traveling without a map? Ridiculous.

As I shut the glove, I caught sight of some shit in the footwell, all dark and dried like it had been there for weeks. Gross. Empty beer cans and broken glass all over. I tried to shake something out of the cans but they were dry. When I went round to check the trunk, I found an old army rucksack. Plenty of pockets, there had to be something in there. I checked it over too many times to count, each time turning out nothing, not even a crumb.

'Aint gonna get downhearted so soon, are you, Aggie?' I said out loud. 'Hell, no,' I replied. I don't know who I thought I was talking to. I glanced at the map held tight in my hand, and thought of the possibilities it might bring.

I spread it out on the hood of the car, but it was too hard to read in the dark. When I tried to close it back up again, it refused to go. It kept folding and unfolding itself beneath my fingers. Every time I thought I had it beat, another section would pop out. I yawned again, and through watery eyes the yellowed piece of paper folded and unfolded over and over again, until the sun peeked up over the horizon.

Blinding brightness on my left. Road stretching out before and behind; taunting, laughing beneath my feet. The snakes

19

had escaped to the coolness of the thick grass, their long bodies twisting and rolling their way to a gentler darkness. From far behind me, a noise. Its strangeness made me stop. Uneasy, I turned round.

A dot in the distance, getting closer. Gradually, it took on the size and shape of a car. It didn't move like a car, though. Flat tires on opposite sides front and back gave it the up and down motion of a merry-go-round pony. It scraped the ground with a painful screech until it pulled alongside me.

'Found you,' said the driver.

I recognized the voice but I could hardly trust my eyes.

'Jojo?'

I'd never seen her like this before. Like she'd just come off some movie set. Half her face was hidden by a pair of oversized sunglasses, and a white scarf turbaned her hair. Only the mole on the corner of her mouth told me it was her. Funny I'd never noticed that it was shaped like a car.

'I been looking for my cat,' she said. Her lips were real pretty. All painted orange. Orange like pumpkin pie. I was wrong – the mole wasn't shaped like a car – it was shaped like a cat.

'Which cat?' I asked. We had near enough a dozen on the farm. They were good for catching snakes and rodents, but they weren't allowed in the house. *No good getting attached,* Jojo had said.

The door popped open. Sun streamed in through the window like a laser. It bounced off the pink key chain. Bullets of light flew around the inside of the car.

'Jump in.'

Without my say so, my arms and legs began to obey. I brought them into line quick smart and stepped back.

'What way you going?' I asked.

'Get in. You'll find out.' She patted the empty passenger seat.

'I aint going back home, Jojo.'

The little cat-mole beside her mouth had whiskers which

turned down like sad smiles. 'I aint saying we're going home,' she said.

I wished I could see her eyes. I wanted to climb in with her, but I couldn't shake the feeling I'd regret it.

'Don't you care about me, Aggie?'

'I do, Jojo. More than anything.'

'Aint you sad one of our little kitties went walkabout?'

Her nails tapped a rhythm off the side of the steering wheel as she scanned the horizon. An empty cat box appeared on the back seat, a white box with a metal grill on one side. Hadn't seen one there before.

'Jail for pussycats,' she grinned.

Something weird about that grin.

'I need you to get in,' she said.

The turbaned hair, the pumpkin mouth, the dark glasses. She tilted those huge shades down, looked me straight in the eye and smiled. 'Trust me, Aggie.'

I found myself climbing in and we took off, Jojo grinning so wide the corner of her mouth almost touched her ear. The sound of bare wheels on concrete.

'Why don't you come with me?' I yelled at her.

The car braked with such force, I flew forward and hit the dash.

'There she is, my little cat!'

Pulling myself back up, all I could see was grass and rocks spread out far and forever.

'Look, it's Aggie!' she yelled again, but her lips didn't move in time with the words. Everything was wrong, disjointed somehow. Sunglasses like bug eyes and huge, yellow teeth sticking out of a painted mouth turned round to face me. A tiny version of me was trapped in the reflection of her big, black glasses.

'Ready to come home now, little Aggie?' It was her voice, but Pop's face. His hand, or hers, tightened around my wrist and pulled. 'Sub Aggie. It's time to come home.' And her voice again, small and far away, saying, 'Now

21

where could that Aggie be?'

I ripped myself free and woke up lying on the back seat, breathing hard. There was a crick in my neck and a cramp in my foot. I sat up to rub the cramp out and the morning glare stung my eyes and made them water. No noise. No Jojo. No cat called Aggie. Broken glass all over the back seat just like before. I knew because I was lying on it. Scratches tore my leg. The rucksack was a pillow beneath my head.

The earth rattled as a truck thundered past, making the little car jump. The brakes screamed like witches on fire as the contraption pulled over. The driver jumped out and took a piss on the roadside. If he noticed me or the car he didn't show it. He pissed for a good long time.

'Watch out for snakes,' I whispered, and laid low till he moved on.

2.

I started off that second day running. Was good at it too. I'd won school competitions regular on account of my extra height. I was tall for my age. I took long strides, trying to put distance between me and Jojo, as though it were possible to outrun my imagination. My muscles burned but I pushed through it, telling myself the faster I went the sooner I'd get some food in my empty belly. It was building to be another hot day and I still didn't even have water. My tongue and gums stuck together like velcro. But fortune was shining that day, because before I got too far I came to a four-way stop with a service station just beyond it, a sight so glorious it made me fall to my knees.

'Thank you, Lord,' I praised. I scrambled back up again and staggered closer.

I knew it was early on account of the number of eighteen-wheelers still parked up in the lot. Pretty soon the sleeping drivers would be waking up and coming out of their cabs to grab themselves coffee and a bite. All I had to do was wait.

I'd always tried to be an honest child, and not just because of my awkward habit of blushing at the drop of a hat. I obeyed my elders, and never even spoke out of turn unless some kid decided I was fair game. Funny how a single night can change a person. I didn't question what I had to do. It was simple. I needed food, no matter what it was or how I got it, and I had to get it in me before this hunger soared upwards and roared out my throat.

There was no ditch to hide in so I had to brazen it out on the open road and pray no one came by. I scuttled up fast as I could and crouched behind a wire trash can. Took me less than a minute to feel like a fool. I was in plain view of any traffic that might come along so I moved round behind the station itself.

It was a scratchy little lot round the back. Nothing there but old tires and empty gas bottles. I couldn't see the trucks so good and I had to keep peeping around the corner every few minutes or so. There was a shed with a padlock hanging off the bolt. I gave it a rattle and discovered it was for decoration only. That's when I got my first clue that 'sub' though I was, I probably wouldn't have too much trouble putting one over the normal people of this planet. Not if they all went around leaving things unlocked anyhow. Still, only thing I found in there worth anything was a hammer. I'd been around hammers all my life but never till now had I viewed one as a weapon. Never till now had it occurred to me I might have need for a weapon, crazy as that may sound. But this was a good hammer, I could tell. Heavy with soft rubber around the handle. The hitting end was big and flat, the claw sharp enough to scratch my skin when I rubbed my thumb along its edge. My rucksack was gathering contents and it felt good, solid, like I had something to hold on to. Everyone needs something to hold onto.

'Little girly.'

I near enough jumped out my skin. I whizzed round to see a grizzly sort of fella, as big a man as any I'd seen, with a face full of hair so thick you could have kept rodents in there. When he spoke, I hoped it was his lips making his beard move.

'What time's your daddy set on opening?'

'Uh...'

'Run along and tell him he's got business if he wants it. I'm fixing to make a good start today. Aint hanging around.'

He stood aside to let me pass and there, right in front of the gas station, was a little house complete with a picket fence. I hadn't noticed it on account of it being tucked right behind a giant billboard as you approached it from the road. Even though I knew this, I couldn't shake the feeling it had just arrived through some kind of black magic. And now Grizzly was sending me right over to it.

'Uh. Sure, mister.'

My brain did overtime in that short walk from the station to the house and by the time I got there I still had no plan. I cast a glance over my shoulder to see Grizzly stood by his truck, watching and waiting.

I pushed open the squeaky little gate to the front yard and approached the door. It was painted blue and all peeling off. Drapes pulled across dusty windows. All in all, it didn't look too friendly. I was wondering if I could disappear round the back of the house, and let them all figure it out for themselves, when the door ripped open. An old guy – skinny as a rail and with more hair on his warts than on his head – greeted me.

'What you want?' He scowled and spat in the dust.

Before I could reply, he looked over and saw Grizzly waiting. Grizzly raised his arm, you wouldn't call it a wave, and walked behind his truck. The old guy turned his beady stare onto me.

'We aint open yet,' he snapped, though he slammed the door behind him and set off across the road.

I caught sight of a worn old chicken coop in the corner of the yard. I took a look around. The ground was thick enough with birdshit but there was no sign of live chickens. With a quick glance to make sure the old guy wasn't watching, I stooped and put my hand inside the box. My fingers scrabbled among the hay and grass until, right at the back, I felt them. Two smooth, beautiful, sweet little eggs for my breakfast. With a quick apology to the invisible chickens, I withdrew my hand. Now all I had to do was figure out how the hell to eat them.

Over on the forecourt, Grizzly was inside paying for gas.

He'd left the door to his cab open. Looked awful dark in there but it was too damn bright out on the road. His was the smallest of all the trucks in the station and it was easy to climb up and over the seats and slip into the back. I lifted a bottle of water from the dash as I went. My throat was drier than the heart of a haystack.

It was pretty gloomy in the back. A stash of boxes were tied in at the sides with some old gray rope, but there was room enough for me, my rucksack and my two eggs. At first, I didn't know what to do with them, and then I remembered a movie where this guy just ate them raw, so that's what I did. Cracked them on my teeth and swallowed them. Made me gag some but that was okay. Washed them down with Grizzly's water, and scanned the cargo in hope of more food. I used the claw of the hammer to rip a box open. It was full of toasters. I took one out and shoved it in my bag, figuring I'd sell it later. I was shaping up to be a pretty fast learner.

The truck shifted its weight and I knew Grizzly was back. I held my breath, scared he might sense me skulking in the back there. His door slammed shut and the engine growled into life. The worst thought came to me. What if he was going back the way I just came? The truck lurched forwards and I grabbed the rope to steady myself. *God Jesus, please, please don't let him turn left.* When I felt the world tip to the right, I near enough cried with relief. We rumbled on down that road, further from home, my body shaking along with all those boxes, feeling I was finally getting somewhere.

Seemed like we'd been going for days when he decided to stop. A suffocating kind of heat had built up. I was soaked with sweat and desperate for air. Deep red lines scored my hands where they'd been holding the rope. It hurt to ease out my cramped fingers.

When I heard his door go, I climbed up and peeked through the curtain dividing the cab from the truck. I was amazed to see it was still light. I looked out the window and saw dozens of people around the parking lot. Looked like we'd stopped at another service station. It was starting to feel like the whole wide world was made of nothing but road and gas stations. I scrambled over the ledge and was reaching back round for my bag when the driver door opened. There was just enough time for my heart to plummet before I was dragged backwards out the truck and slammed up against the side of it.

'If there's one thing I can't stand it's a sneaking little thief.' He had my shirt all scrunched up under my chin. His breath was hot on my face.

'Please, mister. I aint no thief. Please, let me go.'

His eyes narrowed and he lowered his hands.

'Aint you the little girl from this morning? God damn, you been riding in there the whole time?'

'Yeah, mister. Please, I aint no thief. I just needed a ride. I needed a ride real bad.'

I tried to pull open the rucksack, my fingers thick and clumsy. 'I'm sorry, mister. I aint no thief really. I took this one toaster, that's all. I was thinking to sell it to get me some food. I aint no thief really, I swear. Take it back, mister, take it back.' I practically shoved it in his face. He took it from me, grabbing me meanwhile so I couldn't get away, and tossed it on the front seat. A woman carrying a small child walked close by. When Grizzly dropped my arm like a hot potato, I realized it must look pretty bad, him so big and burly and me such a skinny girl. Once they'd passed, he scratched his beard and turned his attention back to me.

'Aint you worried about your old daddy back there?' he asked.

'That aint my daddy, mister. Truth is I never saw him before. That old guy aint missing me, I swear.'

'Well, someone's missing you. What's your age?'

'Seventeen, mister.' My first lie. 'Aint nobody missing me.' My second.

I could see Grizzly was struggling with his situation.

When all's said and done, my only crime was to hitch a ride. True enough, I'd burst open one of his boxes but he hadn't lost anything. He could just walk away now. I prayed he liked the quiet life.

'Where you headed?' he asked.

'Well, I don't rightly know, sir. Where you headed?'

'You can forget that one right there, little lady. Come with me. Let's get you some food while I figure out what to do with you.' Grizzly locked up the truck and headed to the diner. My belly followed him and so did I.

The station heaved with groups of tourists, all loud and with no sense of personal space. I got bumped and shoved so many times I felt like the silver ball in a pinball machine. Rows of one-arm bandits dinged and winked their pretty lights while groups of boys crowded around and fired pretend machine guns at flashing screens, *bam-bam-bam-bam-bam*! Children shrieked and hollered as tired parents dragged them past those adventures, and above it all on giant screens, TV presenters moved their mouths silently in the din.

I felt his grip on my arm again and he pulled me through it all.

'You need a piss? You better need a piss. You better not have pissed in my truck.'

I hadn't. I was fit to burst.

'You go in there and meet me back here in one minute, you hear?'

I nodded.

The lavatories were almost as busy as outside. I soaked a bunch of paper towels so I could clean myself in the cubicle and joined the back of a long line. We shuffled slowly, as one, towards the cream-colored doors that opened and closed to the unpredictable tune of flushing toilets.

I could feel people's eyes on me as I dripped my way closer to the front. To distract myself, I tried to focus on a girl who was brushing her hair in the mirror. Stroke, stroke, stroke. She was a princess in a tower. She didn't have to wash down there the way I did. She caught me looking, and I blushed.

The constant flushing was like a river rushing through my head. The lights glared, and I swayed on my feet. I grabbed on to the woman in front to stop myself falling over. When she turned to see me with my wet towels soaking my clothes, she looked at me the way a calf does a new gate. I mumbled an apology and gave myself a shake. I'd only been going a day and already I was drawing attention. I looked in the mirror and Jojo was looking back at me. I blinked and she was gone. I was left with just myself, dark hair sitting around my shoulders, and dark lines under dark eyes. Man, I was tired.

Grizzly was antsy when I got back outside.

'A minute, I said.'

He was pissed off with waiting but I was too shot to care. I shrugged my shoulders and followed him to the food court. He chose a table, told me to sit and went to order burgers. He'd asked me where I was headed and the truth was I'd no clue. I didn't even know where in the world I was. How far I was from home. From Jojo.

I squeezed my eyes shut and tried to concentrate. All I wanted to do was go sleep in his truck, but I figured the chances of him letting me do that were slim. I eyed him across the table. His attention was with the waitress who was asking something about the order. The exit wasn't too far away but my body was heavy. My ass was glued to the seat. I willed myself to move but nothing happened. I shook my head and cursed under my breath. Hell, I'd walked all night on my own with only snakes for company and never felt weaker, but now I realized it's people who make you truly weak. You come to depend on them and I didn't want to come to depend on Grizzly, because people will let you down every time. Still, if I could just sleep in his truck a little bit I was sure I'd be stronger when I woke. He came towards me carrying a tray. I craned my neck to see what was on it. Jojo always said with food in your belly and a good sleep, the world always seemed that bit friendlier. Not that you should let that fool you.

We ate our burgers in silence. I had to force myself to eat slowly. Every time I glanced up at him he was watching me. Eventually he said, 'You aint seventeen.'

'So what if I aint?'

I slurped the last dregs of coke through my straw. He wanted to know what my story was but no way was I about to spill my guts to some guy I never even saw before. It might give him ideas. Less people I told more likely it would be that one day it'd just slip from memory, easy as ice turning to water when the thaw comes. I swirled the ice in my cup with the straw and waited for him to speak. The waitress swung by and asked if we needed anything else. I shook my head and kept my eyes down but Grizzly ordered me a pancake with ice cream.

'How's it taste?' he asked when it arrived.

'It's larrupin' good, sir. I sure do appreciate it.'

I wasn't even hungry anymore but I crammed it in anyway. Didn't want to appear ungrateful and didn't know when I'd next eat. I could feel him watching me, hatching some plan. It made me nervous.

'What age are you?' he finally said. I shrugged my shoulders. He leaned forward over the table, keeping his voice low. 'What you expecting me to do with you if you don't tell me nothing about yourself, little lady? What's your name?'

I looked up from my plate. You couldn't tell anything much by his eyes, shadowed like they were by a baseball cap and those eyebrows, but I figured beneath that beard lay a good face. I took a chance.

'Name's Aggie,' I said, my voice suddenly croaky. I cleared my throat and to my embarrassment, tears flared beneath my eyelids.

'Aggie.' He nodded. 'And you aint even seventeen?'

I blinked the tears away and shook my head.

'Sixteen?'

Shook my head again. One fat tear rolled its way down my burning face.

'Shit.' He leaned back in his chair, sighing as he removed his hat and stroked his head. He gazed over me to the sky outside. I remembered Ash, how he used to stare out of my bedroom window when it was happening, seeing but not seeing. Grizzly shifted in his seat, reminding me where I was.

'Well, Aggie,' he said, at last. 'I'm not sure what I'm supposed to do with you. You got no money to go nowhere. You aint got no food but what I bought you. You aint even told me what it is you're running away from. I'll take a guess it aint too pleasant, whatever it is.'

Maybe it was just sugar rush but I decided to be truthful.

'No, sir,' I sniffed. 'Aint too pleasant at all.'

'I hear you, Aggie, but here's the thing. You're a minor. A little girl. I can't just walk away and leave you. Guess I aint got no option but to call the cops. They can decide what to do with you.'

I almost choked on my pancake as he pulled out his cell and started to dial. I reached across the table to stop him.

'Don't do that, mister. I wouldn't if I was you.'

When my voice came out, it was like someone else talking. I barely recognized it or knew what I was going to say, but I was powerful sure no way was I going to the cops. They'd only send me back again.

'I said I wouldn't if I was you, mister.' My voice was harsh and I'd somehow pushed his arm down onto the table. He looked surprised as I felt.

'You call the cops and I'll tell them you abducted me,' I hissed. Pancake crumbs fell out my mouth onto the formica table. 'I'll tell them you put me in your truck and made me do things. I'll say you did things to me. I'll say it, mister. They'll believe me, I know what to say.'

He stared back at me. 'You little whore.'

I could hear the anger in his voice and the change frightened me. Words I never liked to say came tumbling out, words I'd been made to say before, but for the first time I twisted them and used them to protect me.

'I'll say you took your big fat dick and stuck it in me,' I whispered. 'I'll say you made me suck it and they'll believe me.'

He looked so sickened by my lies, I almost felt sorry for him. Inside I was shaking, with fury, nerves, fear, all of that, but I was good at sitting on top of that shit. When I was sure he'd got the message, I changed my tone. It was just business, after all. The business of surviving.

'Now, mister, all I want is some money. I aint greedy. Just enough to tide me over, so whatever you can spare me I'll be grateful for. Bearing in mind I aint got no money at all, no clothes, no nothing. But just whatever you can spare will do just fine.'

I was quite impressed with big Grizzly. Must have been so relieved, he actually laughed a little as he reached in his back pocket and pulled out his wallet.

'Little girl, I wish I'd never have met you.' His eyes locked on to mine and I glanced away. He flipped open the wallet. 'But I do wish you luck with whatever it is you're trying to get away from,' he said, as he pulled out a pile of bills and slid them across the table. I covered them with my hand just as the waitress brought the check over. He sat there with his empty wallet sitting open like he was waiting for me to pay, but I just kept my eyes on the table, too frozen stiff to do much else. The waitress was getting the fidgets and eventually he pulled a card out and laid it on the plate. She disappeared again. He started to get up from the table and still I couldn't look at him.

'Thanks for the money, mister,' I managed to blurt out, and I meant it. If he replied, I didn't hear him. He picked up his card from the waitress on the way to the exit, and a few minutes later his truck pulled out.

You ever felt like you were the center of the universe and all the bad things that happened came from you? I sat at that table for an hour, dollars all bunched up in my fist, tummy all full of burger and pancake, and I wondered what the hell to do now. I got another coke and flipped the waitress a couple of dimes and felt like a big shot. A few tables down from me a woman was hissing at her two sons to behave while her husband was sucked into some game on his phone. Behind the service counter, a girl and guy threw fries at each other and laughed. Outside my window, people poured in on buses and then out again. The clock on the wall told me Jojo was laying the table for supper. Had she let on I was gone yet? Tomorrow was Wednesday, the day they started getting all friendly. I thought about Pop's dirty laugh and his big hands slapping the kitchen table. I thought about that stain on the floor. I thought about Cy and how he stroked my hair as I was washing dishes, and I thought about Jojo drying up beside me, doing everything she could not to look me in the eye. Screw her. Screw them all.

I wandered into the shop that sold stuff for rich folks. By that I mean it mainly sold magazines and candy, but I got a toothbrush and some soap and a washcloth. Just because I was homeless didn't mean I had to be dirty. I stood in line because I had the means to pay and right by the checkout was a basket filled with rolled up picnic blankets. I picked a green one for lying on and a pink one for on top and felt a whole lot better for my evening's prospects.

Outside, the day was beginning to settle. The air was hot and thick and smelled of diesel. I stood at the top of the stairs, people still streaming past but less than before. I thought about Grizzly and how quick he'd backed down when I'd threatened him.

I walked round all the parked cars and over to where the trucks were stopped. I don't know what had changed between then and that morning, but seeing them all beside each other made me think they were a gang. It was too hard to break into a gang. I didn't know if Grizzly had warned them about me either. Behind the trucks was the road leading to the on-ramp and I headed to that, figuring I stood a better chance one-on-one. Took me fifteen minutes to bag a new ride. This time it was a big rig with eighteen wheels that came right up to my shoulder. I hopped on up and pulled the door open, wondering what waited for me on the inside.

The driver was old. Scrawny, too. He was wearing red overalls and a Coca-Cola baseball cap. Little wisps of white hair floated out from under it. He never even looked at me as I belted myself in. I knew because I never took my eyes off him. He sniffed and wiped his nose with the back of his hand. Looking in his side mirror, he signaled to pull out.

'Headed south. That alright?' He still didn't look at me.

'Yes, sir. South's where I'm headed.'

It's mighty fine sitting up front in one of those giant trucks. You're the highest thing on the road, and even though I'd just put myself in a tight space with a strange man, I felt the safest I'd been since starting out. There was almost four feet between me and him and as long as he was driving there was no way he could touch me.

Couldn't see where he might keep his money. No jacket, no bag. Not in sight, leastways. There was a pocket in the arm of his overall but it didn't look big enough to hold a wallet. Maybe the glove was a better bet and I resigned myself to wait. If I still didn't find any then I'd just have to turn on my big teary-eyed act for him and threaten to call the cops.

The thrum of the engine was kind of hypnotizing and I felt myself begin to drift. The sun was hitting the sky from beneath. I always loved that.

But how can it hit from beneath if it's still in the sky, Jojo?

It aint in the sky no more, Aggie. Look, it's falling off the edge of the earth.

And she'd point and show me and there it would be, casting off its orange rays, or yellow or pink or red, the very last edge of sun slipping off the side of the planet, pushed down and chased away by the blueness of night.

I'd dozed off. Couldn't believe I'd been so dumb. I checked my bag and the money was there. So was the hammer. I snuck a look at the old guy. It was like he didn't know I was there. At one point, he looked at me and blinked over and over, like he was surprised to see me, his eyes like water and mud. It was dark by now and all the lights on his dash made me think of space ships. Cars zoomed past far below us but he just kept it slow and steady. His CB went off a few times but he never answered it. Now and then he grumbled a bit out his window – at what I don't know – but apart from that, he never spoke.

When we reached a town I liked the look of, it took exactly sixty seconds to threaten him with a charge of rape and take his wallet. I almost felt bad about it.

3

All my life I'd never gone anywhere and I guess you could say I was making up for it now. Wichita, Lubbock, Abilene, Sweetwater, Brownsville. Got drove so many places, I've forgot more names than I can remember. Learned it doesn't matter how big an eighteen-wheeler is on the outside, it starts feeling pretty tight in there after a while. I was happiest out free on the country, going days at a stretch, seeing nothing or no one but the odd buzzard sailing the sky. It sure was better than the monotony of the drive.

Once you got off the tarmac, the country came alive. It was green and watery and lush or it was dry and dusty and red. Whatever shape it took, it took care to provide nooks and crannies for a child, or young woman, as I now considered myself, to tuck herself away from prying eyes.

I got a good system going. I'd get some cash and build up supplies before holing up somewhere in the desert, not too far from a town or campsite where it was easy to get what I needed: waterproof matches, a lighter, flint and steel. I learned that fire makes a good friend when the lonesome dark falls.

It wasn't difficult to find a cave or hollow to bunk down in, though sometimes scratch marks on the walls made for uneasy thinking. If the cave smelled bad, I knew a bobcat must be using it and I'd keep looking. The night creatures I wound up sharing with didn't seem to mind me, though the same couldn't be said of the morning prairie dogs. I'd be lying still as could be, watching them skip and scuffle about the short grass. As soon as I made any move, they'd sense me and disappear down their burrows, quick as lightning. Wasn't like I was fixing to cook them or anything like that, they were just real jumpy. Guess fear's what kept them little critters alive.

Fear's good for humans too. I never got too relaxed about taking money off those truckers, even though once or twice it was so easy I wondered why they'd never mentioned it as a career option at school.

Stayed away from folks much as I could but every few days I was forced to find somewhere to wash. I kept clean as I could out in the desert. But eventually the sand and dust licks over you, laying on your skin like flies on a sticky trap. I learned to always wash my face with bottled water before heading to a rest stop. Strange that some people won't let you wash if you look too dirty, but the world's made up of all kinds of folks, and some of them are stupid.

I was trying to settle into a new cave, but I couldn't make myself comfortable. The roar of the traffic overhead drowned out the crickets like a bad omen. I slammed rocks hard against the cave wall, trying to make each one crumble into dust.

Trying to chase Jojo from my mind.

Sometimes it felt like she was everywhere; a bird rustling in a bush, a shadow thrown down on the ground, the moan of a low wind. I saw signs. Lights flickering in a store could drive me to call her name out. But she only showed herself in my dreams – a constant murmur of *Where in the world could that little Aggie be?* – chased me round and around. It had been her catchphrase in our hide-and-seek games, and whenever I slept now, she chased me again, but it wasn't fun, like before. I kept pushing her out and she kept forcing herself in and we'd fight in my head and it frightened me. The circles beneath my eyes got darker. My arms and legs started to feel heavy as shovels, too big for my skinny runt's body.

Another rock hit the wall and all of a sudden I felt it. It

came like a flood. I still hadn't got used to expecting it every month. All I could think to do was bunch up some napkins my food came wrapped in and shove them in my underwear. I woke up next morning, jeans stuck to my skin and the ground all grape-colored. It was everywhere; my hands, my ass, my front. Little bits of napkin were all caught up in my panties. Took an hour to pick it all out. I used the last of my water to wash between my legs and stood at the mouth of the cave looking out. No choice but to walk to the nearest rest stop. Had to be at least three miles.

Kicked the blooded ground over with sand and gathered up my stuff, knowing I couldn't risk another night there with that smell hanging in the air. Dumped my green blanket, tucked the pink into my waistband to hide the mess, and scrabbled back up the canyon to the road. Clots oozed out with every step, and nausea took a hold of me. I tried to console myself that at least this time it was only me who knew. Pop and Jojo always wanted to know when my time came. 'Sick fucks,' I called out to no one, then set off strong down the road.

When I reached the rest stop, a black woman manning the toilets took one look at me and clicked her tongue. I thought she was going to send me away so I showed her my blanket, and begged. My face was on fire.

'Stupid womanhood,' she said. 'What's it good for anyway? Nothing but turning sane guys crazy and slowing sad gals down, that's what.'

She fetched some pads and I took them gratefully. She opened up the shower for me, face serious as death, and walked away shaking her head at the sadness of a woman's lot. I locked the door and turned on the water. As I undressed, I was aware of a dark shape moving in the mirror. I didn't dare to look. I stepped into the shower and the water shot down like hot needles. I took the soap, turning it over and over in my hands. A thousand stinging bubbles washed me good, and the water cried red circles down the drain.

It's chicken blood, stupid. Just take it. My sister held out a soiled maxi pad. *Show it to Pop.*

I don't want to, Jojo. Don't make me. Take it away.

He's coming, Aggie. Please. Just do it.

She shoved it in my hands just as Pop walked in from the field. Of course, I did as she asked. I laid it before him and prayed to die when he looked at me with such revulsion, I thought surely he must hate me now. Then with young, jealous eyes, I could only watch as Jojo took his hand and gently led him away.

The days were elastic. Seemed they stretched far beyond their possibility before snapping back to night time. I picked up cheap paperbacks for entertainment, or newspapers people threw away. I arranged my cans in alphabetical order, then by color, then according to the calorie count on the side. When the cans were empty, I lined them up and threw stones at them for target practice. I did handstands against the wall. I lay on my back and cycled the air. I did everything I could think of to do, and when I ran out of ideas, I'd stop moving. That's when Jojo burst into my head. It was a hard job getting her to leave.

Whenever Jojo saw me on Pop's knee, she'd say, *You're too big for that now*, and I'd slide off if he let me, but sometimes he held on.

Little girls never get too big for daddy hugs.

One day, he came in unexpectedly early. Jojo was upstairs while I was sitting at the table, struggling with some number work. Fractions gave me a headache. One day I could do them, the next it was like a different language. No matter how hard I tried, the formula wouldn't stick.

Where's your sister? asked Pop, shrugging his boots off at the door.

I was glad to lay my pencil down. *Changing sheets upstairs. You want some lemon tea? We just made it this morning.*

I scraped my chair back and headed to the fridge, but he caught my wrist and dragged me to him, his strong hands forcing giggles as he squeezed.

I just want my baby girl.

He pulled me tight into him and walked me over to the couch, where we both sat down, my shoulder nestled beneath his underarm, his right hand wrapped around my right forearm, my left hand caught in his.

Don't want nothing in the world except my baby girl, he said again. He kissed the crown of my head and inhaled deeply. As his body deflated on the out breath, I relaxed further into him. He moved my right arm across the hill of his belly.

You aint too big for nothing, are you? he said, almost to himself, and gave me a gentle, reassuring hug. I grinned.

No, sir, I whispered.

A creak on the ceiling above told us Jojo was on her way back down. Quick as a wink, I sprang from the sofa and returned to my schoolwork. When Jojo came in, I was as she'd left me. Pop watched the TV news, his feet crossed one over the other, his big toe peeking out of a hole in his sock.

Want me to fix that? she asked him. Without looking at her, he shook his head no, and turned up the volume. When she turned away, I dared to glance up at him. He was smiling right at me.

I was in a tight hole in a canyon wall when I woke one morning with a start. Something bad happened in my dream. I pushed it away to that part of my brain where I push all the bad things. I stepped outside for a change of scene only to discover a circle of paw prints around my burned-out fire. I took a real good look and my mouth went dry. If they were bobcat prints, it was one hell of a big bobcat. I got a sick kind of feeling inside. My eyes followed the trail as it led off. Bigger than a bobcat, bigger than a coyote.

When I was a little girl, Pop and Cy had stayed out every

night for a week trying to catch a cougar that was taking down the sheep but I'd never thought of it since. Mountain lions didn't like people. Mountain lions kept away. But not this one.

I packed up. The sun was sitting lower every day and I started to think about winter. Snow could rise up to hug your waist, could steal a body and keep it till spring. My funds were low anyway. I needed a new ride. Figured it was good a time as any to take a break from the country.

4

I was sitting in a Dairy Queen, trying to make my coke last, when James squeezed his fat ass into the next table down from me. Empty tables all over but he chose the one where we couldn't avoid looking straight at each other. I didn't mind because I'd been watching him through the window long enough to know he had a van and was on his way somewhere. Happy days. I smiled at him but he looked away and concentrated hard on his food. I waited for him to finish, which he tried to do quickly on account of me staring at him.

'Careful, mister. My sister says you eat too fast you get sick.'

He nodded. Fries poked out the sides of his mouth as he replied, 'Heartburn.'

'Yeah, that's what she said.'

'Well, that's why I drink milk, isn't it.' He lifted his glass up, as though I was too dumb to see it sitting right there beside him.

'I hope I don't never get heartburn. My sister says it hurts like hell.'

Jojo acted as though everything hurt like hell as long as it was a man doing the complaining. She used to fuss over the men like they were babies if they even caught a cold. Made me mad to see her fuss over them and their sniffles like they'd just lost an arm, but maybe she taught me a lesson.

James burped, his chin all shiny from grease and milk.

'Pardon you, mister.'

I handed him a napkin and gave him my best smile, little

orphan Annie appealing to Daddy Warbucks.

'Nothing worse than trapped wind, mister.'

James was in his early forties, but carried the decayed heart of a fading seventy-year-old. The cab of his truck was littered with donut boxes and Dr Pepper cans. He was fairly busting out at the seams. His stomach forced its way past the feeble buttons on his blue-check shirt, spilled over the top of his corduroy pants, and went all the way round to his back when he was sat behind the wheel; a big lumpy cushion of flesh that was making its way back from the coast with a load of fish and lobsters. It was what he did.

He apologized for smelling like the fish. He said the smell never left, no matter how hard he scrubbed. I have to say, he did smell pretty bad, but the guy was prepared to drive me so I let him talk.

His ex-wife had set him up with the driving job and then wouldn't let him in the house on account of the smell. He later found out she'd been having an affair with his boss but instead of straightening the guy out, James had found he needed the wages to pay his ex the alimony the lawyers said he now owed her. He told me how lonely he was, that he had a kid he wasn't allowed to see, that in his darker moments he'd considered taking the kid and jumping off a cliff. It wasn't often I met someone sadder than me.

I sat beside him, eating his donuts, trying to ignore his crying, and when dusk came I asked him to pull over so I could pee. He stopped by the side of the road. There was no place to hide so I figured I'd just do it up against the wheel. I was zipping myself up when I caught him in the side mirror. He was looking at me. My instincts told me not to get back in but there was no place for me to go out there. If I ran, he'd be sure to follow, and if we had to fight I didn't much like my chances. If I got back in the truck, I could pretend everything was normal and wait for my right moment to disappear, so that's what I did.

We'd been driving in a tense silence for some minutes when he slid his big fat paw over my thigh. His hand moved up and down, kneading me like I was made of bread. I sat up straight as an arrow and locked on to the outside world. The first stars were appearing. His hand moved higher.

Lord, forgive us our sins. We know not what we do.

When he dug his hand right in and under, he hurt me. I yelped as my back arched and at last I found my voice.

'James, stop.'

He kept pressing and rubbing, staring blankly out the window. He was breathing out his mouth, almost snoring. A little bit of drool slipped out his fat lips and greased his chin.

'James, please stop!' I hated my voice, so weak and pathetic.

He took his hand away and sighed. All the air seemed to leave him in that moment. His whole body started to shake and he began to cry in huge, gasping sobs. 'I'm sorry,' he said. 'I'm a loser. I'm such a fucking loser.'

He wiped his face with his forearm and the van lurched to the left. If he didn't calm down we'd be off the road. I swallowed the bile that had risen in my throat and placed my hand on his arm.

'You aint a loser, James. You just had some shit luck.'

'Aint that the truth,' he said, and wiped his snotty nose with the back of his hand.

'Luck's got a way of changing, James. Blow your nose now.'

I handed him a napkin and turned my head away as he blew. Sounded like an avalanche. I forced myself to look back at him.

'You can't give up, James. You got a little boy who needs you.'

'But he aint gonna have no clue who I am,' he wailed. I felt a powerful urge to smack him but I sat on it.

'Not if you stick to life on the road,' I said, in my most patient voice. 'But there's other jobs. Get yourself something closer to home.'

He mulled this over. 'Maybe she'd take me back if I didn't smell of damn fish all the time.'

'Course she will, James.'

With his fat fucking face all shiny with tears, he looked like whale meat. I'd heard of people coming to resemble their pets but not their jobs. We were driving on the wrong side entirely now, and I'd spotted lights coming round a bend up ahead. I tugged on his shirtsleeve.

'Stop crying now and slow down, mister. You aint gonna be no good to that family of yours less you get home in one piece now, are you?'

He straightened up and the oncoming car passed us with a blast of its horn. James looked at me with such gratitude it made me want to puke.

'I'm sorry,' he said, wiping his eyes. He blinked hard a couple of times and gave himself a shake – trying to shake some sense into himself, I guess. 'I'm sorry,' he said again. 'I lost it for a minute back there. Jeez, life, huh? Sorry, kid. Didn't mean to scare you.'

'Don't worry about it, James. We all got problems.'

'You're pretty smart, you know that?' He punched me gently on the shoulder like we were old friends. 'What's your story anyway? How comes you're getting into trucks with strange men? That aint so smart.'

'Oh, James, I sure wish you hadn't asked me that,' I said, relieved to see we were approaching another town. Should have stuck with Plan A all along.

He looked at me with surprise. 'How so, Aggie?'

'Because now I got to tell you. Pull over a minute, will you?'

He seemed real interested, and looking for all the world like he hadn't just shoved his hand in my crotch, he slowed down to a stop and parked up beside a drive-thru liquor store. I quickly scanned the streets, decided which way I was headed, and then I gave him the routine.

Shocking how much a fat face can crumple. I felt bad

about it. He was one of life's prime losers. But the heat of his hand still burned into me and that made me mad. Besides, I knew he'd get a paycheck and then another after that, and it was all going to his bitch ex-wife anyway.

I finished speaking and waited. I wasn't totally surprised when he laughed. I'd had that before. Some guys were actually impressed with me. I normally liked them best.

'Oh, that's a good one, that is. That's a good one.' He banged his fist down on the wheel and bared his teeth.

'Don't get your hackles up, James. I tell you what, just show me your wallet. I won't take it all.'

'Won't take it all.' He laughed again and hung his head like a dog in mourning. 'You women would make me a slave to y'all the rest of my days.'

'Oh, James, don't be like that. Biggest burden to bear is a chip on the shoulder.'

Well, they say you can't teach an old dog new tricks, but in that moment, James sure learned himself a new tune. He picked up his CB and said, 'Y'all, I got a little teenaged lady in with me right now. About five eight, long dark hair, skinny as a bone. I'd advise you not to go picking her up less you want to meet a little witch who'll burn you soon as look at you. Act just sweet as a daisy and then claim you got indecent with her. She's a regular little con artist after your money, y'all.'

With every word I lost my grip, my means of holding on. When he finished he turned to me, grinned an ugly and said, 'Aint no trucker in the state gonna pick you up now. Not with good intent, leastways. Maybe some of them'll be looking for you. Teach you a nasty lesson, how about that?'

I grabbed for the door but before I could open it, he slammed the truck into drive and we took off.

'I'm sorry, James. I didn't mean you no harm. I made a mistake. I was just fooling with you.' My voice trembled as my bravado trickled away. I prayed for a red light but we hit greens the whole way out of town. I thought about jumping but we were eight feet off the ground and picking up speed.

I pressed myself up against the window, trying to draw attention before the houses and stores disappeared behind us. The speed signs told us to go faster and pretty soon we were back out in the middle of nowhere.

'Where we going, James?' I said, but seemed he'd lost interest in conversation. His CB was jammed with people responding to his message and he turned it off. The sudden silence and thickening darkness outside made me panic. I raked through the belongings in my bag looking for the hammer.

'Fucking little whore. What you got? You got a fucking gun in there?' James snatched my bag over onto his lap. He drove with one hand and with the other began to empty it out. He snorted when he discovered the hammer and slipped it down between his seat and the door. After making sure there was no gun, he shoved the bag back at me. With a weird snigger, he opened his window and began throwing stuff out – the bread I'd bought the previous day, a couple of apples. The few bits of clothing I had were whipped out the window and lost to the night. My throat seized as he whooped in triumph. This guy was fucking nuts. I cast my mind back to the last town. Did anyone see me? Could someone point the finger at him if they found me dead on the road tomorrow? Would Jojo ever know? We drove for an hour before he stopped.

'Alright, bitch, get out. Teach you to mess with me in a hurry.'

I grabbed my bag and clambered down. Even in the night, the heat wrapped itself around me, suffocating. If I managed to walk away from this I swore I'd get a gun.

I waited for his cab door to slam, for him to appear from round the side of the truck, in which case all I could do was run, but to my eternal relief he took off at a great rate, kicking up a cloud of dust in the process. I threw my head back and screamed after him.

'You fucking fish-dick! I'm so fucking happy your wife left you! You hear me, asshole?' I punched the air and stamped the ground, my anger falling uselessly into nothing. I kept track of him until far off in the distance his red tail-lights were swallowed whole by the inky night.

Dark, dark, darkness all around.

Above me, a rash of stars measled the sky.

Could be I was hunted now. I prayed the road stay straight and I walked.

Walking was a different prospect now I had an idea how big the state really was. No matter how far I got by morning, I knew it wouldn't be enough. The land was impossible on foot. A person could walk all their life in those plains and never come out. The thought rolled out my head and slipped into my stomach like the dead weight of a viper's nest. I thought of the cowboys who'd tamed this land generations ago and envied them their horses. Every mile or so, I came up on a sign that made my blood boil: *Rough road ahead.*

Ha fucking ha.

5

Walking and walking and walking till walking turned into a limp caused by a moon-sized blister on the ball of my right foot. I slowed to such a pace that a little armadillo kept up with me, until he spied something tasty and disappeared down a hole. I clutched my empty flask, as though any minute I might stumble upon a fast-shrinking river and have to catch its last few drops in a hurry. The straps of my rucksack cut into my shoulders. Gradually I emptied it of the little James had left me; newspapers, magazines, little stones I'd picked up here and there. Like a Texan Gretel, I left a trail behind me, and while I cried along with the distant coyotes, I didn't know if I was running from a witch or straight into one.

Around mid-morning I saw a rise of buildings in the distance. My excitement lasted till I drew close enough to realize it was just a rest stop. No shops, no place to eat; only toilets and a storm shelter. Still, I was thankful to escape the sun. Hungry and thirsty was bad, but hungry, thirsty and burned was a disaster.

I made a short prayer as I turned the handle on the restroom door. When it opened, the tears that had stayed just beneath my eyelids all night long finally rolled. *Thank you, Jesus, oh thank you, sweet baby Jesus.*

I fell on the faucet and drank until I gagged.

Now please just send me a gun, Lord.

I didn't recognize the girl in the bathroom mirror, though she looked as sub as ever she had. So dirty with dust, the only white skin showing was the tracks left by tears. I washed my face and drank some more and when I looked and felt a little more human, I made my way over to a shady picnic bench and tried to sleep, but every time I dozed off, Jojo's face rose up before me.

Pop had been drinking all day when he said me and Jojo could go camping. I was fresh in my pajamas and cock-a-whoop at this unexpected turn of events. Jojo, not so much. But we climbed into the truck and Pop drove us a good distance before dropping us with a warning to look out for rattlesnakes.

They're on the move, he said.

We stood in a rocky clearing surrounded by trees, and watched the truck disappear in a haze of dust.

Snakes, Jojo?

She laid her arm around me. *Ssh. Don't worry.*

My eyes were drawn to the darkness of the woods. The ragged outline of the tree-tops was still clear against the darkening sky, but what lived beneath? The harder I looked, the more I saw fast-moving shapes dancing behind the tree trunks, waiting for their time to slip out into the open.

A loud rattle sprang up from some nearby bush. A second later it was drowned out by the sound of my wailing.

It's cicadas, Jojo whispered, and it might have been true, but it didn't matter, because dark was closing in on us, creeping from the woods and sweeping along the ground to where we stood. Something brushed my foot and I screamed and jumped. Jojo yelled and whipped round and grabbed me. Our voices echoed around the canyon. Jojo held me tight.

Aint nothing there, Aggie. Shit. Reign it in, will you?

I thought I felt something I mumbled, feeling a fresh batch of tears brewing and kicking myself for being such a baby.

Look, sit up here, will you? She hoisted me on to a high, flat rock. The cicadas rattled on and on, so much it seemed impossible there wasn't a snake or two watching us. *This is the test, okay? Pop wants to know if we're smart. Look all around. We got everything we need right here.*

I looked doubtfully around me. *I guess we might make a den.*

Jojo's face lit up, and from her back pocket she took her penknife.

Good girl, Aggie! Come on, let's get fixing.

We searched the edge of the woods for fallen branches, Jojo cutting thinner ones from the trees, saving anything we could use to make a shelter. We built it beneath the trees and huddled in, almost forgetting we didn't want to be there, and snickering at our small victory over Pop. Bet he didn't think we'd do this.

Why'd he do it, anyway? I asked.

No answer. I tried again.

This aint such an adventure, really. Is it?

Sure seems like one to me, she said. *How many girls get to stay out on their own at night?*

Far off there was a deep rumble of thunder. I hoped it wouldn't get any closer. Jojo twirled the point of the knife round and round her palm.

Guess you don't remember, Aggie, why would you? But do you know what today is?

No school, no Scripture, meant it was Saturday.

No, I don't mean that. I mean...

I heard her swallow.

It's seven years to the day that Momma left.

Momma. The magic word. Even the cicadas seemed to stop singing. I knew I was supposed to appreciate the moment. I searched myself for any sign of emotion, but all I found was frustration. Whenever Jojo mentioned Momma, I'd nod and ask questions, even though I'd long lost any interest I might have had. Normally, I went along with the game because it made her happy, and afterwards I'd ask myself why I was such a terrible person that I couldn't find any feelings at all for the person who'd given birth to me.

But that one time, sitting in the tight night air, reeling from the shock of imagined rattlesnakes, I couldn't do it. My eyes filled with tears again, but this time they were hot and angry and felt better than the little-girl tears I'd cried earlier.

I didn't ask nothing about Momma, Jojo. I asked why Pop would leave us here. And don't say again that it's an adventure, because it aint. We got no tent. No food, hardly. No blankets, no nothing. Why'd he do it?

Why do you think he did it? she snapped. *Oh hell. Maybe if you weren't such a baby, you'd understand. Grown-ups have shit to deal with too, you know. It aint all about you, all the time. Shit, now look what you made me do. Damn knife gone and cut me.*

My nine-year-old head was smart enough not to point out that's just what knives do.

The slamming of a car door brought me back to the present. I heard footsteps on the gravel and then the swing of the toilet door. I lifted my legs off the bench and gingerly stood, putting weight gently down on my sore foot. Shit. I still wasn't good for walking. I hobbled myself round to the car park and saw a white pick up in the lot. I was weighing up the odds of me sneaking over, climbing in the back and hiding, when a female voice came from behind me.

'Excuse me, miss. Is there a vending machine here?' I turned round to see a girl just a few years older than me, real preppy, with Bermuda shorts and boat shoes and her hair all tied up in a ponytail. She must have walked the whole way round the shelter in order to come up behind me like that.

'Uh, I don't know. Sorry.'

'You don't work here? My gosh, I'm sorry. I figured you worked here.' Then she frowned and said, 'But where's your car?'

'I had a fight with my boyfriend. He drove off.'

She looked at me in amazement, which I must have mirrored because I amazed myself with my quick lies.

'He drove off? Oh my God!'

Another girl appeared behind the first. 'Did you find any – oh, hi!'

'Hey,' I smiled, plan forming fast.

'Lori, can you believe it? Her boyfriend just dumped her here!'

'What? Oh my God. You poor thing. How long you been here?'

'All night, I guess. You folks are the first to pull in.'

I had them. I knew it. And they were the kind of girls who oh-my-Godded over everything.

'He took my wallet,' I said.

'Oh my God!' they said.

'I think he's been seeing my sister,' I said, just to test my theory.

'Oh my God!' they said.

The one called Amy declared my boyfriend a total dick, and the other one, Lori, offered me a ride straight off.

Sitting hunched up with their bags in the back of the pickup, my story came as easy as one of their T-shirts sliding from their bag to mine. Me and my boyfriend had been set to wed and were running off to do it today. When we'd stopped for gas, he thought I'd been flirting with the guy behind the counter. One thing led to another, we'd had a fight and he dumped me. I couldn't face going home, seeing everyone being real sorry for me, or laughing and saying I told you. So I was a free agent and they could just drop me wherever it was convenient.

I could tell they didn't like the idea of just dropping me off some random place with no money, and though they seemed like rich kids to me, they were college kids, not exactly dripping in gold. Not exactly the smartest, either. When they asked my name and I told them Aggie, they screamed like they were on a roller coaster. I had to cover my ears.

'Are you thinking what I'm thinking?' Amy said.

'It's a sign,' Lori replied. 'Got to be. Hold on, Aggie.

53

Everything's going to be alright.'

Lori grasped the wheel with both hands and floored it. Amy plugged her cell into the car and music came out, real modern with a hard beat and no words. Outside, the plains, wide and wider. Felt like we were going nowhere real fast.

They were farm girls like me, only their farms were big and for cotton. They talked about Daddy filling his plane from oil sprung on his own land, and for a moment I felt a stab of sympathy for Cy. Ambitious Cy. Always talking about the guys he'd grown up with and how he wanted to expand the farm. Said he felt a regular laughing stock in company. Pop batted him away each time, like Cy was no more than a fly buzzing around his hat. Pop told Cy to content himself. Said greed wasn't God's way.

Sitting behind Lori and Amy, I got a good look at greed. Greed gave you thick, soft hair and bracelets jangling on your wrists. It gave you proper shoes for walking in and gold sunglasses to shade your eyes. It gave you long brown legs, smooth with no blemishes. It made you smell of flowers and coconuts. Gave you glossy lips. Made you pretty. I decided one day I'd give greed a try. In the meantime, I contented myself with twenty bucks taken from a roll of eighty in the side pocket on the bag beside me. Just enough to make them wonder, but not enough to be sure.

Outside, nodding donkeys jacked up and down, robbing oil from the ground just as easy as the turbines above them stole wind from the sky. The sun burned hotter and hotter. On the road ahead, pools of water appeared and disappeared like silver magic. Amy switched the air con to high. I didn't ask where we were going and I didn't care. I'd been catching rides with truckers for going on six weeks. I could handle this pair.

They told me I was their lucky mascot and when we got to where we were going I'd understand why. I just smiled and nodded, not wanting to seem too happy on account of my recent breakup, but for the first time since leaving I did feel a little excitement, or hope, or expectation, fluttering in the pit of my stomach. The happiness and contentment sitting in the seats in front of me was contagious.

I didn't have to talk too much. They took my quietness for grief and were quick to fill in the gaps with their own experiences. They'd both had bad boyfriends in the past, though Lori reckoned she had a good one now. The look Amy flung over her shoulder towards me made me doubtful, but neither of us disagreed, especially when she said her good boyfriend might give me a job.

'He works in a pizza place, right? And one day he gets a call from the manager who's been having, like, major personal issues lately, and he just leaves him in charge! Like, of the whole place! I mean, it's small but still, you know? How does that work out, I asked him. He's an undergrad, know what I mean?'

I didn't have the first idea but I nodded anyway.

'Final year. He can't be managing a crummy pizza place in his final year,' said Lori.

'It does do the best pizza, though,' interrupted Amy.

'Oh my God, to die for,' agreed Lori. 'But he plays football too, know what I mean? There's no time for pizza. Of course, he won't let his boss down, because he's a decent guy. But I told him he needs help. He's on the team. The actual team, for Christ's sake!'

Amy turned round and rolled her eyes at me again. I guessed she heard a lot about this boyfriend in his final year with his football and his team and his unreasonable pizza manager.

'He's not on the team today,' Amy said, and the air in the car turned electric.

Lori exploded. 'That's because he's working in a shitty pizza place doing a shitty job that a fucking monkey could do for a shitty manager for shitty money!'

Amy was suddenly fascinated with something outside the passenger window and didn't reply. It was time for me to bring the subject back to point.

'So you think he might have an opening?' I said.

'Well, that depends.' Lori was obviously pissed now. 'Do you have experience?'

'I thought you said a fucking monkey could do his job, Lori?' Amy was back in the game. 'If a fucking monkey could do his job, then Aggie can do it. Aggie! Hell, the girl was made for it!'

For reasons that were unclear to me, they both laughed again and the air was cleared. They were confusing, but at least I never had to answer if I'd experience or not.

6

The place was College Station and the school was Texas A&M. They couldn't believe I'd never heard of it, like it was the center of the earth.

'Oh my God! We're a premier school!' said Amy.

'Like, haven't you even heard of the team? They televise our games all the time!' said Lori.

'Oh my God!' said both of them.

I just shrugged. They were squabbling again by the time we arrived, on account of Amy, or Lori, depending who you listened to, making them both late for the game which was playing that afternoon.

'Sorry for dumping you, Aggie,' Amy said, as they dropped me at a full parking lot and hurried elsewhere to find a space for the car.

'Tony's place is down there on the left, opposite the Army & Navy.' Lori pointed out a street fifty yards away. I thanked them and waved as they drove off, but they were already fighting again and didn't wave back. They took a left at the corner and then they were gone.

I took a look around. I was disappointed. From where I was standing, College Station seemed a quiet place, small. Nowhere to hide. But if I could stay even a week or two and get some money together that would be awesome. Plus, I'd never had an opening before. Seemed like the universe was sending me some help at just the right time. If I doubted it, there was even a public bathroom for me to wash and change in, and make myself presentable before going to ask about the job.

Fresh in my new T-shirt, I approached the street that had been pointed out. A group of tourists cleared to reveal a statue a few feet away. I stopped to check it out and nearly fell down. So that's what they'd meant. In front of me was a young guy built out of black metal, and he was carrying an axe. The inscription said: *Aggie Spirit, The Tradition Lives.* How about that? Maybe I was going to like this town after all.

I found the pizza place, opposite the Army & Navy just like she'd said. It was nothing special. Just six empty tables and a high counter with a bored-looking blond guy behind it. His eyes were focused on a TV sitting on one of the tables. As I pushed open the door, he hollered and punched the air so abruptly I almost wet my pants.

'Oh, what!' he cried. 'No way! I thought we had it.'

'Uh, hi,' I said.

He looked at me for the first time and I gave a little wave. 'Did you see that?' he asked, pointing at the TV. 'I mean, did you *see* that?'

From the way the TV was angled there was no way I could have seen it, but I remembered Jojo saying to me one time that when it comes to men and sport, it's best to be sympathetic.

'I'm sure it'll go the right way next time, sir.'

'Yeah, yeah, I'm sure,' he said with a scowl. 'Anyway, you need a slice?'

I fingered the twenty rolled up in my pocket and tried not to look at the different types of pizza all laid out begging me to eat them: Hawaiian, pepperoni, one with chunks of red pepper that made my tummy growl just by looking. The twenty stayed in my pocket.

'I was told to ask for Tony.'

'Well, I guess you just found him. What can I help you with?' He seemed to kind of inflate like some jock puffer fish as he rolled his shoulders and flexed his pecs at me.

'Lori sent me. Said you needed some help here.'

He gestured towards the empty seats. 'Does it look like I

need help here?' He flicked a dishcloth over his shoulder and his eyes drifted back to the game. I came round to look at the TV screen with him.

'She told me you were missing the game. Said you might miss the whole season. My name's Aggie.'

His eyes snapped right back to me. 'Are you serious?' He began to laugh.

I nodded. 'Lori said to say she's sent you a lucky mascot.' No, she hadn't, but what the hell.

He shook his head and chuckled to himself. 'You got any experience with pizza, Aggie?'

'Sure,' I replied. It wasn't a lie. I'd eaten plenty.

'Cool,' he said. 'Listen, I'm kind of busy right now.' He nodded at the TV and I gave him my most understanding face. 'Can you come back later? Say six? We start getting busy then.'

And that's how I got my first job. Easy as pizza pie.

Second time Pop drove me and Jojo into the canyon, he said it was to test us. He said books and schooling had its place but they were no substitute for the country smarts. Jojo said he never would have done it if he'd known the storm was coming, but even Cy said it was a wicked thing, storm or no storm. We huddled together between some boulders. The rain didn't dampen the rattle of the cicadas.

Cicadas, Aggie, remember? Just cicadas.

I pressed in tight to her. The rain poured down so hard we could barely open our eyes. When I tried to talk, I had to spit water after every second word.

Let's build another den, I suggested, my throat hoarse from some infection or other.

Rain'll kill it, Aggie. No point.

Can't we go take cover in those trees? I asked, but I already knew the answer was no. Trees weren't your friend in an electric storm.

We're safer out here, she yelled. *Those trees over there will take a lightening strike before we do.*

She pulled me in even closer, squeezing loose some water trapped in my fleece. Tiny cold rivers trickled down my back and sides, worse than the general flood we were experiencing. My teeth chattered and I bowed my head to let the water pour off without getting in my eyes. I'd been sent home sick from school that very day. A cough gathered in my throat and I gave in to it, adding my germy spray to the general wetness. On purpose, I didn't cover my mouth. If she cared she didn't say, but I imagined I could feel her grow harder, more distant from me. She was already mad with me from earlier that day. She'd tucked me on the sofa and given me a book from Momma's pile to read. 'You be real careful with that one now,' she said, though I didn't need the warning. The book felt like gold dust in my hands. I settled back on the sofa for the afternoon, gently turning the pages, in awe of my treasure, a real life connection with Momma Who Ran Away.

Guess I'd fallen asleep. Somewhere nearby was Pop's voice and Jojo's. I turned my head to see, and a flannel fell from my forehead. I caught it in my hand. It was warm and dry, all coolness long gone.

My head pounded and a sudden pain in my ear made me roll over and cry out in pain. Then Jojo was in front of me, opening a bottle and pouring a foul tasting medicine onto a plastic spoon. I swallowed it down in one, eyes screwed tight shut, as though I could block the flavor, then the second spoon arrived loaded with strawberry jelly to take the taste away.

How's my girlie? Pop appeared from behind Jojo, sat down beside me and pulled me onto his lap. He put his hand to my forehead and it was so hot he made like he burned himself. I giggled, even as Jojo frowned.

She aint well. Go easy.

I will, he replied. *I'll go easy, won't I, sugar pie?* And he tickled me then, and made me squeal, despite my sore throat.

Y'see? he laughed. *She's cured already. Its a goddam frikkin miracle!*

I wriggled to get away, but his hands were so big, it was like trying to get out of a locked gate once Pop had you on his knee. His fingers squeezed my waist and dug into my armpits and I bounced myself hard as I could to escape him. Finally he let me go. I tumbled onto the sofa, then jumped right back on his lap and wrapped my arms around him. His overalls were unbuttoned and he smelled of sweat and tobacco and work.

Aggie, get down, Jojo said. She stood back from us, medicine bottle in one hand, jelly jar in the other. *You're too big for that now.*

Like hell she is, said Pop, giving me an extra squeeze. I clung to him, defiantly rubbing my head on his chin.

She bent to pick up the little plastic spoon, and when she stood again, she gave me a look you couldn't argue with. *Well, seeing as you're so cock-a-whoop, young lady, maybe you could see your way to giving me a hand in the kitchen.*

Pop let loose his grip on me. *Ah, hell,* he said, *the child's sick, Jojo. I'll leave her be. If I'd known you'd get yourself so aggravated about a little horse-play. We was just fooling, aint that right, Aggie?*

He pushed me down, arranged a cushion behind my back, and pulled the sheet over me, leaving grubby finger marks on the graying cotton.

Happy now? he asked Jojo, as he stepped away. His boot twisted on Momma's book as he left, leaving pages fanning out from the mangled cover.

Jojo gasped and bent to snatch it up. To my horror, it fell apart in her hands. Pages swooped to the floor and scattered at her feet.

Why did you leave it there, Aggie? Her voice whiny and accusing.

You said I could read it, I croaked.

Well, I was a fool that time, she said, and followed Pop out. I followed her journey as her footsteps stomped up the stairs.

I'm sorry, Jojo, I called after her. The roughness in my

61

throat made my eyes water. I heard her yelling at Pop, and sitting in the dark, pummelled by rain, it struck me now that maybe she was the reason he'd driven us out here.

Least your skin's waterproof, Aggie. Gotta look on the bright side.

Another lesson I learned from Jojo. Look on the bright side, sure. But don't make it so bright the dazzle blinds you from the truth.

Tony's manager hadn't left him with hire-and-fire privileges, so he had to pay me out of his own pocket, which he did nightly. He was apologetic about it but of course it suited me right down to the ground. Amy had been right about the pizza. It was amazing. I ate so much in the first three days I had to track down some Ex-Lax to loosen me up, but after I learned that lesson, I was happy as a pig in shit.

I spent the nights in a nearby park, climbing the fence after dark. It wasn't what you'd call comfortable, but it was quiet, and felt safe. I slept in an empty water fountain and passed the time counting bats. When I was done with that, I counted the bills in my pocket. They were stacking up. I'd be able to get a room some time soon, and then I'd relax. When you've got your own four walls around you, you can be a real person. Maybe I'd send for Jojo, show her she didn't have to put up with that shit anymore. Maybe she could be a real person too. I gave myself a shake. It wasn't the time to get wrapped up in fairy stories. In the morning, I'd stash my bag in the bushes and wander the streets until it was time for work.

Lori and Amy came by the pizza place a couple of times to see how I was doing, but they didn't invite me to hang out with them. I hadn't known I could be offended and grateful all at the same time, but maybe they were put off by the fact of their T-shirt on my body beneath my pizza apron.

Anyway, College Station was my town. I'd no doubt I'd finally found my home. It was bigger than I'd first thought, yet everywhere I went I saw my name. Aggie was what the university kids called themselves. Frikkin weirdos. I'd have picked a cuter name if I were them, but I understood why Amy and Lori had taken me as their mascot. Aggie bookshops, Aggie coffee shops, Aggie T-shirts in every third window. I went into shops that sold Aggie dishcloths, Aggie golf tees, Aggie frikkin snow globes and Aggie Christmas baubles. It was like looking in a mirror and having the world shout your name back at you.

What bowled me over most was the huge water tower. It stretched a hundred feet to the sky and it welcomed the whole wide world to Aggieland. I spent hours just staring at it, fascinated by my own name, while the college kids walked, ran, learned, loved and lost, all day every day around me.

It was night, I was in my dried-up fountain, and something had woken me up.

'Miss? Are you alright in there?'

A white beam swung down onto me and a hand clasped my shoulder. I knocked it off and scrambled away.

'It's alright, miss. I'm sorry. I didn't mean to scare you.'

The beam of light swung away from me and onto the face of the person carrying it. Actually, there were two of them, both guys, both looking a lot like students. The one without the flashlight held his hands up to show he didn't mean any harm. He'd have to forgive me if I didn't believe him.

'Can I help you?' I said, wondering which way to escape to. They were between me and the park gate, which was probably locked anyway. I'd head for the trees behind me.

'We just wanted to check you're okay,' said the one with the light.

'Yeah, I was until you woke me up. What you do that for?'

'I'm Mike,' said the one with the light.

'And I'm Dan,' said the other. 'We're with the Christian Fellowship. Just wondering if we can help?' He offered me a flyer with a picture of five men standing up to their waists in water with a fishing net spread wide in front of them. What were they hoping to catch?

'I don't want it,' I shook my head and backed away from them.

'Hey, that's cool,' said Dan. 'No pressure. I'll just leave this for you to check out later.' He held the flyer out like it was a bomb about to explode and laid it carefully down in the fountain, the whole time holding his other hand in the air so I could see what he was doing. Then they both took a step backwards and the amount of relief that one step brought me almost removed the need for Ex-Lax.

'I'll read it in the morning,' I said.

'We're here to help. We can give you shelter, help you get back on your feet. We're almost full every night, but if you get there early enough we'll see what we can do,' Mike said.

'Oh. Right.'

'So you'll come then? The details are all on there,' said Dan.

I nodded, keen for them to go. When they still didn't move, I leaned over and picked up the leaflet. 'I'll check it out,' I said, waving it as though they were chickens who could be easily chased.

'We've room for all God's children,' said Mike. 'You are very special. You are loved.'

'Yuh-huh. Um, thanks.'

'All you have to do is let Him in. God's grace will deliver you.'

And with that, they were gone, or at least I couldn't see them anymore. I gathered my stuff and went to look for a good bench, Dan's words ringing in my head: *God's grace will deliver you.*

I chose a wooden bench to sleep on. I spread my blanket and lay down, once more using my bag as a pillow. I listened to the bats rushing through the trees and turned my head in case I could spy them in the moonlight. I spent a long while watching them dance around the thick steeple of a nearby church. Together, they climbed the night and disappeared into darkness. Alone, I discovered I'd been concentrating on the bats so much, the idea of whispering a prayer had slipped into my mind, settled and festered.

I'd no memory of ever being in God's house. Momma used to take us weekly, but once she'd gone, Pop put a stop to it. We didn't need busybodies poking their noses in. We'd be good Christians under Pop's instruction.

When the mood took him, he'd gather his four children around the table and we'd take turns reading Scripture aloud. One Sunday, he passed me the Holy Book, my page marked by a dried flower taken from a vase upstairs.

That's for you, he said. *Keep it.*

I began to read and everyone listened about the angels who came to Sodom, and Lot who protected them from an angry crowd, and Lot's daughters who were given up to save the angels.

That's enough now, said Jojo.

Pop slapped her across the back of the head for being so disrespectful and told me to read on.

The eldest daughter said: Come, let us make him drunk with wine, and let us lie with him.

I stumbled over the words. When I finally finished, the room was different, or maybe it was just the people. Jojo's face was scarlet, just as her knuckles were white from the effort of pressing her hands together. It didn't look like prayer. Ash had his head so low, he might have been asleep, but Cy was looking at me strange. Shifty, almost. Before I could put the pieces together, Pop placed his hands upon my head and offered a blessing.

Lord God, look down kindly upon our family, and give particular care for our little Aggie, for she be a woman now.

Hard to believe how much I flushed with pleasure.

The day after Dan and Mike had offered me a place in God's house, I was working alone. The place was dead, which was fine by me because I hadn't slept much on that park bench. My eyes were stung with tiredness. It was Saturday afternoon and Tony was back playing football. The TV had been brought out in case customers wanted to watch but it sat there, screen blank. Every now and then I caught a glimpse of myself reflected in its darkness; an aproned girl with a white net hat was strange company.

Every available surface was covered with tiny mounds of pizza toppings. I'd chopped every tomato, onion, mushroom and pepper I could find and discovered there weren't enough containers to pack them in. I'd grated too much cheese and rolled more pizza bases than we'd ever need in a day. They were stacked in piles of a dozen. It occurred to me Tony might not be happy with my work today, which seemed unfair given I'd done so much of it. I took a trip over to the window and looked out. The streets were empty. Maybe I could catch a nap.

I pushed four chairs together to make a bed and lay down. The park bench had been a better arrangement. A stack of free newspapers on the floor by the window caught my eye. One of them was called *Missing*. I'd resisted looking in it before but today I sat up and lifted a copy without even thinking about it.

Inside were pages and pages of people who had disappeared. People who had other people looking for them. Idly, I scanned the pictures, imagining the stories behind each face. I thought mostly they'd be dead – suicide or murder most of them, maybe an accident or two – but surely there'd be one or two like me, somebody who just woke up one morning and decided to take a walk out of their life. That thought was crazy, that there were others like me, other subs who refused to take it anymore, subs who preferred to be a nobody instead of a useless, used somebody.

A girl on page five caught my eye. Same age as me, long brown hair like me, dark eyes like me. Her name was Chanelle. Her mommy missed her. Mommy wanted her to call. Mommy just wanted to know she was alright. Mommy missed her so much. I flicked through to the end and then turned back to

Chanelle; big lips, big doe eyes, big fucking deal.

I took all the papers and placed them one by one in the pizza oven. I sipped a cherry lemonade while I watched all the people burn up. Then I took Dan and Mike's church flyer out of my jeans pocket and watched that burn up, too. Bye, bye, Jesus.

I headed out leaving the door unlocked behind me. The sun was high and the world was roasting. The water tower poked up through building roofs. Its huge burgundy letters, *WELCOME TO AGGIELAND*, seemed a little sinister today. Somehow it drew me, and I crossed the main road to the campus.

The place was deserted. The big yellow buildings looked like a movie set. It was like I was seeing them for the first time. With no one around, I was brave enough to enter one of them. I ignored a sign forbidding me to walk on the grass, and crossed a patch of lawn between two roads. When I reached the building, a dark pane of glass slid silently to one side, inviting me to enter.

The air con rushed me like an ambush, stealing the sweat from my body. Taking my first decent breath of the day, I stood for a minute just to absorb the grandness of the place, all marble floors and chandeliers. I trailed my hand along the cold wall as I made my way down the hallway.

The reception desk was big and empty. A couple of brown parcels invited attention but not from me, not today. My heart lurched when I saw the next desk was security, but there was no guard, and I continued past the ladies restroom and past the elevator taking you up to the rest of the building. A Plexiglas map on the wall told you where everything was but I didn't feel like I could stop, or maybe I just didn't care to look. My shoes flip-flopped with every step. I passed a huge lounge with brown leather sofas, too big and plush to sit down on. More chandeliers dangled inside, not just one, several. Cy used to mock me and Jojo because we liked to read. He said education was a luxury. Now I knew what he meant.

The next unit was a Starbucks and I went in just to feel normal. The girl behind the register didn't even look up which was just the way I liked it. The coffee shop bled into a gift shop and I went through. Once again I was amazed by the amount of stuff in the world with my name on: Aggie pens, Aggie teddy bears, Aggie salad bowls, Aggie jewellery, notepads, pencil cases, hats, cups, corkscrews, wallets, all things everywhere singing *Aggie, Aggie, Aggie.* Aggie in all sizes. Aggie infants, Aggie toddlers, Aggie teens, Aggie women, Aggie men. And then a bookstore selling *The History of the Aggies, Aggie Escapades, The Aggie Fightin' Band,* Aggie this, Aggie that, till all I could see, hear and breathe was my own name.

'Howdy, miss. Anything I can help you with today?' He was suddenly in my space, probably just a student trying to put himself through college, but in that moment, Satan couldn't have rattled me more. He grinned. Saliva shone slick on his braces. At the corner of his mouth was a mole, just like Jojo's.

'I'm good, thanks,' I said, slipping back out to the corridor, heart thumping. Down the hall, a security guard was talking on the phone. A pane of dark glass moved in front of me and I stepped back out into the day's white glare. A single gull keened, swooping crazily in the windless sky. From a far off place, a train horn sounded.

As I'd done once before, I looked left and right. Left would take me back to Tony's. I went right, trying to ignore my name written all over the walls, when a roar ripped the air and I realized I was right outside the stadium. Behind that wall with my name on was eighty thousand people, and me, here, alone. I looked around me and blinked in surprise. I wasn't too alone after all. Sleepy guys sat behind stalls selling banners and flags. Gig 'em, Aggies. Rows of tents lined up behind cars and trucks, with tables set out under white cloth, and on the cloth buckets of ice to keep bottles and bottles of beer cool. This place was about to go apeshit. I was tempted by an unattended car, but before I made it over I was distracted by a statue of a guy – they were always guys – and he was holding what I thought was a turtle but turned out to be a baseball cap. I stopped reading the inscription when I got to Aggie. It was the second damn word.

The doors to the stadium burst open and the world was born. People spilled out, thousands of them, all dressed in burgundy looking like agitated fire ants. They swarmed around me, not even seeing me, waving giant flags and foam fingers and everywhere my name was ringing through the air: *AGGIE, AGGIE, AGGIE*.

I shoved my way through the crowds and something grabbed my arm. I looked down and saw a hand wrapped around me. I followed its body to find a red-faced monster grinning like a loon.

'Aggie!' it said. 'It's Mike! From last night. Remember me?'

I dragged my arm free and pushed past him. Past a thousand others all yelling the same thing and ran, ran past the stadium, past the parking lots, ran until *AGGIE* was drowned out by the fearsome bells and horn of an approaching freight train. I didn't make it over the track in time. The train penned me in with eighty thousand voices calling my name.

I waited for it to pass; red carriages, black ones, green, yellow, blue, but it didn't pass, would never pass, and behind me and inside me, *AGGIE, AGGIE, AGGIE*, and through the gaps in the carriages I could see the world I would never get to, and before I knew what I was doing, I grabbed the nearest handle and jumped.

7

It was night but the city didn't know. All lit up and spread out like a magic carpet, it sparkled like jewels. Buildings stood so high, they blocked out the moon and made you think the sky was only above, not all around like it was at home. Not a star in sight. In the city, all the brightness is on the ground.

The city stinks. It's a place you can keep your skin clean but not your soul. It's a hellhole, a maze of deceitfulness. I wound up staying longer than I wanted to just because I couldn't find my damn way out again. People scurry like rats down sewers, home to office to malls to home again.

I missed my Aggieland. I'd burned that bridge the day I walked. Shouldn't have left the restaurant lying open, but at least I hadn't cleared the register. I soon got to thinking I should have done.

As a homeless person, there's no dignity in the city. I got fresh clothes from a thrift outlet and then tried to find a job. At first, I was hopeful. I'd done it once, right? Figured the one advantage I had over others was I wasn't fussy. Coming from where I came from, I'd do just about anything. I tried every restaurant's back door, thinking sooner or later someone would let me wash their greasy dishes but no one ever did. I tried until I grew desperate and then I knew my chance had gone. Nobody likes the smell of desperation.

It rained three days solid and the only luck I had was finding a decent size of gray tarp to hide under, though in truth all the difference it made was I got wet from the feet up instead of the head down. The cardboard I laid out on was soaked through. My ass felt like a sponge.

I was hunkered down in a little courtyard surrounded by offices. The only way in was through a back lane, the likes of which only rats and dogs might nuzzle down. I slipped down after dark and felt safer there than the guys I'd seen in doorways being kicked and spat at and moved on by the law. I crouched under that tarp like a mouse in a hole and made like the sound of rain popping on plastic was popcorn in my kitchen. Jojo used to complain about my overactive imagination but out here I was learning to use it for good. I closed my eyes as the rain came down and the smells returned to me, clear as comfort; smells a body never forgets, a toasty, buttery sweetness down my throat. She, standing with one hand on her hip, the other holding the lid of the pan down while an army of jumping jacks pinged inside. She, telling me to fetch the plastic bowl with the blue strawberries on to put the popcorn in. She, beside me on the couch watching fuzzy *Cosby Show* reruns on the old portable, and outside a storm whipping up to keep the men gathering scattered sheep for longer.

The rain was soaking through the tarp, there must have been holes there somewhere, and I was only getting wetter and wetter. Eventually I got to thinking I might as well just take a shower right there in that courtyard. I knew it was stupid, because I didn't rightly know when I might get dry again, but I eased the tarp back and lifted my head to the heavy sky. The water on my face felt good, something natural in the most unnatural of places. I closed my eyes and let it wash over me.

Thought I heard something. Snapped my eyes open and looked quick around the courtyard but the rain was coming down so hard it was difficult to see. Seemed I was alone but still, I had a bad feeling. At last, a voice cut across the night.

'Take your clothes off!'

I dived straight back under the tarp and balled myself up

underneath it, willing myself invisible. No one approached but I'd definitely heard it. My breath caught somewhere between my lungs and darkness.

But nothing happened and I got to thinking I was imagining again. I peeked back out. There, spinning like some ghost or angel or moonchild, was this creature all white and glowing in the night. I counted two arms, two legs and a head before I realized I was looking at another human being. A female one at that.

'Take your clothes off!' She screeched and spun round in the rain, arms stretched out at her sides, naked as a newborn, cackling like a hyena. Outside of a dream it was the strangest sight I ever did see.

I did not take my clothes off.

Instead I sat dumbstruck as this white witch skipped and jumped and hopped all over the place. She had long, crazy pink hair and she whirled it around so much it came to look like the whirring blades of a helicopter. She splashed in puddles and came close enough for me to make out the blue Care Bear tattooed on her ankle. Then she was gone, dipped behind a rusty yellow dumpster, and then there she was again, flipping over the side and down into it.

I sat there half blind with rain wondering what the hell I'd just witnessed. A moment later, a big bag fell out of the dumpster and landed on the ground with a thud. There was some scuffling and some swearing, and then two white hands appeared over the edge and hauled their body back over into the courtyard. She was dressed this time, wearing blue jeans and a long-sleeved T-shirt. She tucked a jacket in between her legs, leaned over sideways and began dragging her fingers through her hair. I still hadn't budged an inch and was now sitting in a puddle which threatened to become a lake. My jaw hung so low that if a boat happened to sail by it would have sailed straight on into my mouth.

'My name's Freak,' she said, tying her hair back in a tight ponytail. 'What's yours?'

'Uh. Aggie.'

'That your real name?'

'Uh-huh.'

'Well, you're dumb for telling me your real name, Aggie. Don't tell nobody else your real name, y'hear?'

I nodded.

She slipped her jacket on and pulled some jewelry from its pockets. Grimacing, she shoved her dangly earrings in, and her plastic bangles made a noise that later on I could tell from fifty yards. She had at least one ring for every finger, including her thumbs.

'I been watching you two days, Aggie.'

She glanced up at me expecting some reaction but far as I was aware my face was still frozen in solid shock.

'I been living in that dumpster whole time you been here and you had no clue. What if I'd been some bad guy, huh? I could have taken you like that.' She snapped her fingers and with the other hand she made like she was drawing a blade across her throat. She raised her eyebrows at me and nodded, waiting for a response. I nodded back.

'You gotta sharpen up, Aggie. You're new, huh?'

'I been living out country ways,' I said, offended she thought I was a newbie. Like to see her sleeping with snakes and spiders.

'Country, huh. Well, this aint no country. Things are different here. Jesus. What piece of shit is this?'

She marched over and snatched the tarp.

'Look, it's all ripped up, y'all. This bitch aint never gonna keep you dry.'

Too damp to be angry, too cold to care, I let her scrunch up my little home and toss it aside. She didn't look too dry herself and I told her so but she didn't seem to hear me.

'This weather's a real goddam turd-floater. How about we go find somewhere better?'

She stood over me, crazy, scary, different. When she stretched out her hand, I reached up and took it.

8

Freak talked a little bit like she was some sergeant in the army. When she asked a question, it came out like a command. She was only little but seemed to me she'd been practicing making herself big as possible. She swaggered to go forwards. One foot pointed to two o'clock while the other went to ten. Made no sense to me but that's just how Freak was. Told me she was eighteen but I reckoned she wasn't much older than me. Claimed she wasn't a runaway; she was just out having an adventure. When I asked if her parents didn't mind, she told me her family were good, clean-living folks who reckoned it was fine for her to do some traveling, so long as she didn't forget who she was or where she came from. Strange, since all I wanted to do was exactly that. Next time I opened my mouth to speak, she told me to quit with the questions.

But she knew where she was taking me that first night. She led me through the wet city streets until the skyscrapers were behind us and the roads gave way to smaller complexes. She took me through streets with names all misleading; Pine, Maple and Beechnut, but hardly a tree in sight. Reckon we walked an hour before turning into a modern development, so new they hadn't even finished building it. The house we stopped at was the nearest thing to a palace I'd ever seen: a townhouse with three storeys, four if you counted the storage room at the top. Looked so grand from the outside I near enough bolted, but Freak grabbed my arm and dragged

74

me up the six or so steps to the front door. She banged on it hard but the place stayed silent.

'Goddam it.' She peered through the opaque glass and banged again. Curtains in the house next door twitched and a woman peeped out, face more miserable than the weather. Freak flipped her the bird and she disappeared, pulling the curtain tight behind her.

'Adrian!' Freak yelled. 'Open up!'

The house stayed dark.

'I know he's in there,' said Freak, and she continued to bash away on the door like she was trying to knock it down. More curtains opened and silhouettes stood watching us from windows up and down the street.

'Maybe we should go,' I said, just as a window above our heads flew open. I tried to see through the driving rain but all I could make out was a white face and long black hair.

'Piss off, Freak-face,' it said. 'You're not wanted.'

Weirdest accent I ever heard.

'Aw, come on, Ade. We're freezing our asses off here.'

She wasn't lying. The rain hadn't eased off one bit. Freak rattled with shivers and I wasn't far from joining her. Our itsy faces must have looked like two drowned moons looking up at him.

'Who's your friend? Another little thief?'

'Naw, Ade. Don't be like that. This is Aggie. She's fresh. Needs our help.'

'Need our help, do you?'

I looked from him to her and back at him and I shrugged. Freak jogged up and down on the spot. 'Aw, come on, Ade, just open up. Please.'

'You have rotten taste in friends, do you know that, Aggie?'

The holler that came from Freak almost sent me down the stairs in shock. She threw herself to the ground and thrashed like a toddler in a supermarket. Her head smacked off the concrete floor and her fists pummelled the iron stair railings.

I didn't know what the hell to do with her. I looked up to the window for guidance but the guy had gone and the window was closed. I tried to protect her head by cradling it in my hands but all I got was a punch in the mouth for my efforts. The neighbors were coming out to watch on their porches when the guy opened the door and hissed, 'Freak! The fucking neighbors!'

Her whole body went limp. I was fixing to ask someone to call an ambulance when her eyes snapped open and she flashed a grin. She hopped right up from the ground and strolled through the front door like she was some rich lady and Ade just the doorman at a fancy hotel.

I stood alone on the steps, unsure of what I was getting into. I was soaked to the skin and so cold it hurt. Ade stared at me, a tall, gangling kind of guy with matted black hair and clothes scruffy as mine. Not exactly what you'd call respectable.

'Cell phones are banned.' His weird voice again. 'If you have a cell, you have to leave. Now.'

'I don't have a cell,' I replied, confused.

'No cell. Are you sure about that?'

I shrugged and nodded. It wasn't a hard question. I spread my arms out. All I had was a plastic bag with a change of clothes in.

'Mister, if I had a cell phone I can tell you I wouldn't be holding on to it. I'd be selling it to buy me some new shoes.'

He looked down at my sodden tennis shoes. When I wiggled my toes, it felt like they were in an overcrowded goldfish bowl.

'You do need new shoes,' he agreed.

'Indeed I do, sir.'

He stared at my shoes, as though he was real sorry for them. Then he looked up and said, 'If I find you with a cell or a laptop or any type of electronic device, you'll be asked to leave. Got it?'

He was a whole new type of crazy, but I was so cold I just nodded.

He glanced back up the street and then up to the sky before moving away from the doorway. 'Come on then,' he said. 'Are you in or out?'

The door he held back was thick and made of solid wood. The hallway inside was dim.

I was trying to decide when a bunch of loud folks came running down the street and up the stairs I was on. They pushed past me, and amid a chorus of *Hey Ade's*, a light snapped on in the hallway. The place came alive with the sight of people shaking water off their shoulders. A pizza box was opened up and the contents disappeared in a flash. Freak came running out to see what was going on and when she saw me still on the stoop she reached out and dragged me in.

'Sorry, I should have warned you about him,' she hissed in my ear. 'You did right to say you had no cell. We all do that.'

She pushed a towel into my hands and as I wiped my face and squeezed my hair dry, the door clicked closed behind me.

1

The hall alone was the size of my entire downstairs back home. A staircase made of solid oak twisted up from the middle and doors went off at every side. The smell of paint hung thick in the air, and the walls were decorated with graffiti and stencils. No furniture to speak of and no carpet either. I followed the crowd through to the back of the house and found the kitchen. It was even bigger than the hall, with a breakfast bar that wouldn't have been out of place in any drinking joint. The back wall was made entirely of glass so you could look out at the garden.

'We got a pool,' said Freak in my ear.

'Seriously?' I replied.

'Yeah,' said Freak. 'Aint got no water in it, and it's full of junk, but it's there. Sure beats a soaking-wet alley, huh?'

And then just like a truck had knocked her into next week – she was gone. Shouts and jeers started up and I was bumped and shoved as people crowded around. Through the huddle I caught glimpses of Freak being hauled around the room by this beast of a woman, all chains and big black biker boots. She'd wrapped Freak's hair around her fists and tugged her clean off the ground. Freak's arms flew all over the place but she couldn't land a touch on her. Looked to me like her head couldn't stay on her shoulders much longer. I pushed my way to the front to try to help but by then they'd stopped. Freak was on her back with a boot on her chest.

'Where's my money, you fucking whore?' grunted Beast

Woman. She had silver bracelets jangling up her arms, and a tattooed snake that slithered its way down from under the sleeves of her T-shirt.

'Fuck you, Marjorie,' Freak moaned.

Beast Woman lifted her leg and looked fit to stamp down when Ade appeared out of nowhere and pulled her back. Freak was on her feet in a flash, spitting nails.

'Dirty fucking bitch, coming at me from behind like that.' She lunged for Beast Woman, but Ade grabbed the back of her jacket and stepped in between them. 'Fucking behave!' he roared. He was such a puny-looking guy I was amazed when they both shut up and calmed down for him.

'What you let her back in for, Ade?' demanded Beast Woman. 'She's no good.'

Freak let out her ponytail and shook her hair loose. A little bit of blood oozed from a cut somewhere in her scalp.

'I got your fucking money, Marj. Here.' Freak took a wallet from her jeans pocket and threw it in the woman's face. It fell to the floor and the two of them stood, each willing the other to pick it up again. It was Ade who settled it.

'Pick it up, Marjorie. Count it.'

Freak kind of snorted as the woman bent to pick up the wallet. 'There's extra in there for goodwill,' she said.

'For interest,' Beast Woman growled.

'Is it all there?' Ade asked. Beast Woman nodded.

'Freak, you need to apologize to Marjorie now. Do it.'

Freak's face turned blacker than an ace of spades.

'She got her fucking money. What more does she want?'

'I need an apology, Freak. I need an apology real bad.' Marjorie drawled the words, clearly mocking, but Ade seemed to miss the tone. Folks around us were starting to laugh a little.

'I'm fucking sorry, okay?' Freak said, looking more mad than sad.

'And, Marjorie, your friends need to leave. Now.'

The laughing faces changed to dismay.

'Fuck sake.' Beast Woman muttered, as some of the crowd shuffled forward. Ade stood back to let them pass, while Freak smiled at Beast Woman and Beast Woman continued to glower.

'Right. Everybody's friends again. Good.' Ade clapped his hands. Marjorie barged her shoulder into Freak as she left the room. The others drifted off after her until it was just the three of us.

'Freak, see me later for a refresher course on the rules of this place,' Ade said.

Freak shrugged and sucked her teeth. He turned his attention to me.

'Don't worry, it's not usually this exciting. What did you say your name was?'

I'd already told him Aggie but the fight had shocked me and Freak's words from way back in the alley were ringing in my ears. *Don't tell anyone your real name.* I heard myself say, 'Jojo,' and Freak exploded into exaggerated laughter.

'When I said don't tell people your real name, I didn't mean make one up after you've already told them!' she hooted.

Heat and redness prickled up my neck into my face. I managed to stammer out my name.

Freak howled. 'Told you she was fresh.'

I wished the ground would open up and swallow me. Ade looked real pissed and told Freak to can it, she was on her last warning. She shut up. He turned his attention to me.

'Alright. This is how it works. Do you know what a squat is?' I shook my head and he started talking about something called adverse possession. Freak leaned against the kitchen counter and rolled her eyes. I zoned out until I heard him say, 'I'm the boss. That a problem for you?'

'No, sir.'

'Good, but don't me call me sir. Look, I have no problem throwing you out if I have to. This is our home. We treat it with respect. No mess, no thieving. As for our neighbors, we blend in with them. We don't alienate them.'

I looked away from his wannabe dreadlock hair and Freak's mane of pink that made her look like something from *My Little Pony*. I nodded. 'Blend in. Got it.'

'Main rule is: any trouble and you're out on your arse.'

'Arse?' I couldn't help myself, his voice was too weird. Freak started giggling again and he just looked even more pissed and walked out.

'Arse?' I said again, making Freak laugh even more.

'Shut up, he's British. Can't help it. Least he speaks American. Come on, I'll give you the grand tour.'

We were to treat it with respect, but as Freak showed me around it was clear the place was pretty fucked already. All cables and wires had been cut, whether they were hooked up to something or not. Power was limited and came from a generator out back. The windows on the upper floors were covered by silver foil.

'Ade's nervy.' Freak shrugged.

It was a house intended for rich folk. Ceilings so high you could almost fly a kite in there.

I ran my fingers over the smooth wooden handrail and imagined walking down the stairs in a Cinderella gown.

'Hey, daydreamer. Up here.'

I followed Freak up to the final landing.

'You'll be in here with me,' she said. 'It's small, but at least you won't end up sharing with anyone else. Careful coming in. The floorboards aint nailed down.'

I stepped inside. It was tiny. We'd be able to lie down but that was about it. I took two steps over to the high round window. It was still raining outside.

'Take this.' She shoved a sleeping bag at me. 'It was here when I moved in. It might smell.'

'I don't care,' I said, as tears pricked my eyes. 'Thanks.'

Freak grinned. She wrapped her arms around me and gave me a tight hug.

'Come and meet the others,' she said, and vanished again.

I wiped my eyes and followed the sound of her footsteps

back down to a large rectangular room where a small group of people sat around a marble fireplace. Conversation stopped when they saw us. Beast Woman scowled and I turned to go, but Freak grabbed me and pulled me in.

'Everyone, this is Aggie.'

I almost forgot to breathe. I'd never met so many people at once.

'Hey, Aggie.' A black woman with a crazy frizz of hair smiled at me, revealing a gap where her front teeth should have been. 'I'm Tawanna. Sit yourself down, honey, and tell us all about yourself.'

'Or don't,' a guy with a guitar said. 'Tawanna thinks she's a talk show host.'

Tawanna frowned. 'I didn't mean anything by it. You don't have to tell us nothing if you don't want to. But you been living on the street, huh?'

I nodded.

'Come sit here.'

I sat down beside her and she shuffled herself closer to me. She gave me another gummy smile and opened her mouth to speak when the guy with the guitar cut across her.

'Leave her alone, Tawanna.'

'Jeez, Monty. You wanna try being friendly. It won't kill you.'

'I'm friendly enough.' He shrugged. 'But you're too friendly.'

She laughed. 'What can I say? I got love inside. Where you from anyway, Aggie? Stay calm, I'm just teasing,' she said, before Monty could say anything.

She leaned over and bumped her shoulder into mine. It was alright.

Freak had taken up residence beside Ade, who sat on a beat-up sofa with his nose in a book. On the other side of him, Beast Woman swigged from a bottle of Bud, and stared at Freak hard enough to bust her eyeballs.

Tawanna rocked and hummed gently beside me like she

was trying to soothe all her questions to sleep. I concentrated on the fire, trying to ignore the fact that everyone was looking at me, trying to size me up. Monty continued to pick out a tune on his guitar. A long white arm extended itself. I looked beyond it to find its owner, a woman, tall, slim, white. She was older than the others but I couldn't pin an age on her.

'Virginia,' she smiled, and all the lines in her face stretched and deepened. 'Aggie, is it?'

I shook her hand and nodded. She folded herself onto the floor beside me, tucking her orange tie-dye skirt behind her.

'That stuff'll kill you,' she said, as Tawanna lit up a cigarette.

'Yeah, yeah, so you say.'

'You a smoker, Aggie?'

I shook my head.

'Thank God for that.' She leaned in and smiled. 'I need a little back up here. Look at all these cancer dodgers.'

Freak, Ade and Beast Woman were all rolling cigarettes.

'And that there is Brandon.' She nodded at a thick-set guy with brown curls. 'He's a smoker, too. You won't get conversation out of him.'

Brandon nodded at me without smiling.

'I don't mind smoke. Everyone at home's a smoker.'

'Oh, really? Where's home then?' Tawanna asked, shuffling closer.

Monty laughed. 'Down, girl! Let her settle in before starting with the questions.'

'Oh, it aint my fault, honey. I'm just excited to meet someone new. Been hanging around this bunch of jokers too long. Hey, Lloyd, come on over and meet our new girl.'

I looked over my shoulder. Two new guys had arrived. Lloyd was black and turned out to be married to Tawanna, and the other, Ricardo, was Mexican.

'You legal?' The words were out my mouth before I'd even thought of them. Ricardo's brown face turned purple. Tawanna tipped her head back and laughed.

'And you think I'm bad?' she said to Monty.

From the sofa, Ade was frowning at me.

'Sorry,' I said, horrified. 'I didn't mean anything by it.'

In my head it was Pop's voice that said it.

'I don't give a shit. Honest,' I continued.

Ricardo mumbled something and left the room. Tawanna was still laughing, but I caught a glance fly between Monty and Virginia, and Ade still looked unhappy. If I was going to be spending any time with these folks, I'd better sharpen up my people skills.

You heard talk about the Mexicans all the time. We were lucky we lived in the north and not the south. Pop had been to El Paso one time and said they had more Mexicans than roaches in that town.

Back home, the only Mexican I ever met was a guy called Eduardo. Cy got tight with him for a while, more than likely trying to annoy Pop. Eduardo barely spoke a word of American, but somehow he'd got himself a job on a nearby hunting ranch. I didn't see the sense in being friends with someone you couldn't talk to, but Jojo said sometimes that was the best type of friend. Pop was so mean towards Eduardo, it got so he wouldn't set foot on the farm. He'd wait for Cy at the bottom of the track and if Pop was in a good mood, he'd yell from the porch, *Come on up and I'll show you my gun. No need to be scared, you fence-hopping border bandit!*

No need to be scared at all.

One time, after they'd been out together, Cy came back full of excitement. Eduardo's boss had gone on vacation with his family, leaving Eduardo in charge, and Cy, being the good friend he was, had left Eduardo drunk in town, having swiped the keys to the ranch.

Cy wanted it to be a boy thing, just the two brothers and Pop, but Pop said us girls had to go along. Of course, the farm couldn't be left empty so Ash had to stay behind. Just another random way of Pop making himself feel big. Ash accepted it without a word, but me and Jojo didn't want to go, and Cy was mad. But Pop had laid down the law and it must be obeyed. Me and Jojo bundled up together beneath a blanket in the back, Cy sat in pissed-off silence in the passenger seat, while Pop ranted about something or other the whole way there.

Eventually we arrived at a big metal gate and Cy jumped out to open it before we'd even stopped moving. It was pathetic how desperate he was to impress Pop.

This is one of the biggest in the state, Pop. We got deer, hog, birds and bobcats to choose from.

Pop grunted in response and switched on the truck's work lamp. A wide pool of light spilled in front of us, illuminating rows of trees standing guard on either side of a wide track. We trundled through the gates and Cy stayed behind to lock them. He ran to catch us up but Pop took off, going through a stop-start routine of swerving the truck into Cy, and laughing at his panicked attempts to climb back in. Me and Jojo held on tight in the back until eventually he picked a good spot, flicked the light off, and ignored Cy when he finally managed to climb back in. We stared into the blackness and I thought of all the wild animals, all fenced in, all ready to be taken down.

They got any hog candy laid out, boy? Pop asked, after a while.

Naw, Pop. He said the traps are clean.

Pop snorted.

This better not be a waste of my time, boy.

It felt like hours passed before there was a flurry in the undergrowth and we heard a whisper of what sounded like birds taking flight. Cy switched on his headlamp, and he and Pop leaned forward and peered real hard out the window.

There! Cy whispered. *There by the bush.*

Me and Jojo craned our necks to see what he was looking at. Just a few feet away, a dozen or so hog had gathered around an old trap, burrowing the ground for traces of old bait. Pop's door clicked open and his seat creaked as he shifted himself out. He bid us follow him but before me and Jojo had untangled ourselves from the blanket, a shot blasted the night and the air came full of terror and the rush of tiny hooves scattering.

Cy whooped and hollered, his headlamp casting crazy strobe shadows in the undergrowth, as Pop closed in on the injured animal.

Oh yes, Pop! You drilled him! Cy yelled.

Hush, now. It aint finished yet.

He went that way, Cy said. He was tracking blood on the ground. All four of us set off after it. Me and Jojo kept back but a strange kind of fascination took over, and I was eager to see what they had. Fifteen minutes later we found it. A male hog. *A shame*, Pop said, *because the females were tastier.* I shivered. The hog stared right at me with eyes too intelligent for the present company. In my head, I said sorry.

Cy lifted his shotgun for the final shot but Pop put his hand up and pushed the gun down.

Don't waste the bullet, he said.

Cy dropped the rifle straight away but it was clear he was pissed. *Come on*, he whined. *Are you the only one allowed to shoot a gun around here?*

Pop pulled a knife out of his pocket and flipped it open. *We do it this way*, he said, and offered the knife to Cy.

Cy looked at it and shook his head. *Keep it. I got this*. And from his rucksack he pulled out the scariest-looking knife I'd ever seen. Looked to be about seven inches long with a gut hook on the end of a drop-point blade.

Suit yourself, said Pop.

They approached the animal, which had taken shelter beneath a mesquite tree. It pushed up against the trunk, trying to hide but there was nowhere to go when the knives began to fall.

Strike after strike after strike the animal squealed, but not loud enough to disguise the sound of steel stabbing through flesh. Cy's knife looked a lot more effective than it was, or maybe it was the way he used it, back and forth, arm up, arm down, puncturing the skin over and over but never killing it.

Jojo grabbed me by the arm, pulled me back. She picked up the rifle, walked right up to the beast and shot it between the eyes. After the blast, the new silence was louder than anything else we'd heard that night.

What the fuck you do that for? Cy burst out. *I was doing it!* Blood spattered the front of his clothes, little flecks all over his face; he was nearly crying like a child.

Jojo stared at the hog like she didn't know where it had come from or why she might be in a dried-up creek past midnight with a rifle in her hand. Pop took three steps over and took the gun from her. I was frozen to the spot waiting for him to blow up, but instead he grinned like a jackpot winner. He nodded at Cy, who seemed to wither and shrink before him.

Now that, Pop said, eyes gleaming. *That's how you kill a pig.*

I'd spent two nights in the attic room with Freak, and a bucket to catch drips, when the rain finally stopped. It occurred to me that I should be on my way, but Freak frowned and shook her head when I mentioned it.

'Not unless you want to?' she asked.

We were hanging out in the backyard, surrounded by trash, which Freak was arranging into piles.

'What you doing anyway?' I said, avoiding her question.

She rolled her eyes.

'Ade makes us do this. He thinks if we send the trash out wrong, the authorities will use it as an excuse to get a warrant.'

'Huh?'

She suddenly got super focused on a bag of empty cans.

'Nice job, Freak,' called Monty, walking out from the house with Ade, who looked less than impressed. Ade upturned a box of empty cans, scattering them at our feet.

'How many times have I told you? You've got to CRUSH them.' His hair swung along with his arms as he stamped down.

Monty reached out and placed a hand on Ade's arm.

'It's cool, bro. I'll take care of it.'

Ade looked up from between the greasy curtains of his hair. I thought of the time Ash sleepwalked into my room. I hadn't known not to wake him up. Ade had the same look of fear.

Monty nodded and smiled, gently. 'I'll take care of it,' he said again.

Ade frowned, and at last, nodded. 'Reuse everything. The less we throw out the less we need to bring in.'

'Sure, Ade. Sure.'

'The less we bring in the harder it is for Them.'

'Sure, Ade. I understand. Come on.'

Monty slipped his arm around Ade's shoulder and walked him back to the house, while I helped Freak pick up the cans and plastic bottles.

'Ade can be a little intense from time to time,' Monty said to me, when he came back.

'Aint that the truth,' replied Freak. 'He needs to chill the fuck out.'

'What's his problem?' I asked. I'd seen a lot of crazy in my time on the road, but this was a whole new level.

Monty took the box from Freak and began flattening the trash beneath feet so big they could have been made especially for it.

'Ade's okay,' he said. 'He just gets a little anxious about the times we live in, that's all. We all got a common enemy, you see.'

'Shit. Who?' I asked, and they laughed at me.

'He means the government. He aint being serious though, are you, Monty?' Freak threw another can over, which he caught with one hand. His hands were big, too.

'That's why we aint allowed cells or computers,' Freak

continued. 'Cameras, bugs. That sort of thing. Nobody listens to him.'

'Not us, not the CIA, not nobody. Easiest thing is not to get into it with him,' said Monty, and passed me a can which I stamped down on.

I'd heard of the government being our enemy before. Pop hated those bastards. Went on about it a lot. He was no fan of technology either, and I wondered if he'd like it here, but as Monty wiggled a finger through the quarter-sized hole stretched into his earlobe, and Freak squealed, and I giggled, I reckoned he probably wouldn't feel quite as at home as I was beginning to.

10

When I was a child, I had a lot of bad dreams. When I woke up, Jojo was always there. I'd sit up and cry in her arms and she'd hush me by kissing my cheeks and stroking my hair. She'd ask me what was wrong but I could never find it in me to tell her. I didn't want it out in the real world. And what to say anyway? Truth was my dreams were nothing. No monsters, no big bogeyman. Just dark.

And fear.

Fear of what, I didn't know, but it sank inside and made like it would never leave. This was way before any of that shit started on me but I know now it was happening. Had always happened in that sub little family of mine.

I woke up so many times crying, eventually Jojo put a lock on my door. Told me only I could open and close it. It meant she couldn't sneak in at night the way she used to. Meant we couldn't cuddle anymore. One night after I bolted it, my dreams changed. It wasn't me in the dark, it was Jojo. And I'd locked her in there myself. I never used the bolt after that.

Freak was sitting on top of me, squeezing my breath out and shaking me like I was pancake mix. I struggled and she rolled off but kept her face right close.

'You okay?'

I sat up, nodded, tried to get my bearings.

'You were crying.'

I looked around, took in the bare walls, the wooden

floorboards. It was our room. Just our room.

From the darkness in the hallway, an unwelcome voice sniggered.

'Freak's got a freak for a friend. Figures.'

'Fuck off, Marjorie,' Freak said, and Beast Woman cackled her way down the stairs.

'Did you unlock the door?' I asked.

Freak shook her head. 'Naw, it was like that. What were you dreaming, Aggie? Tell me. I love scary stories.'

I got up and shut the door, sure I'd locked it earlier. I slid the bolt in place and rattled it to make sure.

'Nothing. Didn't dream nothing.'

Freak snuggled back down.

'Must have been good, whatever it was. Crying like that? You sounded like a little kitty cat.'

I slipped back inside the stinky old sleeping bag Freak had dug out for me. She was asleep in seconds. It was a talent she had.

The moon wormed its way through the clouds and shone bright outside the window, bleaching out her crazy pink hair. She looked softer when she was sleeping.

I lay on my back and counted the cracks in the ceiling. There were more than ought to be for such a new house. When that was done, I rolled over and counted the webs in the window. A dried out fly dangled and spun. Guess some spider forgot about him. Such a sad thing to die for nothing.

Freak taught me a lot about the city. We didn't much like being criminals, but once you realize that some people are so stock-stupid they're just asking to be robbed, and especially when your belly's rumbling, it's not always easy to be a good girl. Freak taught me there's satisfaction in teaching people the error of their ways. Everybody knows you don't put your wallet in your back pocket but still they do it. And you shouldn't leave your bag sat there, wide open. After a while, it got too easy and we started doing stuff just for fun. We'd go into Starbucks or some such place and mosey around the counter, waiting for someone's coffee to be made. When it landed on the counter, and if the waitress was too busy to be paying attention, we'd take that double-shot, skinny, piece-of-shit drink with sprinkles for ourselves. If they objected, one of us would politely inform them they must be mistaken as we'd been in the queue in front of them. We always backed each other up. They just accepted what we said. I have no idea how long most of them stood waiting for some coffee that was never going to come. Sometimes we drank the coffee, but sometimes we just put it straight in the trash. A person has to find their amusement somehow.

'You're getting good at this shit,' she said, one day.

I'd never considered myself bad at it, but I took the compliment anyway.

'Reckon you're maybe ready for something bigger. We get you shopping in the department stores, I can set you up with someone to sell it to. If you wanna make some money. Regular money, that is. You can't always depend on a fool leaving their purse open just because you're hungry.'

I turned the idea over and over. Stealing from a store wasn't like taking a man's wallet. No amount of pretty tears would stop them calling the cops if they caught you.

'No pressure,' Freak said, 'but the guy I use is sweet. His name's Duke. Looks after me real good. He's got a lot of sympathy for street girls.'

Is that what I was? A street girl? Freak read my mind.

'Hell, Aggie. We can't stay at Ade's forever.'

Her words struck home. I suddenly worried I might be overstaying my welcome, so I offered to wash everyone's clothes. Ade was the only one who didn't take me up on it, which was annoying because he was the only one who counted. I washed everything in two big basins in the back, one for scrubbing, one for rinsing. I was happy because I'd got a stain out of Freak's cream top and I knew she'd be pleased with that. I laid everything over chairs and crates and waited for it to dry. There was a bare patch of earth alongside one wall. Too small to be useful, I made a mental note to ask Ade if I could plant a climber there. It could look real pretty, I thought, as I folded the dry clothing.

As I entered the hallway with the pile of laundry, the dimness made me temporarily blind. I stood for a second to let my eyes recover and heard a strange shuffly type of noise. I glanced across the wall the staircase ran along. Whatever the noise was, it came from the understairs closet. I placed my ear against the wooden door. The air smelled of paint.

Steadying my bundle with one hand beneath and my chin on top, I raised my fist to knock, but the door suddenly swung outwards, bashing my head and causing me to drop the clean clothes all over the floor.

'Jesus, you scared me.'

It was Tawanna, her eyes and nose puffy from crying. She knelt to help me gather everything up. I was flustered, like I'd been caught doing something I shouldn't.

'Sorry,' I said. 'I thought I heard something.'

'You did. Me.'

She folded a pair of Freak's jeans and placed them on top of my pile.

I glanced over her shoulder into the cupboard.

'Uh, what's the attraction?' I asked.

Her eyes grew wide and she did a little laugh of disbelief.

'Aint no one told you about this yet?'

'Nuh-uh,' I shook my head.

Before I could object, she grabbed the laundry from me and pushed me in. It was empty apart from an old towel and a can of paint with a brush lying across the top.

'This is where we let go,' she said, whispering like we were in church. 'Look closer.'

I walked into the center and up to one of the three and a half walls until I almost touched it with my nose. The paint fumes were strong enough to make my eyes water. Beneath the fresh white paint, I made out a faint scrawl of writing.

'It's like a house rule. Whatever's bugging you, you put it on there. Just get it all out. It was Virginia's idea. She wanted a whole room but Ade gave her this cupboard instead. Makes no difference, we'll never run out of space. You just write and write whatever the fuck you want. Nobody's gonna judge you, cos when you're done, when you've got it all out, you just pick up the brush and paint it all out. See? Easy.'

Now I saw it. All over the walls, beneath the whiteness, lines and lines of anger and hurt and sadness. I counted at least three different styles of handwriting.

'Does everyone come in here?'

'Mostly, at some point.'

Which was Freak's?

'But anyway,' she said, 'that there wall is wet so if you wanna use it you gotta wait. Or use that smaller side there.'

I looked at the clean white wall.

'Aint got nothing to say,' I said, as I grabbed the laundry and pushed past her.

The dreams kept coming. Jojo always. A desert with no rocks or plants, just bright yellow sand, stretching as far as the eye can see. Fenced in by sky, we're like tiny figures in a giant snow globe.

Except if you shake us you get sand instead of snow.

'Take my hand,' I offer. 'Walk with me.'

I can't, Aggie. You know I can't.

She pulls at a thick rope that I now see is knotted around her waist. I look along the length of it – it seems to take forever – and of course there's Pop holding the other end. He's so far away yet I can make out everything about him: ice-blue eyes, white wiry hair, his tobacco-stained teeth, the deep burn of sun on his skin.

He binds the rope around his fist and begins to draw her in.

Aggie.

No, Jojo.

Aggie.

No.

'Aggie, wake up.'

And I realize I'm in two places at once and I have to choose where to be.

'Wake up, Aggie,' says Freak, and I fight to find her. I'm not in the desert any more. I'm in my room, the door is in front of me, my hand is on the bolt.

I blink the last of the dream away.

'Jesus, Aggie. That was some creepy-assed shit.'

'What the fuck just happened?' I asked her, clutching the bolt, grappling with the fact that only seconds before it had been so purely, so completely, Jojo's hand.

'You were sleepwalking,' said Freak. 'You were doing your kitty cat thing again and then you just got straight up and opened the door, fucking weirdo. You should have told me you did that. Coulda put a bell around you for safety.'

A noise in the hallway made me look up in time to see Beast Woman coming towards me. I slammed the door and pulled the bolt just in time. With my back against the door, I shuddered with every thump she gave on the other side.

'Get your ass out here, Freak-face,' she demanded.

Freak had moved as far away from the door as it was possible to do in that small space. First time I ever saw her scared. Finally, it got quiet. There was nothing to do but climb back inside our sleeping bags.

'What's her problem with you, anyway?' I asked.

'Aint you figured it out yet?' she sniggered.

'She still mad you took her money?'

She shrugged. 'More likely she just don't like the way Ade looks at me.'

'Are they going together?'

'Naw, but I reckon she'd like to. Aint you seen the way he looks at me?' she smiled. I shook my head, aware my heart had picked up pace.

'Do you like him?' I asked.

95

'Maybe. Not sure if he's worth it. She's a stupid bitch, though. Might just do him to piss her off.'

'Stupid Beast Woman,' I said. We snickered like children, which, after all, is what we were, and we didn't talk about Marjorie any more that night.

'Aggie?'

We were facing each other so I didn't need do more than raise my eyebrows to answer.

'What happens to you in the night?'

'I don't know.' So quiet I hardly heard myself.

'Is it like… monsters, or something?'

Had to give that one some thought.

'Something like that.' And then I changed my mind. 'It's my sister but she aint no monster. I don't know why she comes to me like she does.'

'Huh,' said Freak, surprised. 'You never said you'd a sister. Where is she?'

I faked a yawn and turned over to face the wall but she didn't take the hint.

'If I'd a little sister, I don't think I'd ever leave her.'

She probably said it on purpose and it worked. I rolled over in a flash and it rushed out of me. 'She aint my little sister, alright? She's my older sister and she's big enough to take care of herself.' I smashed my fist down on the rickety floorboards. 'She's damn near enough thirty and aint nothing in the world she needs from me, alright? Aint nothing in this whole wide world that I can do for her. Shut up about it, just shut up!'

Freak sat up, eyes wide, hands raised in defense.

'Jesus, Aggie, sorry. I didn't mean anything by it.'

I hunkered back down but I was wired. I sensed Freak was still sitting up, waiting for me to talk some more. Eventually she gave in, just like I knew she would.

'What's her name, Aggie?'

Jo-Jo-Jo-Josephine Jones.

'Jojo, huh? That's a pretty cool name.'

Hadn't realized I'd said it out loud. Confused wasn't the word. And then for some reason, I suddenly became hyper aware of the tiny little room we were in. A crack I'd been studying for weeks had spread across the ceiling and was making its way down the wall. Everything was all a dusky shade of blue apart from Freak's pink hair and her face which, peeking out the top of her sleeping bag, looked like a little moon.

'You look like an alien.' We giggled, though nothing was funny.

And then I told her my story. Parts of my story. Some parts I left out.

After I finished, she was quiet for a time. And then she said, 'Where was your momma?' and I told her about Momma being a whore who had skipped town.

'I used to think she'd run off with pirates.' I grinned, and next thing I was telling her about when I was little and Jojo used to put me to bed with a stubby scented candle tucked under my pillow. *Tropical Seabreeze*, she'd called it. Once upon a time that candle smelled of something good but it had long gone. Still, Jojo always wanted to know that I could smell it, and I'd nod, even though there was nothing there, and she'd seem satisfied and say that's where Momma's gone. Living on the high seas, Momma was gonna get rich and then she'd be back for us all. Such a gleam in her eye right then. Told her I believed it as well. I smiled, trying to cover up that familiar emptiness. She'd smile and curl into me, and hold my hand, stroking my hair over and over till finally, behind the raggy curtain, the sun was gone and I was in the land of sleep.

For the first time, I noticed something wrong with this story. It was Freak who said it.

'How come your momma's so precious if she was such a whore?'

I had no answer. The ceiling crack was going down the other wall too, I noticed.

'Guess you were lucky you had such a big older sister. Guess she was like your momma, huh?'

My words were stuck. There was something inside me and I didn't know what. Far off I heard the cry of gulls, birds I'd seen so rarely on the farm, but had dreamed of my whole childhood.

Freak rolled over and fell asleep. Just like that. I was surprised with how open I'd been. Wasn't like I trusted Freak all that much. I'd kept what little money I had tucked away in my bra. And I'd forgotten all about that memory with the candle, hadn't thought of it in years, it just rose up from nowhere. Wonder if Momma really had made it back to the ocean? Jojo and Ash seemed convinced of it. We'd spend long hours in *Jack King*, them swapping stories about Momma while I acted interested, but all the while quietly bored with my lack of memory.

Freak's breathing came slow and rhythmic, like waves on the shore. I settled down beside her, but spent the whole night wide awake, trying to remember my momma. Try as I might, it was only Jojo's face I saw. Just the way it had always been.

She wanted me to put on her Sunday dress. It had hung at the back of the closet all these years, waiting for the time it would fit me.

But Jojo, we don't go to church no more.

She kneeled before me and tried to pull my T-shirt up. I kept my arms rigid.

Don't you want to look pretty? she said.

I want to look like you, I sulked. *I aint never seen you in such a dress.*

Well, that's cos I'm grown now. But this was mine when I was your age. Little girls should look pretty sometimes. It's fun. Come on, just try it. It'll only take a minute.

I let her pull my T-shirt over my head and I wiggled my arms through the holes.

Don't like it. It scratches.

Oh hush now. And look here, these are the shoes I wore.
See if they fit.

She pulled my foot onto her thigh and slipped the navy blue Mary Janes over my bare feet. She spun me round to zip up the back and I caught sight of myself in the mirror and gasped. Jojo rested her chin on my shoulder and grinned at my reflection.

Now, child, aint you a thing sweeter than stolen honey?

I spent many a fine afternoon preening, sashaying and twirling for Jojo. The way she laughed made me enjoy it almost as much as she did.

Aside from doing everyone's laundry, I also took to working in the garden. Back home at this time of year the ground would be thick with snow, but here it still gave up salad and carrots, kale and potatoes. The builders hadn't got around to putting down lawn so it was just soil. Almost the entire backyard had been given over to growing food. I made soup for everyone, just the way Jojo showed me. It wasn't the same as hers, something missing, but it was good enough, and people tolerated me. Most people, anyway.

One day Marjorie found me picking zucchini in the garden. She made out like she'd just been passing but I was right in the furthest back corner and there was no place for her to pass to. The day was pulling in and the sun was about to disappear behind the house.

'Smoke?' She smiled as she offered. When Marjorie smiled, it was just plain weird. Made me think of crocodiles. I shook my head, squinting with the last of the sun in my eyes. She lit up and took a draw. Through the sun and smoke I saw straight up the sleeve of her T-shirt. The tattooed snake twisted around her arm, up to her shoulder, and disappeared down her back. No saying where it stopped. I got a shiver and carried on digging, trying to ignore the smoke as it blew in my face.

'What's your story, little freak-friend?' She'd called me

this ever since that first night. Freak said it was because she felt threatened by us. It didn't bother me, because privately I still thought of her as Beast Woman.

'How come you've made friends with such a freaky little whore?' she wanted to know. 'Can't be good for you.'

I stopped digging and looked at her. Four of me could probably fit into one of her. She reminded me of one of Cy's bulls and I didn't like my chances if it came right down to it. Her eyes never left mine as she flicked some ash in where the kale and carrots were growing.

'Don't mind if I do that, do you?' It wasn't a real question. I shrugged.

'Good for compost.' I'd dug plenty back home and knew my way round a vegetable patch.

'You like it here?' she asked.

'Some, I guess. It beats the street,' I added quickly, in case her plan was to get me to leave.

'Guess it does. Where's your little freak-friend gone then?' She spat on the ground.

'I aint her keeper.'

'You'd do well to make new friends, Aggie.' Her cold eyes cut through the gray smoke. 'I'm being nice now and warning you, alright? I'd worry for you if you keep on keeping bad company. Don't you say you didn't get no warning, that's all.'

She ground the butt beneath her heel and flicked it into the soil.

'Ade don't like trouble,' I said. 'He'll throw you out if you touch a hair on her head.'

She got right up close to me, nose to nose. Marjorie's breath was fouler than a dog's. I tried to stare her out but eventually I had to breathe so I turned my head away. I think she took it for weakness.

'Ade aint throwing me anywhere, freak-friend. But I want Freak gone and I want you to tell her. She's bad news. I'd hate for you to get caught up in the crossfire.'

As she walked away, I asked myself if she was right. I

pushed the thought away as soon as it arrived. I wasn't in the business of being disloyal to my friends. Besides, if Freak was bad company, I must be, too.

It was a week before Christmas and Freak said it was time I left the house. I'd holed up in there living off carrots from the garden for so long she said I was in danger of not only going soft but also turning orange. I was sitting up at night to avoid any more sleepwalking; it always sparked an avalanche of questions. As a result, I had that kind of heavy tired that just sits inside, the kind where you'll do just about anything anyone says and agree with anybody over anything. So when Freak took me shoplifting, I couldn't find it in me to resist.

We hopped the bus uptown, wearing clean clothes and looking just like two regular girls. Freak's hair was the only thing that made us stand out, and she'd tucked most of it away beneath a cowboy hat. A little boy in front of us stood on his momma's lap and I played peekaboo with him till they got off. Looking out the window, everything was so pretty. People had gone to town on decorations, flashing lights everywhere. Block after block all you saw were giant nativity scenes, donkeys and everything, spread over roofs, windows, parks and gardens.

The mall had a tree taller than four buses. So many shiny sparkles on it, you could have gone blind from looking too long. Shoppers busied in and out of stores like elves, carrying more bags than Santa on Christmas Eve. I'd never seen anything like it. Back home, we'd pulled out the same plastic tree we'd had my whole life. By the time I was six, I was bigger than the tree. Santa paid us a visit till I was seven years old and then he stopped. The only presents in that house were between me and Jojo.

The first store we went to, Freak steered me towards the make-up counter and made me sit down on a stool. It was right by the escalator and I felt a fool as I let her paint my face in different colors while crowds of people stared down at me. The assistant lady came over looking like she wanted to give us trouble but when Freak told her we didn't need any help she backed off quicker than a bear from a hornets' nest. Guess it was just the way she said it. When she was done, she let me look in the mirror. It wasn't too bad in the end. I was expecting something clownish but there was a pretty golden glow slicked across my eyelids, and a shimmery kind of peach on my lips. I wouldn't go so far as to say I liked it, but it was different. Maybe felt a little like fun.

'You should get yourself some of this, Aggie.' Freak was dabbing something else on my cheeks. 'Makes you look older.' And it did. I figured that might not be such a bad thing, all things considered. I checked the price tag. The expense made me mad. It deserved to be stolen. A quick glance told me the assistant was occupied with an older woman who was having trouble deciding between two face creams. It found its way to my pocket.

'And you should definitely get some of this.'

Freak breezed her way round the counters like a millionaire, picking stuff up, trying it, putting it back or keeping it, and the whole time just chatting away. I could practically see her halo.

Sixty minutes later we were back on the street, our pockets and bags full as they could get without giving us away. Freak had shown me a neat trick. You go to the returns desk saying you've seen something in store that you want but the right size isn't there – so would it be okay to look here? The stuff on the returns rail has already been taken home by somebody so the security tags are off. If you see something in your size you can just slip it in your bag. I took a pair of jeans and she got a dress, as well as some random stuff we were going to sell to her contact, Duke. We giggled on the bus ride home and I joked we were rich enough to have fried chicken every night, but she didn't get it and I felt like a hick. Seeing my blush, she took my hand, which only made me blush more.

'You know that pink dress?' she said. 'I was gonna keep it, but you can have it.'

'How come?' I asked.

She shrugged and squeezed my hand. 'Changed my mind about it, is all.'

I figured it was because it didn't have sleeves. She'd learned stuff about me from us sharing a room but she didn't know yet it worked both ways. She carried a penknife with her which she said was for protection but I knew it was for something else. All those nights I didn't sleep there was no one and nothing to be looking at but her, and it got me to thinking about Jojo, the way that knife twirled round her palm, the way she dug her nails into her skin, the way a trail of red half-moons sometimes travelled up her arm, the way her fingernails got dark with dried blood.

One night when Freak was asleep, I took the knife and did myself. I wanted to know what it was like, wanted to feel the escape. The edge of the blade was sharper than any tool hanging on the barn wall back home. I liked the way my flesh bulged on each side of the blade when I laid it flat on me. I wasn't sure I could do it. When it split my skin, it was almost an accident. And then I pressed just a little bit deeper and drew the blade toward me.

My blood spilled out, warm and tickly as it circled beneath my arm and dripped onto the floorboards at my feet. For a split second I was back home on the farm, a small girl beneath the kitchen table, watching the bloody juices from meat above drip down to the floor just a few inches away. Then the place where I'd cut began to throb and I realized I had to find a tissue. I cleaned the blade off and tucked the knife back into Freak's bag. I was done with it.

The bus hit a pothole and we grabbed each other to keep from falling.

'Remember that guy I told you about?' Freak said, when we'd settled ourselves back down.

'What guy?'

'The one I run my shopping through. Duke. He'd be happy to meet you, I reckon. Could be good business for both of you.'

'Last time I did business with a guy it didn't go too well.'

'Will you think about it? Please? For me?'

That smile again.

'Sure, Freak.'

We jumped off the bus, my hand still in hers, laughing at some stupid thing or other until we rounded the corner and Freak stopped.

'S'up?' I said.

'You go in first. Make sure the Beast's not there.'

The coast was clear and we raced up the stairs and locked the door behind us.

'Okay, try the dress,' she said, shoving it at me.

'Now?' There was nowhere to hide, no screen or even a wardrobe door I could stand behind.

'Silly,' she said. 'I seen it all before. Just do it.'

I turned away from her and pulled my top over my head. I could feel her eyes like hot lasers on my skin. By the time I slipped the dress over my jeans, and shimmied my jeans down my legs, my face was on fire.

'What you so shy for, Aggie? You got a good body.'

She walked around me, pulling the dress straight where it rode up on my hip.

Not to sound ungrateful but I wouldn't have chosen it. It was pink and strappy with a scoop neck and stopped half way down my thigh. Slutty.

'When d'you do that?' She lifted my arm and ran her finger over my cut. The perfume she'd sprayed on in the store floated beneath my nose. I could almost taste it.

'It was an accident, is all.'

The heat and her scent made me dizzy. She dropped my arm and pulled up her sleeve. It was worse in daylight. Random slashes going all the way up, bright red lines that could almost be pen marks, and others that were ugly and bumpy where the skin had burst and fixed itself unevenly.

'Freak… ' My hands flew to touch her but stopped just short.

From her back pocket she took her knife and flicked it open.

'Give me your arm.' She said it soft but it was a command. Confused, I shook my head no. My arm raised itself anyway. Her fingers wrapped around me and when she cut, she did it quick. She squeezed the flesh and it came thick and fast and right. Then she did herself, finding a last tiny patch of perfect to destroy.

She took my hand and led me, shaking, to the floor. We knelt facing each other, the knife forgotten now, and our blood pooling and mixing as it dripped to the wood.

'Sisters now,' she said.

She stared so hard at me.

'I never had a sister with blue eyes before.'

'Well, sweet girl, you do now.'

She wrapped her arm around me and we curled up together like spoons. Her hair slipped over my shoulder like it was my own. I slept the deepest sleep, but when I woke up in the morning, she'd gone.

Her absence was a real thing I could feel and touch and look at. I lay with my cut arm reaching into her empty space until I was angry with her. Anger was an emotion I could deal with. I made my way to the kitchen, hoping to find her, but there was only Monty and Virginia, fresh from their weird dance ritual in the yard.

'I'm making coffee. Want some?' Virginia asked. I nodded and said thanks. Virginia gasped as I spooned eight sugars into my cup.

'She's young. She can take it,' Monty said.

'It'll catch up with you,' Virginia frowned at me. 'You don't think so now. What age are you? Sixteen? Seventeen?'

'Ask no questions, she'll tell you no lies,' Monty butted in, and I was glad.

Virginia moved her hand protectively over her flat belly. 'Whatever,' she said. 'You'll regret it when you're forty.'

'Ginny, are you so old you've forgotten you can't talk to teenagers about forty?' Monty teased. He picked up his guitar and began singing something folky about being 'forever young'.

Their voices were annoying, and sounded like they were coming through water. My arm hurt from Freak's cut. I lay my hand across it and felt her heat still there.

Virginia took my hand and started to sway with me, right there in the kitchen. I wriggled my way out of her reach.

'I aint much of a dancer,' I said, and backed off into the corner until the music came to an end and Virginia stopped moving.

'Anyone seen Freak?' I asked, in the awkward silence that followed their performance, though maybe it was only me feeling awkward. Monty and Virginia exchanged a look. I was liking them less with every passing second.

'What?' I asked.

'Always somebody looking for Freak, that's all,' said Monty.

'Is everything okay, sweetie?' Virginia wanted to know.

'Yeah, it's fine. I know she likes to take off. I was just asking, is all.'

Virginia poured herself and Monty more coffee. I'd barely touched mine.

'She does this, Aggie. You'll get used to it.'

Monty did a gruff little laugh. 'Yeah, she always turns up again. Like a bad penny.'

'Oh, hush now,' she said. He shrugged and hid his face

behind his coffee mug.

Yeah. I was liking them less and less.

She came back that night, as it happened.

'I brought you a present,' she said, looking so shining pleased with herself, it was impossible to stay angry. 'Close your eyes and put your hands out.'

Something cool and waxy rolled in the palm of my hand. I opened my eyes and looked down to find a pale blue candle. Its label said *Tropical Seabreeze*.

'Smell it,' Freak urged. 'Is it the same?'

I cradled the candle beneath my nose and sniffed. My heart sank – it was nothing familiar. For once it would have been nice to tell the truth.

'Wow. It's exactly the same.'

She glowed with the compliment. Guilt niggled me.

'It's just about the nicest thing anyone's ever got me,' I told her, which was true. 'But you don't have to give me stuff.'

'I know that, dummy,' she said. She smoothed a flyaway piece of hair from my face. Her fingers were light as she tucked it behind my ear. 'But we're sisters now. I can give you stuff and you have to take it. It didn't cost me nothing, anyway.'

'I worried about you when you weren't there this morning,' I confessed.

'Why? You my keeper, all of a sudden?'

The sudden harshness in her voice shocked me.

'No,' I whispered. 'Of course not.'

She softened and touched my hair again.

'Shit, Aggie. Don't be sad.'

'Where you been?' I asked, sounding pathetic.

She sighed, like her patience was wearing thin, and when she spoke, her voice was tight.

'Don't matter where I go, what I do, does it? Long as I come back.'

She had me pinned in her stare. If I turned my head, it was like her eyes controlled it.

'I guess,' I said.

She reached into her bag and pulled out the tiny penknife.

'I'm ready for this,' said Freak. 'Are you?'

Jojo's knife had a pink handle too. How about that?

'I said are you ready?'

Freak's eyes flicked down to my arm and then up again to catch me in that stare of hers. I found myself nodding in agreement.

12.

Christmas came and went. Ade got us all making paper chains. Some of us liked it better than others. I swear we could have swung to the moon and back on those chains. When it was time to take them down, Ade made us sit and cut the sticky ends off so all the paper could go to compost. There were plenty of grumbles about that and I figured that next year people wouldn't be so keen to make miles and miles of paper chains.

Freak kept on with her disappearing acts. I felt like a car without an engine whenever she was gone for more than a day. She'd come back, sometimes with stuff to sell, sometimes not. The presents stopped after that first time, but I was always so pleased to see her, I didn't even notice.

I could tell by looking whether or not she needed to cut. It got so that I hoped she would – not that I ever came to like it, but because it made her happy after. She was good at it. She always chose a place no one would see, like my inside thigh or high up my inside arm, and she never did them as big on me as they were on her. Sometimes she watched the blood come out and sometimes she watched my face.

'Does it hurt?' she'd ask. She'd squeeze hard to make the blood come faster. I closed my eyes tight and felt her strong grip, her nails digging in.

'Yes,' I'd gasp, and she'd let go. She always said thank you after, that she felt better now. As the cuts started to wind their way down my arm, I took to wearing Freak's long-sleeved tops.

'You gonna get your own clothes any time soon?' she said one day.

I had one arm and my head halfway through a yellow sweater.

'You want me to take this off?'

'Not now. You're practically wearing it already.'

I put my other arm through and pulled it down.

'I mean,' she continued, 'you're welcome, and all. But they'll wear out quicker if we're both wearing them, know what I mean? You should go shopping this week.'

'Sure. What day should we go?'

'Jesus. I aint your babysitter, Aggie.'

She was right, but her words still hurt me. Everything I'd done since meeting Freak, I'd done with her. It was part of the reason I was so lost without her when she vanished for days at a time. I tended to lay low until she got back. Having a roof over my head had made me soft.

'Anyway, if we split up,' she continued, 'we'll make a bigger haul. I'll introduce you to Duke, and you can start making money.'

Money. The word gave me a thrill. Maybe that was all the motivation I needed.

'Go to his bar downtown,' she continued. 'You'll be okay as long as you don't try to screw him over. One time, this girl I know tried to pass off a silver chain as platinum. He cut her fingers off.'

'Shit.'

'Don't be stupid. No, he didn't. Jesus, you're so easy to kid.'

'I'd never do that anyway,' I said.

'I know you wouldn't. That's why I'm letting you meet him. He can be a little… out there. Don't let that put you off. He's basically harmless.'

Basically harmless. The words rolled round and around my head until Friday came and I was due to meet him. I'd shopped what I thought was a decent amount of stuff, and

111

Freak had added a couple of her things to bulk it out.

I was just about to leave when my bag burst open. I bent to repack my merchandise, and when I stood upright, my face just about banged into Marjorie's boobs.

'Jesus, Marjorie. I didn't see you.'

She smelled of cigarette smoke as usual but she seemed different. Kind of mussed up.

'Where's Freak?' She put her arm across the door to block my way.

'I don't know. She don't tell me where she goes.'

'Tell her I want her gone for good, alright? Tell her that and maybe I'll let you stay.'

'It aint up to you, Marjorie. Why you want her gone anyway? You hardly see her. She's never here.'

Marjorie pushed her face right into mine. There was a faint smell from her mouth, a man smell, the like of which I was too young to know but wasn't likely to ever forget. Feeling suddenly sick, I covered my nose with my hand as she growled, 'Don't matter the reason, freak-friend. Just do it.'

The door to the kitchen swung open and Ade came out. He seemed kind of startled when he saw us but he gave me a nod as he passed. Marjorie followed him up the stairs and they both disappeared into his room. Marjorie and Ade. No way. Wait till I told Freak. I pushed the sickness back and ran to catch the bus, smug with new knowledge.

The ride downtown was different to the uptown one. Quieter on the weekend. I clutched my little bundle of goods for sale and thought surely I'd be better off going uptown where all the money was, but Freak wasn't likely to be wrong.

The bar was exactly as she'd described it. It sat next to a supermart across the road from a row of empty garages. I pressed the yellow buzzer for the driver to let me off and walked the hundred yards back. Sadie's Place had big green letters lit up on its roof. Some of them were broken so it looked like it was called Sad Place. If I were Sadie, whoever she was, I'd be pretty pissed with that. Couldn't have been that the P and the L were broke. Sadie's ace would have just been too happy for that part of town.

I'd never been in a proper bar before. A bell above the door jangled my nerves as I entered but no one looked up. It was a dingy little place, pretty empty but it was early yet. A woman behind the counter rubbed glasses with a dish cloth, and a guy with razor cheekbones and a slick white ponytail was sitting at the end of the bar holding a book. His nails were long as claws and painted a pretty sapphire blue. It looked weird on a guy, but I didn't think it could be classed as totally 'out there' like Freak said. Maybe he wasn't my guy.

I sat at the bar, ordered a coke and wondered how I was going to do this. In the end, I didn't have to. Blue Claw Man looked over the top of his book and raised an eyebrow at me. I almost choked on my drink. His eyes were red, like the devil.

Colored contacts, stupid, I told myself.

Was I Freak's friend, he asked.

I managed to nod, and he put the book down – *Meditative Weightlifting*. He slid from his stool and came over. That's when I noticed he was wearing a fucking dress. He took my bag, pulled it open and rifled through it. A silver charm bracelet swung on his wrist.

'This it?' he said.

'There's a dress in there retails for ninety dollars, mister. Brand new, never been worn. Some jeans too. Retail says they're a hundred and fifty bucks. Got tags on and everything. There's other bits too. Freak put some earrings in, mister. It's a hundred dollars all in and that's cheap.'

He looked at me like I'd asked to shit in his bed.

'A hundred dollars?' he called to the woman behind the bar. She smirked and turned away. 'A hundred dollars? What am I, a charity or something?'

He went back to the bag and pulled out a long silk scarf. He held it to his face and closed his eyes while he stroked the tassels. 'Mmm, soft,' he said, in a creepy little girl voice. He shoved it back in the bag. 'That's the only decent thing in there,' he told me. Then he opened a little purse hanging around his neck and counted out some bills. 'A hundred dollars, she says. I tell you what, sweetheart, don't piss in my ear and tell me it's raining.' He threw the cash onto the bar. I picked it up. Forty-five bucks. I didn't know how to argue. He tossed the bag over his shoulder and made to walk off. His hips rolled like a lady's and that gave me courage.

'Bag aint included, mister,' I said.

He spun round on his heel, holding my mangy rucksack away from his body like it might give him cooties.

'This?' he sneered. 'You want this?'

It was old and dirty and coming apart at the seams. 'Yeah, mister. It aint the nicest, but it's mine.'

He sashayed back, turned the bag upside down over the bar and pulled the stuff out. He held it between his forefinger and thumb and dangled it in front of me, tilting his head back, as though a bad smell floated beneath his nose. I made to take it but he didn't let go.

'Where's Freak?' he asked.

I pulled the bag from him. 'I don't know. Busy.'

'Oh yeah?' he sneered. He reached behind the bar and squeezed some hand gel into his palm. 'Too busy for Duke,' he said, tossing his head and rubbing his hands together. 'Sad times. What about you? You too busy for Duke, too?'

He fixed me with a stare. I was so busy wondering if there were real eyes behind his contacts that I forgot to answer.

'Forget it,' he said. 'Just... tell her she's missed, okay?' He took another ten out of his purse and gave it to me. For a second I thought I saw a glistening in his fake eyes, but he turned away before I could be sure.

Back at the house, I dropped my precious bag at the bottom of the stairs and went to the kitchen for some water. There was no one around which was just how I liked it. I slurped water from the faucet instead of using a cup, and I took a slice of bread from an unmarked loaf in the cupboard. Their own fault for not putting a name sticker on it. A *National Enquirer* was lying on the breakfast bar. I was reading about aliens and plastic surgery when I heard something from upstairs, something not normal.

I don't know what it was, some instinct that told me to arm myself. I'd lost all notions about getting a gun after landing my pizza job, but once again I found myself wishing I had one. I slipped into the nearest room and grabbed Ricardo's baseball bat.

As I made my way up the stairs, it became clearer that someone was being hurt. By the time I got to the top, I knew it was Freak. I knew it was Freak because she sounded like a child.

All the doors in the hallway seemed to disappear, apart from one which grew bigger than any normal door. I pressed my ear up against it and heard the crying; the safe, heavy weight of the baseball bat in my hand focused my anger.

Slowly, gently, I pushed the door open.

Up and down, up and down it went; trembling skin like plucked chicken. Jojo's voice like a little girl's beneath the weight of him. Freak's hair, spread like a fan across the bed.

She turned her head and saw me. Her face was twisted in pain, her eyes glazed.

The bat was in my hand. A far-off voice was screaming. I'd turn him into a bug beneath my shoe.

And I swung the bat.

When I finished, I turned round.

'Are you alright?' I asked.

'What the fuck, Aggie?'

I tried to grab her but she shook me off.

'What the fuck have you done?'

She fell to her knees and cradled the lump on the floor. She looked like she was crying, but all I could hear was my own ragged breath, and the rush of water between my ears. If she didn't come now, there was nothing I could do for her.

She wiped his hair back from his face and kissed him.

Everything came into clear, cruel focus.

She'd wanted it.

I look down at Not Pop, this not-monster, not-sub of a human I'd saved my best friend from. Hard to tell but through the mess I thought I recognized Ade, though I'd never seen him with no clothes on before. Does every butt looked like plucked chicken? I wondered. He was coughing and gasping and one hand was held upwards, as though to say *No more, no more*.

A torrent of apologies spilled out of me.

'Help me get him up,' Freak said.

But I couldn't touch him. Couldn't bear to look at him.

I was half way down the street when footsteps pounded the sidewalk behind me. I hoisted my bag and ran.

'Aggie! Aggie, hold up!'

I cast a quick glance over my shoulder. Freak had run all the way from the house wearing only sneakers and a T-shirt that barely covered her ass.

'Go away, Freak. Leave me alone.'

The cops would be here any minute. They'd find out my name, who I was, where I came from.

'Aggie, stop, will you?' She grabbed me and spun me round. She put her hands on her knees and bent over, breathless. A couple of kids a few yards down snickered at her bare ass stuck in the air.

'Jeez, you sure can move,' she complained.

I'd almost reached the bottom of the road. There was a bus in a few minutes that would take me uptown. I'd start over from there. I kept walking.

'You got to let me go, Freak. I can't deal with cops.'

'No cops, stupid. Ade said no.'

I turned in amazement as her words began to sink in. I thought of the mess I'd left on the bedroom floor. 'I didn't kill him?'

Freak laughed and I noticed how over the top it was. She laughed like she was vomiting. It came out in a rush. 'Jesus,

Aggie,' she said. 'Quit being such a drama queen. Reckon you got him one, maybe two times. He's shook up but…'

'I didn't mean to hurt him, Freak. I swear.'

'Aggie, you're tall, alright, but you're skinny as a runt. Hard to tell what was you and what was the baseball bat.'

'But all the blood…' I said.

Freak rolled her eyes and tugged me back down the road with her.

It was a trick. Had to be. Any minute now sirens would come flying down the street and cops would have me in cuffs. There was blood. I knew there'd been blood. But Freak had a strong grip on me and I'd a powerful urge to see if Ade really was okay.

As she led me down the road, the normality of the street was strange. The sun was sinking behind the rooftops as a couple of cars pulled in, delivering people home from work. The clunk of doors closing. A dog barking. The snickering kids shooting hoops in their front yard stopped to eye us as we passed their gate. Without saying anything we both speeded up.

The house looked just the same, though everything felt different. As we got closer, the front door opened. I tried to turn back but Freak dragged me on. Monty winked at me as he passed. 'How do, slugger?' he said.

At the top of the steps Freak put her hands on my shoulders and pushed me against the wall.

'Look, I'm sorry. I should have told you about me and Ade,' she said. 'Don't know why I didn't. Maybe I sensed you'd be jealous. You're my sister. I love you but I aint got feelings for you that way, Aggie.'

It took me a minute to unscramble what she was saying, and then I heard her vomity laugh come out of my mouth. Funny how you pick these things up.

'That's the sickest thing I ever heard of. I aint jealous.'

I think I put her nose out of joint, but I was past caring. I was still trying to make sense of it.

'You know he's fucking Marjorie too, right?' It came out spiteful but I didn't mean it like that.

'He can fuck who he likes. No one fucks him like me.'

Freak looked up at the first floor window and waved at Ade, who was looking down at me with such a strange look. Hurt, confused, scared even. Just like a little boy. I doubled over and splashed all over the pavement.

'Jesus, Aggie,' said Freak as she disappeared inside, disgusted.

Everyone apart from Ade was in the hallway. Our arrival put paid to their gossip and they backed away from each other to make space for me. Maybe I was just a skinny runt, but when I swung that baseball bat I hit a hole in that house I could fit into.

There was no blood. I walked right around that whole room and it was dry as bones. I told myself they must have cleaned it. No other explanation I could think of. I got a good whack at him, though. I know because he wore the proof of it beneath his left eye for a week.

In our house, we lived in the kitchen. There was a fire we only lit on the worst winter nights. Across from the fire there was a bashed-up two-seat sofa that could take me, Jojo and Ash, until me or she or he got too big and we could hardly tell whose leg was whose. In the middle of the room stood the table I'd been born on and where we ate all our meals and read Scripture.

Beside the fire was a blue easy chair with a gold trim and a fringe around the bottom. Time was I could squeeze behind that chair when me and Jojo played hide-and-seek. Always took her a long time to find me when I went there, even though I went there a lot.

The gold trim on the back of the blue chair had been near enough picked off. It hung loose around the bottom, a swing for fairies. It would have made me a fine fairy crown if I'd only wound up the courage to ask Jojo to sew it for me. It was wavy and rough and felt different to the chair, which was smooth the way a baby's face might feel if you were allowed to stroke it. I liked to let the fringe fall through my fingers, silky and loose and free. I flicked the fringe with my finger and then breathed on it, pretending my breath was the fairies making it move – just a stupid kid's game. The chair's legs were little iron balls that let you move it around if you wanted to. Moving the chair made the fringe dance.

One time I fell asleep behind there, only waking up when Jojo found me. I wouldn't come out and it made her mad. She yelled at me and pulled the chair away on its little iron balls and dragged me to my feet.

On one side the fire was burning hot, on the other an icy wind rushed in. I gasped as it reached me. I remember all the lights were on.

Jojo, too bright.

Pop was on his knees scrubbing the floor, which was strange because he never did women's work. Jojo was rough and yanked me past him to the door. Jojo was so mad she was crying. I didn't know what I'd done.

I'm sorry, Jojo.

Snowflakes were blown through the open door, making it seem like it was snowing inside. *Like magic.*

Then Cy rose up out of nowhere and blocked our way. Jojo whipped round so fast she almost knocked me over. She dragged me to the back door, again moving round Pop, who was still scrub scrub scrubbing. This time it was Ash who blocked us. I was so sleepy. Jojo picked me up, my face in the crook of her soft neck, her hand on the back of my head.

Don't look, Aggie, don't look.

Ash and Cy like a pair of bookends. Pop's back like the shape of a hill, throwing shadows on the ground, and inside, the snow was falling everywhere.

R

A couple of days after I'd attacked him, I was called to Ade's room.

'Shut the door,' he said, as he sat on his camp bed.

It was the first time I'd been alone with him. I closed the door, leaving enough space to fit my hand around if I had to make a run for it.

'How's your eye?' I said, stupidly. No need to ask. It was taking over half his face.

'Sore,' he said, matter-of-fact, no malice. 'Sit down.'

I crossed my legs and straight away regretted it. I'd just given myself the extra task of untangling myself if I had to move in a hurry. I shifted position so I was half kneeling, half ready to run.

Ade pulled out papers and began building a joint. Seemed he'd forgotten all about me for a minute. Tobacco fell from his fingers like sprinkles. Then he took a tiny bag of weed and rubbed a precise amount evenly over the tobacco. He shuffled it together, licked the papers to close, and lit up. He took a draw and offered me some. I shook my head. The air came full of smoke and musk while he took another couple of deep draws.

Unlike me and Freak, Ade had a decent set up. Aside from the camp bed, he had an upside-down cardboard box serving as a bedside table with a wind-up lamp on it. Behind me was a desk covered with stacks of books and paper with a sheet draped over. A separate sheet was pinned over something on another wall. Underneath you could just make out pins and threads making shapes over various diagrams and maps.

I leaned back on the desk and a folder of loose papers slipped down the side. I pulled it out to place it back, but he snatched it out of my hands and slid it beneath his bed.

'That's private.'

'Sorry.'

'I wanted to talk to you about what happened the other day.'

'I'm real sorry about what I did, Ade. You know that. If I could take it back, I would.'

'Yeah, you said. What I want to know is who sent you?'

'What?'

He looked at me hard, as though trying to decide something. I stared right back at him. His matted hair had given itself entirely over to dreads now. He shook his head and black snakes rippled down his shoulders.

'Nothing,' he said. 'Never mind. Listen Aggie, I've been thinking. I've got a lot of people to consider here. A lot of people living under my roof, you know?'

'Sure, Ade.'

'People are nervous, you know? We've never had anyone be violent here before you arrived. First day you show up Freak and Marjorie fight, and now I'm wearing this.' He pointed to his swollen eye. 'We've got a good arrangement here, Aggie. People who need it have shelter. People just like you. That's a good thing. A fucking good thing, you know?'

He took another draw and offered me again. This time I took it. I lifted it to my lips and pulled. Smoke caught in my throat and stung my eyes but I managed not to cough. I glanced at Ade, embarrassed, but he was already rolling another joint and hadn't noticed how shit I was at this. My second draw was smoother, and everything started to get a little fuzzed up. The light in the room got brighter and softer all at the same time. My third draw gave me butterflies in my tummy. They tickled. Ade's voice broke through my observations. I struggled to pull my attention back to him.

121

'So if there's any more violence from you, you'll be packing your bags. Do you understand?'

'Sure, Ade. I totally understand. I'm real sorry about it, you know? I was set on leaving but Freak pulled me back. Otherwise I'd be gone.'

'I believe in second chances, Aggie.'

'Well, I sure do appreciate that, Ade.'

'Plus, you're a friend of Freak's, so…' He looked right at me and then quickly back down to his papers. Something had changed, just like that. Something heavy and unspoken was in the air between us now.

'Do you believe in God, Aggie?'

'Sure.' I knew God existed because you got a beating if you said he didn't.

'I don't.'

I looked at him in a new way. The only other person I knew who didn't believe was Jojo. I'd told her I'd asked God to send Momma home to us and she'd laughed.

Aint no God, Aggie. If there is, he's a long time dead.

Don't say that, Jojo. You'll burn in hell for saying that.

The only hell there is is here on earth.

'Couldn't agree more,' Ade said.

'Huh?'

'The only hell there is is here on earth. I totally agree. Who's Jojo anyway?'

'My sister.'

Forgive her, God, and Baby Jesus please forgive her, too. She don't mean what she say.

'Where's she then?'

'Back home, I guess.' Cooking Pop's dinner, cleaning Pop's clothes, keeping Pop happy.

I am Your child and You are my Father.

How did we come to be talking about this? I blinked hard and pushed it out of my head.

'You said something about Freak,' I said, trying to steer him back.

'Did I?' he laughed.

'Yeah, you said I was Freak's friend and so...' I trailed off, waiting for him to fill in the gap.

Ade screwed up his face and thought. 'Nope, it's gone. Where's home for you then, Aggie? Where's sister Jojo?'

My head was spinning. 'I don't remember. Where's your home?' Always trying to keep the focus away from me. 'Why did you leave England?'

'Scotland.' He rolled his eyes. 'How many times?'

'Scotland's in England?' I said. I don't know what I said that was so funny but he fell off his bed laughing. We were both on the floor now. I placed my hands either side of me to make sure I knew where I was. The window is there, the door is there, and here is the floor, the floor.

'I'm here because I'm concerned for y'all,' Ade said, in a bad Texas accent. 'Y'all into pounding your stupid Bibles all over each other. I'm here to put an end to y'all's nonsense.'

'And the Lord said to Cain: *Where is thy brother Abel? And he answered, I know not. Am I my brother's keeper?*'

Ade was so surprised his eyebrows almost flew off his face. I was a little surprised myself.

'*The voice of thy brother's blood crieth to me from the earth,*' I said.

'You can actually quote that shit?' He'd have tripped on his jaw if he'd tried to walk.

'Guess it never leaves you...' I shrugged, and then we laughed till we cried, but only one of us was crying with laughter.

'You know what, Aggie?'

I shook my head and Ade leaned in close, a manic glint in his eye. He drew a circle in the air above his head with one finger.

'All around, Aggie. Man, we're up against it. The walls have ears.' He looked at me straight. 'But you know what else?' I shook my head again. 'There's always more than meets the eye, but no matter how much there is, there's never God.'

He laughed to himself, a nasty, quiet laugh. Then he lit another one and lay back on the bed.

'Biggest fucking conspiracy theory there is,' he said to the ceiling. 'Oh, man. This country fucking stinks. I swear it's rotten to the fucking core.'

I sat on the floor thinking I should probably be offended, but I was mainly just trying to make sense of this conversation.

Next day he remembered why he'd called me into his room. He was worried about Freak. So worried he'd got stoned with me instead. Did I know where she kept disappearing to? I had to admit that after all these months of sharing a room, watching her sleep, letting her cut me – no, I did not know where she kept disappearing to.

The days were long and empty in that ramshackle house. I hardly went out in case Freak came back and I missed her. One day I passed her on the stairs. She was carrying a stack of papers and would have gone straight past me if I hadn't stopped her.

'Hey, stranger,' I said.

She grabbed my arm before I could say much more. 'Listen, Aggie, I don't have time right now. I'll come see you later, okay?'

'Sure,' I said. What else could I say? I was rewarded with a smile and a kiss on the cheek before she hurried up the stairs and disappeared into Ade's room.

She was helping Ade with some issues to do with the house but it was hard to say what the specific problem was when only Freak and Beast Woman were allowed into his room. How a guy like that could hold attraction for two such different women was a mystery to me. Not only did he smell kind of funky on account of all the dope he smoked, his hair couldn't have seen water in years. Freak loved the dreads but I thought they were weird on a white guy. But more than this, it just plain pissed me off that he was keeping Freak all to himself. I wondered if Beast Woman was pissed off, too.

Maybe we could help each other. I filed that thought away for another day. I was loyal to Freak and didn't want to get in the way of the big romance she seemed set on.

'Hey there, daydreamer.'

Tawanna smiled at me through the stair rail.

'You gonna stand there all day?' she asked.

I shook my head and tried to smile back.

'That aint a real smile,' she said. 'Now come down and tell Tawanna what the matter is. That's an order.'

With no Monty around to keep her at bay, I moped down the stairs. She put her arm around my waist and pulled me in as she led me through to the kitchen. She was fat and comfortable and I was happy to feel like a child again. She slid a pitcher of iced tea towards me and told me to add sugar while she squeezed some lemon.

'And then you can tell me all about it.'

We poured the sugar and lemon in and I tasted it. It was still warm but would be good in a while. I nodded and said, 'Aint nothing wrong a glass of that won't cure.'

She laughed again and I noticed she seemed different. Kind of sparkly.

'Yeah, it's good stuff. I made some brownies, too,' she said, as she lifted some paper towels from a plate on the counter. 'Try one.'

I was relieved she wasn't pursuing her line of questioning, although if I'd needed proof there was something odd about her, that was it. I took a bite of brownie and made all the right noises, even though I couldn't help notice it was a little dry. Guess I'd been spoiled in my previous life by Jojo's baking.

'They're good, huh?' she said, picking one up and putting it in her mouth whole. She couldn't talk like that so she settled for making noises like they were the best brownies in the world. Her eyes grew bigger and she waved her hands at me, making sure I couldn't look away. Tawanna was a communicator.

She stuffed another two down, one by one, all the time

rolling her huge eyes and waggling her fingers in the air. Eventually I couldn't help myself and I laughed. She looked mock-angry.

'I'm sorry,' I said. 'Are you okay? You seem a little... different.'

Tawanna slapped her hands down on the counter. 'You noticed? You can tell? Oh my God, Lloyd told me not to tell anyone but if people can already tell just by looking...'

Her hands flew to her boobs.

'Is it these? They're getting so big. How big do they go, do you know? I already got a goddam basketball each side. My Lloyd's one lucky guy, oh yes he is.'

She laughed her usual deep, dirty laugh but this time there was a touch of hysteria in it.

'Tawanna, what are you talking about?' I asked, completely confused.

She slapped my hand, as though I was playing games with her.

'Why, Aggie – you just worked it out! I'm having a baby!'

Her lips were parted in a wide smile, her tongue glistened through the gap in her teeth, her eyes shone with a wild kind of happiness I'd never seen before, and still I couldn't find any enthusiasm for her.

'Wow,' I said.

'I know, isn't it amazing?' Her eyes grew moister than her brownies. She leaned over and took a hold of my hand. 'We been trying, Aggie. I mean, we been trying for years. I been on my knees in that hall closet so many times asking God to send me a child and at last he's heard me. God is good, He is.'

'That's great, Tawanna. I'm happy for you.'

'But don't you go telling anyone, okay? I can't believe you just straight out guessed like that. Incredible.'

'I won't tell. But what... Where you gonna go with a baby?'

She seemed surprised by my question. 'We'll stay here, of course. Ade always said we could. I don't see why he'd change his mind now. And this place aint so bad now, is it?

We'll turn it into a palace. Never was much point before but now… well, now we got reason, aint we?'

I tried so hard to reply but I just couldn't get the words out.

'Holy shit, Aggie. Tawanna's gonna be a mommy.'

Her eyes flooded then and her smiling face was swept away in a tide of tears. She apologized and rushed out the room. I heard Freak on the stairs telling her to slow down and then the slam of a bedroom door.

'What's wrong with her?' Freak wanted to know, as she sauntered over to the counter and helped herself to a brownie. I thought about telling her. Up until recently, I wouldn't have thought twice about it.

'Not sure,' I said. 'Think she's just tired, maybe.'

Freak accepted this and made to walk out.

'You wanna do something later?' I asked. I was too eager, I could hear it. She swayed on the spot, like she couldn't decide which direction she was going to move in. There was a look on her face I didn't recognize. I knew she was keeping something from me.

'Naw,' she said. 'I gotta go. See ya.'

I followed her to the front door and touched her gently on the shoulder as she bent to zip her boot. She jumped and brushed me off.

'Jesus, Aggie. You scared me.'

'Sorry.'

'Alright, I'll catch you later.'

She skipped down the steps and disappeared down the street without looking back. I closed the door and leaned against it. The hallway caught hardly any light and was cool and gloomy. Across from me, the door to the hall closet seemed to shine. I hadn't been in since Tawanna had shown me what it was for.

On the floor inside I found a flashlight and a black marker. I picked up the marker and placed the nib on wall. I didn't know what to write, where to start. I closed my eyes and my hand moved without me telling it. When I looked, the same

127

two names were written over and over: one in strong, jagged up-and-down strokes, the other in messy loops.

FREAKFREAKFREAKFREAKFREAKFREAKFREAK
JOJOJOJOJOJOJOJOJOJOJOJOJOJOJOJOJOJOJO

I was embarrassed by myself. I used all the paint to cover their names up, but I still saw them, plain as day. To my mind, they'd break through all the paint in the world.

She had my arm and she cut. She squeezed real hard and her nails dug in. My blood slid between her fingers. She took her hand away and wiped it on a towel. I waited for my reward: her smile, her whispered 'Sisters', but it never came. She still had that look on her face – tense, focused, far away.

'Again,' she said.

Before I could say no, she'd cut me again. She focused real hard on the cut, like she could pull some special energy from it. She pinched the good skin on either side and the open wound gaped. I tried to pull my arm away but she had it too strong. She slapped it in frustration and the blood smeared. She slapped it again, and I couldn't tell if it was the blood smearing, or her hand slapping that made it redder.

'It's not working,' she said, her eyes alive with something I couldn't put words to. With a hard, final pinch of my bleeding arm, she let me go.

There was a time I could only be found in the red barn. We always kept cats to keep the mice down. One of them had sprung a new litter and I busied myself making sure the kitties all got their turn on their mama's teats. I snuck little cubes of cheese out the kitchen for the momma. I also snuck some bread and cookies and milk.

For the momma cat, I said to Jojo, when she caught me red-handed.

Hmm, said Jojo. *Do you think momma cat would like some apple pie, too?* My mouth watered as she removed the foil from a freshly baked masterpiece. I nodded my yes pleases, then set off to the barn loaded down with treats and drool.

She tracked me down later that day when Pop was at auction. She told me to leave the kittens and follow her out to the field. Ash was waiting for us. Without speaking, he swung his rifle off his shoulder and gave it to Jojo. He pointed some way down the field to where a pyramid of tin cans waited on an upturned crate.

Jojo lifted the gun and he settled in behind her to help adjust her aim. She fired. Not a single can so much as bounced.

Again, he said.

When it was my turn, he swapped the rifle for a smaller gun. I lifted it and looked straight down the middle. *Pop!* The first can went down. *Pop!* The second can went down. *Pop, pop, pop!* One after another, all the little cans fell down.

Shit, Aggie. You're a frikkin natural, Jojo whooped.

I grinned at Ash but he was unsmiling, his attention focused on something behind me. I turned around to see Cy watching us. Maybe he'd been there the whole time.

We'll do this again, okay? Ash said, quietly. He gathered the guns in as Cy walked towards us. Jojo put her arm around me and hurried us back inside.

When Cy told Pop we'd been shooting, there was hell to pay. Why was Ash wasting bullets on damn women? As punishment, Ash had to go round the field collecting sheep shit and then burn it. There was no good reason. It just made Pop happy to see him do it.

As a reward for ratting on us, Cy was allowed to go with Pop to auction whenever it was on. He crowed like a rooster to be so tight with Pop. Promotion, he called it. But we didn't care, because on those days, Ash took me and Jojo back out again. Those days were the shooting days.

One afternoon after school, I was sitting behind the barn playing with the kittens. I'd picked a cute little tortoiseshell as my favorite and was trying to decide on a name when Pop's voice suddenly roared out of the sky and landed all around me. I whipped round but he was nowhere in sight. Then the whole barn juddered as something thumped against it, once, twice, three times. One of the kittens was tugging on the hem of my jeans and I kicked it away as I scrambled up.

Through a gap in the wood I saw Cy lying crumpled on the ground, his back against the wall with all the tools hanging on. It was pretty dark but I could tell he was looking up at something. And then I saw Pop. He rained down slaps and punches harder than a stampede.

After a time, Cy stopped trying to protect himself. His hands useless at his side, he lay motionless. Pop growled, *Think you're man enough to go behind my back, do you?* and then, *Think you can take my place, do you?* And he hit him again, and kicked him. Cy moaned and folded over like he was trying to make himself small, and all the time Pop telling him over and over what a joke he was.

The kitten I'd kicked was crying so I picked it up and tried to hush it. When I looked through the crack again, I just caught Pop's back disappear out the barn into blinding sunshine. Cy was flat out, breathing heavy. I was thinking I should go get Jojo when Ash stepped out of the shadows. He must have been there the whole time. He offered his hand to Cy and Cy let him pull him up. The kitten mewed real loud and they were only a few feet away, so I cuddled it closer and told it again to shush.

Cy stood swaying, his head down like he was trying to find his balance. Ash held him by the arms, trying to keep him steady. Their voices were so low, I couldn't hear what they said. Then Ash gave Cy a rough shake.

You should let her be, Cy. It aint normal anyway.

There was a shift in Cy then. His back stiffened, though he still just looked down at his shoes and I reckon Ash missed it. The kitty cried and squirmed in my hands and I kept it tight into me and kissed its head and begged it be quiet. Ash patted Cy on the shoulder and turned to go.

I knew it was going to be bad even before Cy had reached the pitchfork. My mouth opened but nothing came out. Ash didn't know what had hit him. The fork ran through the back of his thigh and pinned him to the ground when he fell.

Think you're better than me, do you? Cy sneered. He dragged himself forward and pulled the fork out. He lifted it high over Ash and I pictured him bringing it down again, only worse this time, but Ash rolled over onto his back and then I heard my brother beg.

Cy lowered the fork but kept it at Ash's throat. *More*, he said. *Beg some more.*

There was more begging, and there was spitting too, before the pitchfork was thrown to the side and Cy limped out of the barn, leaving Ash lying in the dust and muck of the barn floor.

A few feet away, I stood mute in the bright afternoon. I unclenched my hands and looked down to where the little kitty lay, still and quiet at last. That's when I learned that violence can be catching.

14

When the scars come first they're like trace lines, leaving a whisper of what you felt. Then you make them a little bit longer, or a little bit deeper, and your skin bursts red. Red for danger, red for life. Your skin feels everything so inside you don't have to. Lines, little cuts, scattered around in random places; forearm, wrist, then up to the shoulder. Lines, lines, lines. Sometimes you leave it long enough for them to close up and heal, fade to silver white, but one day you have to open them up again, make sure you've still got it, the ability to feel without feeling. You make lines upon lines of hurt on your skin. Each line a scream you never made. Finding out that inside you it's beautiful. Pure, untainted blood; you're human after all.

Except mine wasn't untainted and she knew it. But we pretended like mine was normal. It was good blood, she said. Good and healthy. Sometimes I believed her.

There comes a point where you notice someone is more fucked up than you are and you want to run but you can't. You know you should. But like a crowd around a car crash, you stick it out, and then wish you hadn't.

She'd been walking, she said. Deliberately walking through bad parts of town. Deliberately drawing attention to herself. When she knew they were behind her, she'd led them down a little dark alley and waited. She never had to wait too long.

Freak. Her arms, legs, stomach, feet, all spliced to shit,

her punishment to herself, and now she wanted me to do her back. She stood in front of me, naked from the waist up, waiting for the cut to come.

'C'mon, Aggie. Do it.'

This was the new thing. Using the knife on me didn't help her any more. Cutting herself did nothing. She told me I was the only one she could trust to do it. So I did. Traced the knife all over her arms, joining up old scars. Trying to make them pretty. Turning nightmares into dreams, she'd said. Everywhere you could see on her was dreams now. Except her back, which was flawless. Not so much as a freckle on it.

I'd tried to talk her out of it but she didn't want to know. It got so I was crying and she was yelling. I'd begged her not to make me do it. Her back was so pretty and perfect but what good was that to her if she couldn't see it, she said. For my part, taking a knife to what was already damaged made some sort of sense. But this clean new canvas made me feel bad. I wanted to fix her up, not break her down. Finally, I said that if I was going to cut her it had to be my way. She looked surprised at that. I'd always gone along so meek with everything she said. 'I mean it,' I told her. 'You want cuts, you want me to do it, it's got to be my way.' Don't know if it was the demons inside or if she was just plain curious, but something made her agree. Don't mean I found it easy, though.

'Can't do it standing,' I said, stalling. She sat right down straight away. Her hair was swept round one side, a few short wisps danced around the nape of her neck. Her natural colour was baby blonde. Baby Freak.

She lowered her head and her back curled, all the knobbled parts of her spine poking out of the whitest skin I'd ever seen. I placed my left hand around her rib cage, feeling her heart beat even from there. She took a deep breath and my hand rose with her ribs. With the blade in my right, I began.

Didn't do it all at once. She was good at breathing through the pain but when she started moaning it was time to stop.

133

She didn't want Ade coming to see what was wrong. He'd stopped having sex with her. Didn't give a reason and she didn't ask. My theory was he got fed up washing sheets that were bloody from leaking scars. I knew she still gave him something now and then to keep him sweet. Something that didn't involve her taking off her clothes. Keep him from moving us on, Freak said.

Took six days in all. Freak got kind of weak and shivery and I thought I should stop but she insisted we keep going. Every night I'd do a bit more and she'd spend the next day lying face down on the floor. Bags of bloodied bandages piled up by our bedroom door. The blood soaked through every shirt we owned.

I had to take a picture on a phone she'd sneaked in so she could see what I'd done. I don't know what she expected to see and I didn't know what to expect of her reaction. Instead of the endless lines crisscrossing their way across the rest of her body, I'd carved her a flower. Starting in the curve of her waist, it had nine petals, three leaves, and the stem, when it healed, would disappear down into her jeans. I'd been as gentle as I could.

'It'll look better when it fixes,' I said. It was swollen a furious red. Didn't see how it could ever look better. Freak gripped the phone in both hands, staring so hard at the screen, I couldn't read her face. I'd cleaned it up best I could for the photo but you can't hold back blood. Some of it started to seep out before I could take the shot. It was a mess.

Freak started to shake. Sobs ripped out of her in long, shuddering breaths.

'Oh my God, I'm sorry, Freak. I'm so sorry,' I cried, but she looked up at me, all blue eyes and pink, and said, 'Thank you.'

15

No one asked about Freak. She wasn't missed. I'd been holed up taking care of her for days. I'd never spent so much time with someone and felt so alone. Guess talking's hard to do when you're in so much pain.

It was one of those rare days we were all there, apart from Freak and Ade who had stayed inside. Brandon, Ricardo and Lloyd had split a pack of beer, and Tawanna was beside them, reading Marjorie's palm. It had been a while since Marjorie had posed a threat. I figured Ade must have called her off, because she'd been almost civil lately. Anyway, I didn't worry about her too much. I was glad to be outside, catching a buzz from the impromptu party atmosphere.

We were having a barbecue using an old grill Monty had salvaged, or at least that was the plan until a red-faced, flustered Virginia turned up with a couple of flapping packages beneath her arms.

'I didn't know they'd still be alive,' she said, as she released the chickens into the yard. They scurried to the farthest point away from the barbecue, and began to peck the ground.

'Where's our food?' Monty asked, grill fork in hand.

'You're looking at it,' Virginia waved a hand in the general direction of the chickens, who looked none the worse for wear after their journey. She lifted some bottled water and drained half the contents.

'"Come out to the farm," my sister says. "Take a couple

of birds away with you." Why I thought they'd be trussed and ready for cooking is anyone's guess.'

She poured some water into her hand and patted her face and back of her neck. Monty's shoulders started to go, and then he let it out, a full-on belly laugh. It spread around the group until we were all laughing. Tawanna collapsed against Lloyd, tears rolling down her cheeks.

'Bless your heart, Virginia. Do they do tai chi? You'll have company in the mornings now.'

'What? No!' Monty cut in. 'I got the grill all ready here.'

We sobered up at that, and fell silent. Scratch, scratch, scratch. The birds moseyed closer to us.

'Can't we keep them?' asked Marjorie, looking slightly pale. 'We can always use eggs.'

'Long term, it makes sense,' mused Ricardo.

Virginia shook her head. 'They're rescue birds. Their laying days are behind them. Might get a couple a week, if we're lucky.'

'They could just be pets,' said Marjorie.

'No way,' said Monty. 'I want to eat them. That was the plan.'

'Yeah, Monty, but we didn't know they'd be living, did we?'

'All chickens are living before you eat them, Marj.'

'How do we make them... not living?' asked Ricardo.

We all turned to look at the chickens. One of them pecked the ground at Lloyd's feet. Tawanna had tucked her feet beneath her backside for safety.

'I can do it,' I said. Everyone stared open-mouthed.

'Well, aint you full of surprises,' said Monty. He took two large steps to the wood pile, lifted the axe and passed it over.

'Nah, don't need. Give me the broom instead.'

'I'm going inside,' said Marjorie. 'Tell me when it's done.'

I placed my hands over the closest bird, holding its tail and legs together, forcing it to lie down. I told Monty to lay the broom handle over the bird's neck, and I placed my feet on it, either side of the bird's head, pulling the body towards me until the neck cracked. A collective groan went up around the group.

We were all hungry, so I skinned the bird instead of plucking. When it was ready to cook, I eyed up its friend.

'Anyone know how to play chicken shit bingo?'

Dusk was setting in. The backyard was littered with empty beer cans and paper plates. Monty's guitar gave us music and our bellies were full, though the meat had been tough. Our makeshift bingo board was covered in birdshit, and Marjorie had guessed the right number nine out of twelve times. Tawanna said she had the gift of second sight.

'In that case, I prophesize this chicken is staying alive,' announced Marjorie, cradling it on her lap. 'I wanna play chicken shit bingo every night.'

'Yeah, Aggie,' smiled Monty. 'You sure brought something new to this house. Where was it you fell off the turnip truck?'

I laughed. It was hard to take offense at Monty. He was the goofiest guy I'd known. He could be annoying, but hell, who couldn't? I took in the faces around me: Tawanna, Lloyd, Ricardo, Brandon, Virginia, Monty – all of them dozy and content. Tawanna's hand caressed her round belly, even though it was still no rounder than it had ever been. Everyone knew she was pregnant now and the news seemed to bring out the best in everyone. Even Marjorie seemed almost human, clucking away at her new bird friend. I didn't want to be the one to kill that bird. I'd a feeling it was here to stay.

The peace was broken by loud voices coming from inside the house. I turned just as Ade burst out, his hair swinging wildly around his shoulders as he scanned the group. His eyes settled on mine.

'You.'

He moved towards me, stepping over outstretched legs, discarded paper plates and half-empty chip bags. I stood up. Freak appeared behind him, her first appearance in days.

'Ade, please don't,' she said.

He towered over me, forcing me to lean back until I fell over the crate I'd been sitting on.

Somebody else said, 'Ade.'

I scrabbled backwards but he was bearing down on me. Not so scrawny and pathetic now. His neck bulged with angry veins. His jaw was clenched, teeth bare, his eyes alive with a fury I hadn't thought he was capable of. Over his shoulder, Brandon and Lloyd were standing up in slow-motion. I opened my mouth to speak but before anything came out Ade was lifting me with both hands, yelling, spitting in my face. Afterwards, they said it was like your favorite puppy going rabid. When I hit the wall, the bricks crumbled in sympathy.

In the end, only Marjorie had the strength to pull him off me. I was flat on my back, staring at the sky, blinded by a strange combination of sun and stars. For a moment I was sitting on the sofa with Jojo watching Jerry smash Tom over the head with a mallet, except the birds I was hearing were in the trees above me and not in an eight-inch TV screen. Through the birdsong, I heard Freak crying and then a shadow fell in front of my eyes, making everything dark.

The light came back gradually. When I opened my eyes, Freak was there.

'Hey, she's awake.'

I tried to look in the direction of her voice, but I was stiff as a board. Seemed like I'd forgotten how to work my body. In actual fact, my body wasn't working.

'How's she doing?' a lower voice, and then Marjorie was looking down at me, her face slack with gravity. They both stared like I was some strange creature bobbing up from the deep. I tried to speak but my voice caught in my throat, and my eyes watered with the effort.

'Here, try this.' Marjorie slid a straw between my lips and I sipped. Strawberry milk. It surprised me with its tang. I screwed my face up.

'She don't like it,' said Freak. 'I told you it was too much.'

Freak stroked my forehead. 'I'll get you some water.'

'Screw water,' said Marjorie. 'She needs sugar to get her energy up. And calcium for her bones. And milk for the fat, skinny lil' runt that she is. Trust me. Whenever I got sick, my ma always gave me strawberry milk and I turned out just fine, didn't I?'

I didn't hear Freak's response.

I don't know how long it was, hours, days, weeks, but Marjorie and Freak stayed with me. They'd 'borrowed' a fan from one of our neighbours and kept it pointed right at the foot of the bed. When I could finally talk, the first thing I asked was could they turn the damn fan off. My feet were cold enough for frostbite. Second thing I asked for was a pair of socks. Third thing – what the hell happened to me?

A look passed between Freak and Marjorie and then Freak slipped out of my eye line. Marjorie leaned over and whispered, 'Just a misunderstanding, Aggie. Everything's fine. Don't worry.'

She patted the pillow around my head and gave me more strawberry milk, which I spit out. 'Oh, Aggie,' tutted Marjorie, wiping the milk from my chin and reaching into my neckline to catch the rest.

'No more strawberry milk, please,' I gasped, my voice croaky through lack of use. Marjorie looked hurt. Was the first time I'd seen her look anything other than angry.

'Don't be like that, Marjorie,' I said. 'Seems like you've ruined strawberry milk for me forever. Can't I get some frikkin water? Please?'

Freak was there in an instant. The look of triumph in her eye as she shouldered Marjorie out the way told me whatever peace they'd brokered was uneasy. Standing between us, she poured water from a bottle into a cup.

I didn't recognize the room, or the bed I was in.

'That's because it's mine,' Marjorie said, in a tone suggesting I'd better drink all the strawberry milk she could offer me, but she didn't say anything about the water Freak tipped into my mouth, except to tell her to go more slowly, which I was grateful for. The water washed away the sour tang of the milk and woke my head up a little. I shifted my position in the bed. Marjorie had to help me as my left hand was wrapped in a white bandage. My whole body thrummed tender but at least now I could move it a little bit. I asked again what had happened.

Marjorie adjusted another bandage that I'd been unaware was around my head. 'It wouldn't have been so bad except you hit your head on the way down. Wasn't just you, you know. You killed a fucking plant pot.'

Her face was straight but there was a smile behind it. Freak missed it.

'Screw the fucking plant pot,' she frowned. 'Ade's real sorry, Aggie. I feel awful. It was all my fault. I showed him the flower you did and he got it backwards. I tried to stop him. He knows he did wrong.'

'Damn right he did wrong, hitting a woman like that.' Marjorie's face was rigid. 'He'll be in here begging your forgiveness, Aggie. Don't give it away too easy, okay?'

Felt like a vice was tight around my head. I struggled to make sense of what they were talking about. Freak turned round and lifted her shirt.

'Looks good, huh?'

Her back was running with blood. I blinked hard and looked again but she'd dropped her shirt back down.

'I told him I made you do it,' she said.

Marjorie pulled up the sleeve on my right arm. 'And these? Who made you do these?' she wanted to know. I looked at the dozens of tiny cuts in my skin, and some longer slashes, and felt like I was looking at a stranger's arm. Apart from one little cut, Freak had made them all.

'You girls are a couple of frikkin nuts.' Marjorie shook her head as she applied some lotion or other to cuts that were made too long ago to heal. She rubbed it in gently, far more gently than I would have thought possible. Such a big woman, and delicate fingers. When she finished, she looked at me and pulled her lips in such a way that made me think she must be smiling. 'We're gonna get you better now,' she said. 'Even if you do turn your nose up at strawberry milk.' She turned to Freak. 'Don't go tiring her out, y'hear?' And then she left, promising to return in a while.

'What's happened to the real Beast Woman?' I whispered.

'Who gives a shit?' Freak said, sitting down at my right-hand side. 'Anyway, I can't stay long. I promised to help Ade with something. You should see him, Aggie. He's all over me since he saw what you did to my back.'

'You asked me to do it.'

'I know I did. You shouldn't feel bad about it, Aggie. Ade's gonna take care of me from now on. It made him see, you know?'

'Can you pass the water?'

'I been sleeping in his room and everything.' She passed the cup over and it sloshed down my chest. She didn't notice. 'This whole thing, I don't know, it's opened something up between us. Like maybe it was a good thing. I mean, I'm sorry you had to get caught in the crossfire, though. I never had a guy do anything like that for me before.'

'Your back,' I said. 'Does it hurt?'

'It's kind of hot but it don't hurt. Not really.'

She turned round and lifted her shirt again. When I looked this time, there was no blood. Just the rough outline of a shaky, unidentifiable flower, and the bumped ridges where the cuts had healed. It was grotesque, some kind of evil pretending to be beautiful. I felt like I'd played a sick joke on us both, but Freak stood admiring herself in the mirror.

'It feels a little tight right now but that'll change,' she said, never taking her eyes off it. 'I'm going to get some color in it. Marjorie told me all about this great tattoo place.'

I was embarrassed by the wrongness of it, and angry she didn't feel the same way.

'Since when's Marjorie your best friend?' I asked.

'Oh, she aint. I promise. But I've seen a different side to her lately. Since she cottoned on to…' She dropped her voice to a whisper. 'It all came out after Ade attacked you.' Her eyes went as dark as her face burned red. 'I told them everything. I had to.'

I remembered what she'd told me about going down alleyways and letting guys do what they wanted. If she'd told them that, what had she told them about me?

'Nothing, Aggie. I promise.'

'You best not have.'

She shook her head. 'It aint my story to tell.'

'Aint having people think I'm some kind of slut.'

She flushed then, and immediately I hated myself. Stupid dumb bitch.

'Can you help me sit up?' I said, embarrassed.

Together, slowly, we arranged the pillows higher behind me and I was able to take a look around.

'You want the curtain open?' Freak asked.

The curtain was actually a sheet. Someone – Marjorie, I guess – had made a loop and stitched it so it could slide on a pole. Light spilled into the room and I saw it properly for the first time. Like Ade's, this looked almost like a normal bedroom. As far as homeless people go, Ade and Marjorie were frikkin millionaires. A wooden wardrobe nestled in one corner, a padlock and chain looped through its handles. I realized now I was in a genuine bed, with real pillows. I had a clean sheet covering me and a crazy colored eiderdown folded neat at the bottom of the bed. In another corner was a desk, and behind it a shelving unit, and leaning on the shelving unit, a row of Jesus crosses all standing up in a row.

'What the fuck are they?' I asked. Freak laughed and took one down to show me.

'Marjorie makes them,' she said. 'They're pretty cool.'

I took the cross in my hand, unconvinced of its coolness.

'She makes them out of strips of rubber tire left on the

142

roads after a blow-out. She goes out to collect the rubber and then makes stuff to sell in gift shops,' Freak told me.

'People buy this shit? All this time I'm hustling for cash all I had to do was collect old tires and make stuff?'

'Yeah, she's got them in shops all over, so she says. I love these. Look.'

I rested the cross in my lap as she passed over a tiny, perfectly proportioned, rubber armadillo. I had to admit it was pretty good.

'Marjorie's a big fan of the armadillo. Says she finds their slaughter on the roads of Texas difficult to process. Her words, not mine,' Freak said, as she saw the look on my face. 'She says this is her way of showing respect. There's dozens and dozens of them here. You'll see when you can get out of bed.'

'Who buys it?' I asked. Freak wrinkled her nose.

'Tourists, I think. Tourists and truckers. Truckers are hot for the crosses. They hang them from their mirror. They don't care for the armadillos so much, in real life or in art, Marjorie says.'

Remembering the number of squished armadillo lumps I'd seen lying by the side of the roads, I agreed she had a point.

I turned the armadillo over in my hand. The way it was built, tiny nails holding layers of rubber together, I had to admit it was kind of clever. No way my fingers could have made anything like it. I took another look at the cross. You could tell it was tire rubber, a few layers put together, and the ends cut into points. At the center of the cross Marjorie had stuck an amber-colored stone. Seemed like maybe I had seen one of these before, dangling between me and some guy before I stung him, but I wasn't sure if I was making it up. Inventing memories. Maybe I'd been accused of that before.

'What you two doing?' Marjorie came in without knocking, but then again, it was her room. Before either of us could answer she was over in a flash, grabbing the cross and armadillo and putting them back where Freak had found them.

'We were just looking, Marjorie. Aggie was asking.'

'I don't want you touching them, y'hear?'

The new knowledge about her artistic side didn't make Marjorie any less scary.

'That there's my livelihood,' she continued. 'Now you respect that and leave them alone, alright? Otherwise, I'll have my bed back.'

'I won't touch them, Marjorie. I promise. And thanks for your bed. Hopefully I won't need it too much longer,' I said. 'Where you sleeping?'

'Our room,' Freak replied. 'I've been in here with you. Most nights, that is.' She smiled slyly and nodded at a space on the floor where her sleeping bag lay in a crumpled heap. 'Anyways, I gotta go. Ade needs me.'

She kissed me lightly on the forehead, and waggled her fingers at Marjorie as she skipped out. We heard Ade's room door creak open and then close across the hall.

'You're in here until you're fit and then I'll be taking my room back,' Marjorie said, as though there could be any doubt about that.

It would only be another day or two before I was ready to get out of bed, though I was in no hurry. Marjorie had her room decked out real nice. Little paintings hung on the walls, and she let incense burn if I asked her. I lay in bed watching the smoke coil lazily upwards, drifting in the light reflected by a chain of colored glass dolphins hanging in the window. When I expressed surprise at Marjorie making such a nice space for herself, Freak just shrugged and said she didn't find it too fancy, though I did notice her on more than one occasion stroking the giant blue-and-green peacock feathers sticking out of a vase on the floor.

I wasn't too keen on seeing Ade but I was in no position to walk away from him when he finally decided to visit. He stood in the open doorway and knocked on the wall to get my attention. 'Hello, Aggie,' he said, in that stupid voice of his.

'Hey, Ade,' I replied.

Silence.

I looked at my hands sitting crossed in my lap, unable to meet his eyes which I knew were roving along the bruises on my face.

'Can I come in?' he asked.

I shrugged.

He stayed at the door.

'I was just wondering how you are,' he said. 'Freak says you're on the mend.'

'Better than I was.'

He came in to the room and sat down on the bed. My eyes shot to the door. At least he'd left it open. I wished Freak or Marjorie were here.

'Man.' He screwed his face up – I couldn't tell if it was disgust or concern – and said, 'Your face looks really fucking sore.'

Really fucking mashed up, you mean.

'It aint too bad.'

Silence again.

Jesus.

'It was really swollen before,' I added, and he looked ashamed, and I was ashamed for making him ashamed.

'I understand why you did it,' I said, to help him out. 'I'd probably have done the same thing in your position.'

'I just…' He raised his hands, weighing up his choice of words. 'Freak's back, Aggie… that was fucking shocking.'

Pause for effect. What a dick.

'But I was out of order and I'm sorry.'

My turn now. I took a deep breath and forced a smile.

'What say we make a deal to stop beating each other up?' It was an effort but I needed to lighten the mood. I winked at him, my partner in fisticuffs, causing myself a little pain in the process, but he didn't seem to notice. He pressed his hands between his knees and began to rock back and forth.

'It fucking scared me, you know,' he said. 'That I could do that. I didn't know. I didn't fucking know.'

His rocking picked up speed and sent vibrations up the bed. My body began to bounce along with him.

'I care about Freak, you know?' he continued, oblivious. 'I don't think I realized how much.'

His hands flew from between his knees to under his armpits, but the rocking didn't lessen. He'd thought he'd come to apologize, but he hadn't really. He'd come to talk about himself.

'I care about her, too,' I replied, clenching and unclenching my good hand. He reached out and grabbed it.

'I know you do.'

The rocking stopped, but he had my hand now, so there was no real improvement. He leaned in closer and cleared his throat. When he spoke again, it was almost a whisper.

'She's told me about… you know.'

A meaningful squeeze of my hand.

'No. What?' There was a challenge in my voice that I hadn't intended. He missed it, obviously. He looked at me carefully, waiting for the penny to drop. I was overcome by the urge to spit in his face.

'You mean, the strange men fucking her in the street on a nightly basis?' I said.

That old thing.

He paled and nodded. 'I wish you'd told me.'

'I didn't fucking know, Ade. And then she asked me to do that stuff to her, and I thought it would help. You don't get it. You don't fucking get it, do you?'

I wasn't sure I got it myself, but it pleased me to turn the tables on him. He shrank back from me, hands up in defense.

'You're right. I'm sorry. I don't get it, I fucking don't. But look, it's in the past, eh? And I'm going to make sure it stays that way. Freak's my job now, okay? I'm going to make sure she doesn't do that shit again.'

Good luck.

'There's just one thing I need to ask, I'm sorry.' He gulped and looked wildly around the room, looking for all the world like he wished he could take his words back.

'I just… I don't want to see it happening again and so I just want to check… this wandering about… it's not something you've… ever…?' His eyebrows were raised in expectation, wanting me to fill in the blanks of the sentence he was too chicken-shit to finish.

'Fuck, no.' I wrapped my arms around me, locked myself in.

'Because if it is, there's people you can talk to…'

'Aint no man getting near me that way.'

'Okay,' He nodded. 'That's good. I don't really know… I mean, I'm not very… good at… I care, Aggie. Alright? I just wanted to say that.'

His eyes were all wet-rimmed. It was kind of touching, and a good bit pathetic. Thank sweet Jesus that Marjorie appeared behind him in the doorway.

'Friends again?' Her gravelly voice made him jump.

Ade looked from me to her and back to me. 'I don't know. Are we?' he asked.

We'd never been buddies and I didn't see why we had to be now just because we'd beaten each other up a couple of times.

'Sure,' I said.

'Hey, what is this – party time?' Freak burst in and I sure was glad to see her. In fact, the only one without a smile on their face was Marjorie. Ade got up like his ass was on fire and gave Freak a big bear hug. They stood there clutching on to each other a stupid amount of time. Marjorie looked like she'd rather hug a rose bush than be faced with the new lovebirds smooching in her bedroom.

Ade finally stood back from Freak, but couldn't quite bring himself to let go altogether. He kept hold of her shoulders and smiled down at her like they were the only people in the whole wide world. She reached up on tip-toe and kissed his nose. It was gross.

'Take that the fuck outta here,' Marj said. 'Unhygienic fuckers.'

Later on I said to Freak maybe she and Ade could be a bit more sensitive to Marjorie and cut back on the kissing. She pulled a face.

'Since when did you give a damn about Beast Woman?' she asked.

Lying in bed smelling of lotion, I was surprised she had to ask.

16

Marjorie let me stay in her bed longer than she needed to. I was fit enough for the floor after a couple of days but she wouldn't hear of it. A whole new side to Marjorie came out. Motherly, almost. She moved the bed as far to the window as she could so I could see out. The view wasn't worth it but I didn't tell her that. The best part of staying in Marjorie's room was her books. I'd never even heard of graphic novels before. The days passed in a haze of heroes and explosions and wrongs put right against all odds. I'd just finished *The Watchmen* and was reaching for something else when, behind a pile of comics, I spied a stash of old paperback novels.

I picked one up, carefully, and Jojo's voice was loud in my head: *Careful now, Aggie. What's Momma gonna say if she comes back to find all her books are tarnished and torn?*

Marjorie walked in and I shoved the book back, but she took one look at my guilty face and came over. The book hadn't landed right. She picked it up and threw it on the bed.

'What's wrong? I don't mind you reading it.'

'I don't know, Marjorie. Guess seeing them tucked away at the back there…'

She shook her head and pulled them all out.

'There's some people who'll use anything to poke fun at you,' she said. 'That aint no reason not to read a good book. Help yourself.'

'What if I damage it?'

'You planning on playing frisbee with it?'

She turned away and unlocked the wardrobe while I flicked my way through a selection of Stephen King, Patricia Cornwell and J.R.R. Tolkien. The inside cover of *Lord of the Rings* had an inscription: *To Marjorie, better than Scotch, Ade xxx*. I put that one back and tried to forget I'd seen it.

Beside me on the floor were several cardboard boxes which Marjorie filled with the contents of the wardrobe. Hundreds of trinkets made out of tire rubber: cowboys hats, boots, guns and more of the crosses and armadillos I'd seen earlier. There was so much of it I thought she must have spent her whole entire life making this stuff.

'I like doing it.' She shrugged. 'Anyway, don't want to live like this forever. Reckon if I can get my stuff out there, sell enough of it, maybe I can get me a place on my own sometime.'

I picked up a cowboy hat. It was only about an inch high and two inches wide. I put it on my head.

'Are they for pygmies?' I asked.

Marjorie didn't laugh like Freak would have.

'Aint no saying what people like or what they'll buy, Aggie. I've had these flying out the Stockyard shops. Now I got a contact out of town saying he's interested. Reckon it's time I took a road trip to try and offload some of these little critters.' She picked up an armadillo and kissed its nose. 'Gonna make me some money.'

'Good for you, Marjorie. That's great.' She looked at me suspicious. None of us were used to compliments.

'I mean it,' I said. 'You've got hot-shit talent there. I love the armadillos.'

'They're my favorite, too,' she said. 'Poor little guys. Aint nobody got time for them.' Her whole face tightened and her voice grew thick. 'People just run right over them, Aggie. Evil bastards. Every time I sell one of these guys I'm gonna donate some money somewhere. I don't know. I'll set up an organization. Save the Armadillo. Something like that. I aint got the specifics fixed right in my head yet. Just seems like someone somewhere needs to make a stand, you know what

I mean? All these harmless little creatures lying dead on the roads. It aint right, Aggie. It aint right.'

Jojo once told me there were people who cared more for animals than humans. Given the variety of humans I'd met since leaving home, this didn't surprise me as much as it used to. Besides, Marjorie had done a pretty good job of looking after me, so who was I to criticize?

'You need some help there, Marj?'

She looked at me hard for a minute, trying to decide if I was for real or not. Then, unsmiling, she gave me a pile of tissue paper and told me to wrap the armadillos in pink, the hats in green, the boots in blue, and the crosses in black. We worked in color-coded silence, filling the boxes ready for her road trip.

A couple of hours later she was taping the boxes up and thanking me for my help. She was biting tape off the roll when she said it, so it came out through gritted teeth. She stood back to admire our work

'I never had help before. That was fast work,' she said. 'Even for a cripple,' and she nodded down at my bandaged hand.

'Uh, yeah,' I replied. 'I guess I'm good to return to my own room now.'

She nodded, as though she'd been waiting for me to say this. 'You can choose a book to take with you,' she said. 'And return when you're done.'

That was Marjorie. Always careful.

'Okay,' I said. 'Thanks.'

I chose a book from the pile and lingered in the doorway, awkward.

'What?' she said.

It was hard to walk out. I took a last look around the room, pictures on the walls, scarves over lamps, the sun-catcher that was done catching any sun for that day.

'I guess I just want to say thanks, Marjorie. You know, for taking care of me and shit. That was... that was real nice of you.'

151

She didn't look up as she taped another box closed. I turned to go.

'Aggie,' she said.

I waited but she was quiet. Just the sound of tape ripping off the roll and Marjorie slapping each box as she sealed it.

'Yes, m'am?' I said, just to remind her I was still there.

'I'm gonna need a second person with me on this trip. Don't wanna be leaving boxes lying in plain sight with no one to guard them. You fancy a trip with me?'

Now it was my turn to be quiet. Spending the afternoon with Marjorie was one thing; a vacation was a different prospect.

'It aint a vacation,' she said, reading my mind. 'There's money to be made.'

'Where is it?' I asked, wondering how I could say no without offending her.

'Down on the coast, near Corpus.'

The coast: lapping waves on sandy beaches, gulls sailing on high winds, keening like discordant angels; the coast, a place where Mommas come from, a place where Mommas and honest brothers run away to; the coast, a place where we forget everything.

'Well?' she snapped, her eyes flying to mine for the briefest moment.

'I'm in.'

'Good.'

She began to stack the boxes.

'Only thing is, Aggie – don't call me m'am again. I aint losing teeth yet.'

My first job was to go with her to her mom's place which was twenty miles out of town. Out on the highway, I was reminded of why I never found my way out of this place. If hell was construction, this was it. Gray concrete lanes, stabbed through with orange cones, stretched for miles. Marjorie had got hold of a car for the trip but it was ropey compared to everything else on the road. Marj said the car was called Oprah, because it was big, black and took shit from no one. Squeezed between lanes of pick-ups and long-haulers, I prayed she was right. The horns that blasted us as they passed were louder than anything coming out of the few wires that passed for a stereo in that car. The roads were rough and the ride bumpy.

Eventually we turned off and found ourselves heading down a quiet street all lined with trees and single-storey shacks with chicken wire running around dried-out lawns. Plastic toys lying out told the story of a busy neighborhood, but there was no one to see.

We drove on, leaving the town of no one behind, eventually coming up against a trailer park situated right at the end of the road.

'Nice spot,' I said.

By the way Marjorie slammed the door when she got out, I guessed she hadn't appreciated my comment. I caught up with her as she rattled the gate into the park. A padlock was hung off it on the other side.

'Did they know you were coming?' I asked. I swear I didn't mean it the way it came out.

'Very fucking funny,' was the response.

She stood back and studied the wire fence running round the park.

'There used to be…' and she began to rip out some weeds that had sprouted alongside the perimeter. 'Here it is. Follow me.'

She lifted a section of fence that had come loose from the bottom and climbed under. I followed, catching my hair as I went. I wrestled myself free, leaving a chunk of hair behind me. Fine first impression I'd make.

The trailers were a real mixed bunch. Some of them had curtains hanging up and flowers in pots outside, almost inviting. Most of them were just grubby.

'This is it.'

Marjorie stopped outside a trailer that was bashed all down one side, the reminder of a tornado from a couple of summers back. All manner of junk cluttered the ground outside: an old bath, a rusty bike, a shopping trolley with one wheel missing. 'Ma deals in antiques,' Marjorie said, by way of explanation. She looked around the site and shook her head. 'It used to be a whole lot nicer around here,' she said. I had a feeling she wasn't just talking about the junk.

'Marjorie?' A woman's voice came from inside.

'Yes, Ma, it's me. How come the gate's locked? I told you I was coming.'

There was a small thud and the trailer wobbled as her mom came to the door. Marjorie turned her face to me and whispered, 'If you laugh, or if you're rude in any way, I will dump your ass on the highway and you can walk back. Got it?'

Before I could reply, the trailer door swung open.

'Marjorie!' Marjorie's mom squeaked. And it was a squeak because she was hardly bigger than a mouse.

'Hi, Ma,' Marjorie bent down to receive her mom's hug.

Dumbstruck, I followed the giant woman, who followed her dwarf mother back inside the trailer.

Marjorie pointed at one end of a shabby sofa and told me to sit. I thought of trying to brush the mat of cat hairs away first, but only for half a second. I sank down way deeper than I expected. I pulled a cushion over and wriggled it under my ass. It wasn't great but at least my knees weren't brushing my chin any more.

'Ma, this is my friend, Aggie.'

I struggled back to my feet to shake Ma's hand. I felt like a giant as I wrapped her tiny hand in mine. I shook her fist and a sizeable portion of her forearm gently as I could, while she smiled and nodded like she didn't notice anything strange.

'Pleasure to meet you, Aggie. You can call me George. Short for Georgia.'

She cackled at my attempt to pretend she hadn't said 'short'.

Marjorie rolled her eyes at me. 'Does that every time she meets someone,' she said.

I felt my old blush start to prickle. My shoplifting days with Freak meant I was almost blush-proof these days, but I'd never met a fifty-year-old midget in cowboy boots, skinny shorts and a vest before. I smiled back at George and pretended I didn't know what Marjorie was talking about. 'Good to meet you too, m'am,' I said.

'Oh, honey, call me George,' George said. 'Aint losing teeth yet.'

I sank back down into the sofa as George busied herself making coffee. She had a row of stools lined up along the counter that she used as steppingstones between cupboards.

'Hank'll be happy to see you,' she called over her shoulder. 'He'll be back any minute.'

'Sure he will,' Marjorie said, beneath her breath to me. 'Happy as a clam at high tide.' And then to George: 'No coffee, Ma. We aint staying long,' but George shooed her out of the kitchen and insisted she sit down.

Marjorie's weight collapsed down on the other end of the sofa and I almost shot straight up in the air. I tried to catch her eye to laugh about it but she kept her eyes trained on George the whole time. I had terrible giggles just bursting to get out but somehow I kept them on lockdown.

Unlike Marjorie, George could talk a blue streak. After she'd filled us in on the comings and goings of most of her neighbors, expressed regret over her cat's recent disappearance (turned out I was sitting on all she had left of her poor kitty. She didn't want to clean up the hairs but didn't mind me sitting on them, natural dispersal being kinder than a vacuum), and cursed the weather inside out for over an hour (when would it damn well ever rain?), she finally fell silent, but kept looking between me and Marjorie, smiling a weird grin as she took sips of what must now be stone-cold coffee.

'And how you been keeping, Ma?' Marjorie asked in a serious voice. George didn't reply. 'Still bad?' said Marjorie.

George twitched her nose and nodded, eyes glassy, grin rigid.

Marjorie reached into an inside pocket of her jacket and pulled out a small bag of dope. She placed it on the coffee table. From another pocket she took some folded bank bills and tucked them into her mom's hand.

'That should do you until I get back,' she said. 'Don't let Hank smoke all of it, y'hear?'

'Oh, Marjorie. He's a good man,' said George.

She lifted the dope from the table and began to crumble a little bit into papers.

'Sure he is,' Marjorie replied, picking bits of rubber from under her nails and flicking it on the floor. 'The best.'

George took three or four good long drags on her joint. Everything was focused around her face as she breathed in, lips pursed, eyes tightly closed. It wasn't just her face that changed from rigid to relaxed; she sank into herself, looking a little bit the way my seat felt.

The door to the trailer pulled open and an old guy aged around sixty came in.

Weirdest walk I ever saw on a man. John Wayne to the power of a thousand. Marjorie told me later that Hank spent his whole life on a Harley, and as a result he couldn't stand up straight. Take his bike away, he stayed in the exact same shape. Only time he came off the bike was when he was filling her up. He'd waddle in to pay for the gas like he was wearing a full diaper. True enough, it was the worst cowboy impersonation ever. Biker leathers, a long blond moustache and a red bandana around his head completed the look. He bent down to kiss George on the mouth and I swear I heard Marjorie growl.

'Sweetheart, we have visitors.' George waved vaguely in our direction before letting her arms flop at her sides. For a second, I thought he was going to come over. Marjorie had taken position behind the sofa so I was closest. If he laid one finger on me, I'd bite it off.

'Good to see you, Marjorie.' He sat down and helped himself to George's papers and the dope.

'That there is for Ma. Alright, Hank?'

He sat back straight away, holding his hands up in defense as though she were about to punch him, even though a sofa and coffee table separated them.

'Sure, Marjorie. Whatever you say.'

'Don't be silly now.' George waved vaguely in the direction of the stuff on the table. 'Go on, Hank. Marjorie don't mean it.'

There was a split second of tense silence, broken by the creak of leather when Hank flexed his arms beneath his biker jacket. He leaned forward with a sly smile on his face and a wink for Marjorie. 'Just a small one, Marjorie. Couples gotta be on the same wavelength. You'll find that out yourself one day when you find a man of your own.'

'Oh, Hank.' George giggled. 'He don't mean it, sweetheart.'

'What I want a man for? I can smoke my dope all by myself.'

'Oh, Marj,' said George. 'Relax, baby.'

George took another toke and offered it to Marjorie, who shook her head.

'It's yours, Ma. For the pain.' She said those words pointedly at Hank but he was already building the next joint.

George looked at Marjorie, begging with her eyes not to say any more. Marjorie shrugged her shoulders and George sank back in her chair.

'Do another for me, honey. Will you?' she asked Hank.

Hank patted her bare thigh. 'Already on it, babe.'

I wished the sofa would swallow me up. The overhead lights were on full and the glare seemed to exaggerate every expression, every look that passed between them. George pointed at me.

'What you do to your hand there, honey?'

She took me by surprise. I lifted my bandaged hand and my mouth fell open, though nothing came out.

'She ran into a door, Ma,' said Marj, dryly.

'Translation: mind your own damn business,' said Hank.

'Nice way to speak to your mother.'

'You got any family, Aggie?' George smiled brightly, and kicked her little feet up and down in front of her like a kid on a fairground ride.

'Uh, no. Not really.'

'Not really, huh?' said George, sadly. 'Kids, huh, Hank? When they're little, they sit on your lap. When they're older, they sit on your heart.'

'Aint that the truth, George. Aint that the truth.' He patted her thigh, and shook his head in sorrow.

Marjorie looked at me, eyes blazing, her mouth stretched tight. Her cheeks were starting to crowd her lips. When she was old, they'd hang lower than her jaw.

'Hurry up with that toke, Hank, will you?' George said. 'I got an awful ache today.'

Marjorie got up from the sofa arm and stepped over the coffee table on her way to the door, causing Hank's papers to fly up and the tobacco to spill.

'Aggie. Time to go.'

She kissed her ma on the head before she left. I followed, and as I closed the door behind me I heard him cursing.

'He's an asshole,' Marjorie spat out the window as we pulled away from the trailer park. I didn't speak, fearful I'd say the wrong thing and bring her wrath down on me.

'Smokes all her weed all the fucking time. It's fucking medicinal for Ma. Medicinal. And he smokes it all. Such a fucking asshole.'

She wasn't shouting about it, just stating it all as fact.

'For a week last month, she couldn't get out of bed. A whole fucking week due to the pain in her joints. And where was he? At some fucking rally somewhere on his precious fucking bike.'

'Your ma seems pretty stuck on him,' I said, as the road disappeared beneath us faster and faster. We were passing the houses with kids' toys but she was making like we were on the freeway. 'You wanna maybe slow down, Marjorie?'

She slammed the brake on and we shuddered to a halt. She turned to me with wide eyes full of worry.

'Did you see that?' she said.

'No, what?' I asked, but she was already out the car.

I jumped out after her and walked behind the car. There, a few feet ahead, Marjorie was crouched over something lying by the side of the road. My instincts were screaming at me to get the hell out of there.

'Did I hit it? Was it me, do you think? Aggie, do you think it was me?'

I edged closer and saw it was just an armadillo with its back end squished. Marj looked up at me and the anxiety in her eyes crushed any joke I'd been about to make. I placed my hand on her shoulder.

'I didn't feel anything, Marjorie. I don't think it was you.'

She nodded back towards the car and told me to go open the trunk.

'Do you see a blanket?' she called. I rummaged among the junk until I found a real nice wool blanket tucked away at the back.

'Bring it over,' she said.

I watched in disbelief as she bundled up that dead armadillo, wrapping it like a baby in finest wool, before carrying it to the car and laying it down.

'We'll bury him on the way back,' she said.

'Hell, Marjorie, don't you know your skin can fall off from touching them varmints?'

'Naw, you mean leprosy. You gotta be careful is all. You can catch a lot worse from humans.'

'Aint that the truth.'

She closed the trunk but she looked at me oddly, like maybe she'd never considered I'd had a life before winding up at the house. 'What you mean by that?'

I shook my head. Hadn't meant to say it. I pulled open the passenger door but she caught my eye over the car roof.

'You got a Hank in your life, too, huh?'

159

'Hank's nothing compared to my folks.'

'He aint just a freeloader, Aggie.'

Her words sat heavy in the small distance between us.

'It gets so you recognize it,' she said, 'I missed it with Freak, I guess because it's so damn hard to get past the fact she's a sneaky little thief. But you? I saw it in you alright. Those cuts on your arms. It aint out of boredom, is it?'

A noise came out of me. Something somewhere between a snigger and a sigh.

'I don't hear no mirth in that laugh, Aggie.'

She'd got it so wrong.

'Fuck off, Marj. You don't know what you're talking about.'

She was a bear of a woman, an ugly bear at that. Who'd do anything to her?

'What, you think it could only happen to you? Think cos you're pretty?'

Shame prickled my cheeks, and my tongue felt over-large in my mouth, but a door had been opened, and we talked the whole way back, listening to honky-tonk at a low volume out of respect to our deceased passenger. I confessed the story of my whore mother, who ran away from my Bible-loving father, and my brothers who fought, and my sister who raised me.

'Brothers, huh?' said Marjorie at one point. 'They single?' She roared with a laughter I hadn't known she possessed. 'I'm sorry,' she said. 'I aint right. I'm so fucking bad, man.' But the laughter kept coming until she remembered the corpse in the trunk and clapped a hand over her mouth. I couldn't not smile along. I didn't bother to explain that Cy was a bastard and that we'd no clue where Ash was, that we'd woken one morning to find him gone. Jojo cried and I ran outside to see if he'd taken *Jack King*, but the boat was still there. My young mind still believed it would take us to Momma.

We pulled over to bury the varmint beneath some trees in a public park. She did the whole thing herself.

I never found out why Marj wanted me to come with her on that trip home, but I sure as hell began to see a whole other side to Beast Woman.

H

We got back to the house to find Freak and Ade playing cards by candlelight at the counter in the kitchen. Freak lit up like a firework when we walked in.

'Hey, Marj,' she said. 'Ade and me are playing strip poker. Come sit with us a while.'

'It's normal poker,' said Ade, with a look to Freak.

'No, thanks,' Marjorie scowled. 'You want a sandwich, Aggie?'

She took some bread out and inspected it before picking out a couple of moldy areas and spreading cream cheese across what was left. I told her I was all set for moldy sandwiches and Freak did her forced vomity laugh. I didn't mean for it to be like that. I'd been making a joke but I could tell Marjorie felt foolish. I felt bad.

'Where you been?' Freak wanted to know. I hadn't had a chance to tell her I was helping Marjorie out with her armadillos. Somehow I knew it wouldn't go down too well. Marjorie seized her opportunity.

'Me and Aggie's been over seeing my ma. Just hanging out, you know.'

Freak turned to me. I shrugged and nodded. Didn't see why I should be feeling weird about it. I hardly saw anything of her these days. I'd have told her if I'd seen her.

'Sweet,' said Freak, looking back at the cards in her hand.

Marjorie left her sandwich and moved closer to Ade. She

bent down and in a low voice said right in his ear, 'Ma said to say hi. She misses you.'

I didn't remember George saying anything like that, but Ade was interested now which I guess was the point. He put his cards face down on the counter and turned to us.

'How's George doing?' he asked.

Freak concentrated real hard on her hand.

Marjorie shrugged. 'Same old, Ade. How you doing?'

'Uh, I need to speak to you actually,' Ade replied. Freak's head shot up faster than chilli through a hound dog.

The faintest flicker of a smile passed over Marjorie's face. 'Anytime you need me, Ade. You know that.'

Freak threw her cards down and stormed out the kitchen, banging into me as she went.

'Reckon you should go see what's up with Lil' Miss Scarface, Ade,' Marj suggested, mildly.

He frowned in disapproval but did as he was told.

'I'll catch you later,' he said, as he left. 'It's about what we were talking about earlier.'

'Sure thing, Ade.'

Marjorie returned to making her sandwich. 'Sure you don't want one, Aggie? Else this bread's only good for trash.'

'Nah, I'm good. Don't throw it, though. It'll do for ducks.'

I took what was left and headed back to my room. Ade had asked me to take Freak out the next day. He thought she was sticking to the house too much. Said there was a balance to be struck between wandering the streets at night, and clinging to his shirt-tails through the day. Of course, Freak didn't know about that conversation and I'd no intention of telling her, especially as Ade had given me thirty bucks to entertain her with. Not that Freak needed the money. I knew she had a big stash of rolled bills under a board in our room. I figured she was smart to keep that quiet. I figured I was smarter not to let on that I knew about it. She was lucky I was an honest person, though I'm sure she would have disagreed with that.

Next day we were kicking around the streets downtown.

Ade's thirty bucks didn't last long and soon we were stuck for something to do. Mid-afternoon Freak said she needed to visit the Sad Place to see Mr Dee about something. I thought maybe Ade would be so happy she was showing a bit of independence, he might give me another thirty bucks to take her out again sometime. We arranged to meet up later and I took a walk. The heat had sent everyone indoors. Only signs of life were the cars. You stayed cool in a car, as long as it didn't go by the name of Oprah.

Beneath my feet, sunk into the stone of the street, were the names of dead people. Born, raised and died in Dallas, now their names were part of the city forever. I liked that. It was proof they'd been here.

Maybe I'd put one in for Momma. *To Marilyn, with love from Aggie.*

It struck me then that my thought wasn't real. I had no feelings. It was Jojo who made me love Momma. All the talk of how she read books and baked pies and sang songs. In my head was a big empty space where Momma should be, and beside it, like a misshapen jigsaw piece that just wouldn't fit, stood the Disney momma Jojo had built for me. I'd try harder to love her. That was how I'd been trained, I thought, as my feet pressed down on all the names, on all the people who'd been loved enough to be remembered.

I waited in the shade of an office block for the lights to change so I could cross the road. The only other person in sight was a tourist, a fact made obvious not only because they were out in the midday heat but also because they stood in the full glare of the sun while they waited for traffic to stop. Behind them were beautiful long shadows cast off by two-hundred-foot buildings. They'd catch on eventually but not before they turned lobster pink. Their problem, not mine.

I crossed over and headed downhill to the park where there was plenty of shade. I approached a bench until I saw a pair of feet in black socks sticking out one end. Someone else who had nothing to do and nowhere to go. I got closer and saw a middle-aged black guy whose snores told the world he was unconscious. A couple of sleeping ducks kept guard on the ground in front of him. Some lookouts they turned out to be.

I walked to the bridge over the river. Nothing much of anything to look at. Behind me, a phlegmy cough. The guy on the bench stood up, wandered over to a tree and spat up the contents of his lungs. He kicked dust over the top, removed his shirt and sat back down again. If he saw me, he didn't care.

Something crashed in the trees next to me, and I jumped clean out my skin.

'Y'alright, honey?' called the guy on the bench.

'Yes, sir,' I answered back, feeling ridiculous.

Sitting under a tree big enough to shade a circus, I looked out. The old guy on the bench slumped like he was drunk but I knew it was just the heat. It made the whole day drunk. Even the air swayed and trembled under the weight of the sun. Birds sang. High up in the dark bushy trees they could afford to be cocky. Their chatter mixed with the sound of distant construction, and when a plane flew low overhead they didn't budge from their shelter. They just sang even louder. I liked that.

Birds slowly gathered around me and I threw Marjorie's moldy bread for them. One duck in particular, its brown eyes framed in a red face, got up real close. Ignoring the bread I put down, it tipped its head to the side and stared at me till I blinked and looked away. I'd never lost a stare-out with a duck before. A warm wind blew over. The duck came closer and closer. It must have learned to trust humans. Humans tend not to hurt ducks. Sure, they'll eat them, but they won't kick them or anything like that. Just feed them bread and crumbs. More than they'll do for each other in a lot of cases.

More ducks arrived and settled down beside me. One real ugly one, with bumpy red eyebrows and a black face, fussed and gasped like it needed water.

'Stupid duck,' I said. 'See? There's a whole river right there. Go get a drink, stupid duck.'

It waddled right over and sat down at my feet, gasping the whole time. Hard to feel sorry for something so ugly and stupid. Unless you're Marjorie, I thought. And I remembered Jojo shooting that hog. Well, I wasn't Marjorie and I wasn't Jojo. I stamped my foot and it flapped its wings. I stamped again and it got up. I stamped and chased it all the way to the river, but when it realized what I'd done, it stopped and tried to run back through my legs. We did a kind of dance and eventually I won. It dropped in with a splash and dipped its head up and down in the rolling water. I'd never seen a happy duck before and before I knew it, I was laughing.

I threw the last of the bread in and turned around, taking in the whole park. Squirrels jumped between trees and the occasional passing cyclist reminded me there was still enjoyment to be had from life. Enjoyment that didn't involve stealing from folks. I straightened the bandage around my wrist. I wasn't looking forward to getting back to work.

Freak was in a good mood when she came back. Mr Dee had slipped her some dough.

'He's kind of like an uncle to me,' she said, spreading the money out and fanning herself.

Money didn't excite me the way it did Freak. For me it was a tool. It was just what you needed to get by.

'What you gonna do with that?' I asked.

'I got plans. Confidential.'

'You could buy something for Tawanna's baby.'

'Yeah, right,' she laughed. 'But here, you can have this.'

She pulled her cell from her pocket and held it out.

'He gave me a new one.'

I took it without question, although I was nervous of upsetting Ade any more than I already had.

'Now you can get hold of me whenever you like, see?' she grinned.

She took me to a place called Cindi's and I took forever to choose between pancakes and waffles, mousse cake or cheesecake. I took so long because Cindi had eight fans

166

whirring away in the ceiling, and the coolness rushed down on top of me. The wetness on my back tickled as it dried up. Eventually I chose coconut meringue pie. Freak made so many funny faces while I ate it, I almost choked myself to death.

18

Marjorie said she was past sleeping in cars. We weren't going anywhere till there was enough money to pay for a few nights in a motel. I didn't care about the motel and told her so. Said I'd sleep in the car if it meant we could leave sooner. I guess I was kinda forceful, because she advised me to pipe down.

'I'm sorry, Marj. I'm just excited is all. I've never seen the ocean before.'

I might as well have told her I'd never seen the sun set, or water come out of a faucet.

'Never seen the frikkin ocean. How can you never have seen the frikkin ocean?'

'I don't know. I just aint. Is that weird?'

'I aint judging. But yeah, it's weird. Didn't your folks never go nowhere?'

Yeah, we did, I thought. A memory of me and Jojo covering the inside of *Jack King* with pages torn from travel magazines surfaced. She ripped them out and chose their position. My job was to secure them with sticky tape. The boat was still pretty solid then, except for a small hole in the bottom that we made wide enough to stand a broom handle in. We tied a sheet to it and sailed for miles, mermaids and sea creatures diving along beside us.

They know the way to Momma's island, Aggie.

'Listen, child, I'm in as much a hurry as you are. You think I want to stay in this place all my days? Well, do you? Living with strangers, locking my cupboards, stuffing ear plugs in every night just to drown out some old hippy's guitar?'

I'd no answer. I always figured everybody in the house felt as fortunate to be there as I did. Maybe it depended on what your alternatives were. If it came to a choice between street-living, Pop-living, or crazy-assed, paranoid, recycled house-living, there was no contest.

'I got my eyes on an apartment in Greenhall,' Marjorie continued. 'Guy says I need to get a month's rent down to make sure he don't give it away.'

I didn't know what to say. I'd never heard of anyone moving up like that. She might as well have told me she was moving to the White House.

'An actual apartment?'

'The real deal, Aggie. All I need to do is offload enough of my little friends and we'll have enough money for the trip. We make the trip, I sell all my stock. I sell all my stock, I'll have enough for the deposit on Greenhall. I get to Greenhall, then I'm out of this place and the future's brighter than bright. You see how that works out, baby doll?'

Easier said than done. We were kind of like business partners now. I'd stay in the car to watch the stuff while she went into shops trying to sell. She wasn't as successful as Freak had made out. Store after store she carried a box in, only to carry it straight back out minutes later. I felt pretty sorry for her. When we pulled up at the next place, she just stared out the window trying to find the energy to go in.

'Want me to go?' I said it without thinking.

She blinked in surprise. 'Really?' she said, her voice like a little girl's for the first time. Well, a little girl who smoked forty a day. And without waiting for me to answer, she jumped out the car and opened the trunk. I went round back to join her and she shoved a box in my hands.

'The crosses are seven bucks a piece. They usually retail around fifteen dollars but tell them they can charge whatever. The smaller pieces, the hats, the boots, are all five bucks. The armadillos are ten. I know it seems a lot but point out the work in them, okay? Make sure they know everything's handmade by a local artist. They love that shit. They can have this entire mixed box to trial for two hundred dollars.'

I raised my eyebrows at that. I may be rookie but I knew no one would take a two hundred dollar gamble on shit made out of old tires. She caught my look. 'Always worth asking,' she said.

They didn't take the two hundred dollar box, but I did walk out lighter and with cash in my pocket. Marjorie was pleased with me. It was the same in the next place, and the place after that. She looked at me like I was a puzzle needing figured out. 'Must be something about you I don't have,' she said. 'What do you say to them?'

Truth was I didn't say anything much, just what she told me to say. I thought maybe it was Marjorie's general demeanor that made the difference. I hadn't seen it but I could imagine her pitch coming off like she was bullying people into parting with their cash. It was easy to misread her. 'I don't know, Marj,' I said. 'Do you smile? I mean, are you friendly with them?'

'Of course I'm fucking friendly,' she said.

I decided to change the subject.

'So when will we be ready to go?' I asked. 'You got cash now, right?'

'I got some but it aint enough. And I need to get my belongings into storage first.'

'Storage, why? Did Ade say that? How long you figuring on us being gone?'

'Quit questioning me, Aggie.' She shook her head from side to side. 'It's just… other shit going down. With the house and all.'

This made me pay attention. 'What shit?'

'Man, I aint supposed to tell no one,' she wailed, as though I'd caught her out unfairly.

'You're putting all your stuff into storage? And you want me to come with you and just leave all of mine behind?'

We both knew I didn't have anything worth a pig's shit to leave behind but that wasn't the point. I thought about Freak's stash of cash. Did she know something was going down? Had Ade told her? I didn't appreciate being kept in the dark.

'What the fuck's happening, Marjorie?'

'Jesus, you may as well know. Bank wants the house back. Serious this time. Hot-shit lawyers.'

Ade had found some obscure law that let him take ownership for thirty bucks, so it was no surprise to learn he had a fight on his hands. Even still, the idea of being back on the road, alone again, filled me with a fear I only got in my dreams of Jojo.

'But they've had lawyers before,' I said, feebly.

Marjorie shrugged. 'Yeah. Sure. Ade's all over it. It'll be fine.'

We turned the corner into our street.

'But I'm putting my stuff in storage anyway,' she said.

I went straight upstairs and banged Ade's door. Freak opened it and I pushed past. The room was as I remembered it. At least he hadn't started packing yet.

'Where is he?'

'What the fuck, Aggie?' Freak stood with her arms spread wide. Her hair hanging loose made her look like some sort of punk-angel.

'Did you know?' I asked.

'I aint a mind reader, Aggie. Know what?'

'About the house?'

Freak looked at the ceiling in frustration, like she was dealing with a child. 'What about the house, Aggie?'

'Quit playing games with me, Freak. Marjorie already told me.'

'What the fuck does Marjorie know about anything?'

'Someone say my name?'

Freak spun round to see Marjorie leaning against the doorframe.

'This is bullshit.'

'Aint no bullshit. Just the truth as I see it.' Marjorie shrugged. 'Ade aint gonna win this one, Freak.'

'The hell he aint,' Freak replied. 'He's meeting someone right now. He's gonna fix it.'

Marjorie came further into the room. It was starting to feel a little crowded with the three of us in there. She lifted the sheets to take a look at all the papers on Ade's desk, and the charts on the wall, and shook her head. Seemed maybe a little bit sad. 'He still into all this stuff, huh?'

'Get your hands off that!' Freak grabbed a folder out of Marjorie's hand and the paper inside spilled out all over the floor. I bent to pick it up. Rows and rows of names and addresses, all handwritten. Must have taken somebody hours. Days, even.

'What is this stuff?' I asked.

'Evidence,' said Freak, gathering the paper back into the folder. While she was doing that, Marjorie pulled back the sheet on the wall and it came down. I recognized the images straight away. It was the road JFK got killed on. The whole world had seen these pictures.

Freak finished picking the papers up from the floor and saw us looking. 'Shit,' she said. 'You have to get out of here.' And she tried to cover the wall with the sheet which had fallen beside the baseboard.

'Take it easy, honey,' said Marjorie. 'Me and Ade go back a long way, remember? I've seen all this stuff before. It's old news.' She took a little turn around, taking it all in, yawning to show how little it meant to her.

'Yeah, well that was then and this is now. Things have changed,' Freak said. 'Y'all need to get out of here before Ade gets back.'

'I aint going anywhere,' I said. 'I want to know if I've got homelessness coming at me.'

'Course you aint,' Freak replied. 'Ade's got a plan. He's gonna work it all out.'

'Sure he is,' Marjorie said. 'Just as soon as he's finished

solving the mysterious case of who shot John F. Kennedy.'

'What?' I couldn't believe what I was hearing. I had Ade down as a thinking type of guy, but I always figured he was working on something to do with the environment, otherwise why did we recycle every piece of shit that came into the house?

'Who shot what?' I said, as though it could all be reframed to make sense, if only I was stupid enough.

Freak looked set to murder Marjorie. 'Aint none of your business, Aggie.'

'You mean, you didn't know?' Marjorie was enjoying herself. 'You didn't know that Ade's set to blow apart the establishment when he publishes his findings on JFK? It's gonna be big news, girl.' I could see that Marjorie couldn't help but smile.

'Shut up, Marjorie. You don't know what you're talking about. He's uncovered something new. Something big.'

'I doubt that, sweetie,' Marjorie ran one ring-clad finger down the spine of a thick, black book.

'He has,' Freak continued. 'He's almost finished the book and when he does there'll be enough money to buy this house. Hell, there'll be enough money to buy this whole street.'

My heart sank. He was one of those. We were fucked.

Seemed only me and Marj weren't convinced of Ade's ability to beat off the bank. Monty told us he'd seen a similar situation in the newspaper and that guy wound up alright due to some loophole in the law. No good talking to Freak about it, because she was Ade's right-hand man. Wouldn't hear a bad word against him. Tawanna kept on with her refurbishment program, tidying one room at a time and leaving color charts wherever she went, all the time ignoring the bigger jobs, like exposed rafters and floorboards that needed nailed down and walls with holes in them. Lloyd stayed out all day with Ricardo, working when he could – he was stressed about the baby coming. Virginia was doing some detox shit and wasn't allowed to speak, but I did notice her meditation time increase, which made me think she wasn't as calm as she made out.

I sat in Marj's room, quietly skimming her books, while her fingers flew and cut and glued and stitched. Dozens of little rubber trinkets began to stack up, waiting for me to wrap them and carry them to the sea.

ᛝ

I was on the shore and Jojo was swimming far out. I called for
her to be careful. She shouted at me but the waves crashing
around my feet drowned her out. *Be louder*, I urged. She had
something to say. *Be louder.*

Something tugged on me and I became aware of Freak's
voice on the outside, distracting me from what was happening.

Be louder, Jojo.

'Aggie. Aggie. Wake up.'

I tried to keep a grip of it but it was no use. I was back
in my own room on a hard floor. The night felt too real and
Freak too close. I scooted backwards, which was hard to do
without putting weight on my damaged wrist. Freak flicked a
flashlight under her face.

'It's me, you dumbfuck. Don't act so scared.'

'I know it's you. Dumbfuck yourself, stupid bitch. I aint
scared. I was sleeping. What's wrong?'

'Aint nothing wrong, stupid Aggie. Why's there always
gotta be something wrong?'

We'd been getting more and more snarky with each other
lately. Every time we saw each other we just picked up our
arguing where we'd left off.

'What time is it?'

'Aggie, listen. I need your help. Will you? Will you help
me?'

'What's wrong? What is it?'

'I told you, Aggie. Quit saying something's wrong when

175

there aint nothing wrong. Alright?' She shone the light straight in my face and I squirmed to get away from it.

'Dammit, Freak. What do you want?'

'Ade's asked me out.' Her grin could have electrified a fence.

'You woke me up to tell me that? You've been screwing him for months.'

'Shut up, Aggie, don't spoil it. He's taking me out. Like on a date. To an actual restaurant or some shit like that.'

I rubbed my face awake. Looked like this was the type of favor that required a conversation. 'Wow, that's great, Freak. So what, you want me to help pick out something to wear?'

'No, that's not it. It's tomorrow. He wants to do it tomorrow. It's the only day he's got free.'

'But he hardly goes anywhere!' I laughed. I couldn't help it. The notion that Ade was some wheeler-dealer guy dashing between appointments was a joke.

'Jesus, Aggie. If I'd known you'd be so awkward about it, I wouldn't have asked.'

'I aint being awkward, Freak. You aint asked anything yet.'

'Well, Jesus, be patient and I will!' she snapped. I sat in the dark and waited, obedient. When she was satisfied I wouldn't interrupt, she continued. 'I'm expected at Sadie's tomorrow. Mr Dee wants to see me. I need you to go in my place and spin him a story about why I aint there. Say I'm sick or something.'

My body was still sore. The Sad Place seemed a long way to go just to make excuses.

'Can't you call him?' I asked.

'I tried that already,' she said, and became all sweetness and light. She tipped her head to the side, clasped her hands, pouted her lips and said, 'Please? He's going into town tomorrow anyway and he's said I can go with him.'

I realized then that Freak had made this date up in her head. She looked like she'd just realized it too, as the smile ran away from her face.

'Sure thing,' I said, and the smile returned, like magic. 'Now can you turn off that light?' And she backed out and tiptoed down the stairs to Ade's room. I got up to bolt the door. I'd been leaving it open in the hope she'd decide to spend a night with me.

It was happening again, just like with me and Jojo. Me and Freak had got closer than two people should get, and now it was as if we repelled each other. The fact that Ade had bashed me for her had turned him into a hero. She spent all her time locked up in his room with him. I didn't miss the cutting – not one little bit – and I was glad she wasn't night-wandering anymore, but it still felt like things were going down a bad road and I couldn't say why.

I lay back down to sleep but I was alert now. I tried to relax, tried to bring back the feel of the dream I'd been having but it was no good. My mind wandered back to the time after Ash had left. Jojo and Cy were spending more and more time together, and that suited Pop down to the ground. His thick fingers would crawl through my hair as we watched Jojo follow Cy out to the fields. Ash being gone opened up a space for her and she was real happy to put jeans on and be out of the house a while. Pop grew his beard longer and longer, as though his extra manliness could counteract Jojo's new independence.

The floor beneath me felt more hard than usual and I couldn't settle. I rolled over and over and back again, my good arm getting tangled in the sleeping bag. I pulled it free and let my hand rest on my stomach. I thought about praying. I screwed my eyes up tight but instead of praying I felt the urge. I tried to push it away. Pop's voice. His grunting. I made a tight fist of my hand. I didn't want to do it, but something else always took control. A feeling of power, of no power, of having it all and having nothing. Of being everything to someone, making them moan with happiness. *The second angel poured out his bowl into the sea. And it became like the blood of a corpse. The third angel poured out his bowl into the rivers. And they became blood. And the angel in charge of the waters said. Just are you, O Holy One, for you brought these judgments.*

The scratching, slow and steady, and the rush, and the tears and the thank-yous, and the reality after when not one person in the house looks you in the eye because, after all, you're just a little whore like your momma.

I turned over and waited for dawn to break.

20

Next day I took the bus downtown to Sadie's Place. The bell jangled as I pushed the door open and Duke looked up from the end of the bar like normal. The place was dark and dead, like normal, too.

'Hey, hey, little Aggie. What you got for me today?' He closed his book, a Jackie Collins, rearranged his charm bracelet, and went behind the bar to pour himself a drink. His pinky finger stuck out while he knocked it back in one, and then he sprayed breath freshener in his mouth. He waggled his jaw around, the way a sheep chews the cud. He was wearing suit trousers and a shirt. He'd left the top few buttons undone. I'd never seen him look so normal before. Only his contacts marked him out as different; they were green today, Emerald City green. I stood in the space between the door and the bar and shuffled like a fool.

'Nothing today, Duke.'

I scanned the empty booths in case Mr Dee was sitting in a darkened corner. Duke glanced up at me and a spark of interest flashed across his face as he took in my bandaged hand.

'What you do there, sugar pie?'

He played with his glass on the counter and examined his nails while he waited for my reply.

'Uh, I ran into a bit of trouble.'

He looked suddenly serious and turned his fake eyes on me. 'Duke don't like trouble, Aggie.'

'Not serious. Just domestic shit. You know how it goes.'

'Sure,' he smiled and turned to refill his glass. 'Duke knows how it goes.'

'Could I get a coke?' I asked, as I forced myself closer to him and hopped onto a bar stool. He bent down and got a can from the fridge behind him. He pinged back the ring and passed it over. I took a swallow and the bubbles made me burp. He grimaced.

'Excuse me,' I covered my mouth too late. He shook his head in disgust and went back to his book. I took a good look around the place. No one here but the two of us. 'I gotta meet Mr Dee, Duke. You seen him? I don't know what he looks like.'

In the dingy half light of the bar, the intensity of his gaze almost pushed me off my seat.

'Mr Dee, huh?' he said, quietly. He laid his book face down on the counter. In tiny writing, sandwiched between the giant letters of the author's name, was the book's title: *Sinners*. I felt heat prickle my chest and redden my cheeks.

'Tell me,' he continued. 'How's Freak these days?'

'She's real sick,' I lied. 'That's why I'm here. She sent me.'

Duke laughed but not in a humorous way. 'Did she? Interesting.'

I crossed my arms over my chest. He wasn't even trying to disguise it. His eyes were all over me. 'Freak keeps real bad health, don't she?' he spat. 'That's more than once she's let me down.'

Saliva flew from his lips and found my face. Something had shifted and the air felt dangerous.

'She just ate some bad chicken,' I offered. 'It aint serious.'

'Oh, I'm afraid it is serious.' He moved along the bar towards me and my heart hit my boots. 'Thing is, she's overdue on a payment, Aggie. She's been owing Mr Dee for some time now.'

I took a few gulps of my coke, trying to get my thoughts

in order. Freak hadn't said anything about owing money. I'd been too sleepy to think of asking. I kicked myself for being so dumb.

Duke leaned over the counter and I couldn't help but see down his shirt. I had to admit his pecs were pretty good for a guy his age. He might have a fondness for dresses, but he obviously worked out. A carpet of white hair ran from his neck and disappeared down into darkness. I flicked my eyes away and kept them focused on my coke as the smell of cologne and alcohol floated over me. Evidently, the freshener hadn't worked.

'I don't know anything about that, Duke. All she said was she had a meeting with Mr Dee today and she's real apologetic about not making it.'

'Because she's sick,' Duke said, drumming his blue nails on the counter. 'And she's sent you instead.'

'Uh – yeah,' I replied.

He leaned in real close. A smattering of gray pores speckled the grease on his nose.

'What she tell you about Mr Dee, Aggie?'

'Nothing.' I shrugged. Keep it casual, keep it easy. 'Just he's real important, I guess.' I glanced up to see if I'd pleased him but I couldn't read his face. Another burp threatened to burst out of me. I swallowed it down but it caught on my throat and made my eyes water. He ran his middle finger round and around the rim of my can, his wrist gently touching my hand.

'Mr Dee,' he murmured. 'You want to see Mr Dee, yes?' His fat tongue pushed between his lips, making them wet. His teeth were white, too white. He must have had them done. He grabbed my chin and pulled my face up so I had to look him in the eye. 'Mr Dee is a very special friend of mine, Aggie. A very close friend. Would you be respectful if you met him, I wonder?'

I let the can go and leaned back far as I could without toppling off the barstool.

'I would, of course I would,' I said.

'Not like Freak. Freak just takes the money. That's all she wants. It's sad.'

He moved round from behind the bar to stand beside me.

'You're tight with Freak, right?'

The way he said that made me want to vomit. He was close enough now to be touching me, just lightly, not enough for me to complain about but enough for me to get the idea. I nodded, eyes fixed on the bottles behind the bar. So pretty, green, blue and purple.

'You should tell her that Mr Dee is very unhappy. He wants paying. If she doesn't pay, Mr Dee will take what's his some other way. But maybe that's what Freak wants him to do.'

He slipped his hand onto my leg and down in between as he moved behind me.

'Does Aggie understand?' he breathed. The smell of him caught in my throat.

He pulled me up by my waistband, forcing me over the bar, my feet only just balanced on the rung of the bar stool.

Bottles, green, blue and purple.

He reached over and pulled up my sleeve. With one hand still holding my waistband so I couldn't move, he gently ran the back of his hand over the mess of scars on my arm.

'You're the same,' he breathed.

The bell on the door signalled someone arriving and he let me go. He stood back and stretched, letting out a huge, fake yawn. I jumped off the stool and put some space between us.

A young woman came in, skinny with boobs and boots. Her stride faltered for a split second when she saw Duke and me.

'You're late, darling,' he said. Her eyes met mine briefly, and she ducked her head as she clicked behind the bar and disappeared through the back. Duke resumed his position behind the bar and thwacked the counter with a dish cloth.

'You have a special quality, Aggie. Duke likes that. You ever want a job, make sure you come to me first. Now scoot.

And tell Freak I'm not happy.'

I stumbled outside fast as I could. The sun made my eyes water. I walked fast, putting that place behind me, ripping the bandage off my wrist as I did. No need to let people know I had a weak spot. I pounded fifteen blocks before I got a straight thought in my head, and when it arrived it told me to pull my phone out. Business people filed out of the building beside me and gathered in the lot across the road. I didn't care if they heard or not.

'What the FUCK did you just send me into?'

If she'd been standing in front of me I would have killed her. I hadn't left my sub folks behind just to wind up sub for someone else. People bumped into me and I pressed the phone hard to my ear in order to hear. Sounded like she was crying.

A fat guy in a gray shirt started moving me on. Fire drill. Jesus. I couldn't make out what she was saying. I hung up. I tried to push my way through the hundreds of people pouring out the building but in the end it was easier to move with them. I waited for half an hour in amongst the normal folks and managed to bag four wallets in that time. And that was me being cautious. When they were allowed back in the building, I jumped a taxi home.

I'd decided what to do. I'd head to the coast. No more stalling. If Marjorie was ready to go then good. If not, I'd go myself. I'd help myself to some of the secret cash Freak had put beneath the floorboards. Not all. Maybe half. I'd call it compensation for trauma brought on by Duke's foul breath down my throat. Fuck him. Fuck her. I'd take all of it.

I took the stairs two at a time. I had to speak to Marjorie first. I banged on her door and rattled the handle but she wasn't in. I took the stairs again up to my room and spread all my shit out. Not much to show for a life. Jeans, boots, a few books belonging to Marjorie. A sleeping bag that had seen better days. A sleeping mat. Make-up. Good. I didn't need to carry a shitload of crap around. I'd go light. Move fast. Do it myself. I'd done it before. Where the fuck was Marjorie? I sat down and waited.

Outside, the light was fading. There was a knock on my door. I watched it swing open to reveal Freak, mascara staining her cheeks, nose like Rudolph. Just looking at her made me tired.

'Why you knocking?' I said. 'It's your room, too.'

She came in, sliding along the wall like a human slug, snot running over her lips. She wiped her face with her sleeve and sat down on the floor beside me.

'Aren't you going to ask what's wrong?'

'I know what's wrong, Freak. Don't have to fucking ask what's wrong. What's wrong is sending me to that fucking creep without a word of warning.'

'Did you tell him I was sick?'

'Yes, I fucking told him!' I grabbed her collar and pushed her down so I was sitting on top of her, yelling in her face. 'I fucking told him you were sick right before he tried to have sex with me!'

'Big fucking deal. He tries to have sex with everybody. Don't mean you're special.'

I smelled it again, that alcoholic smell, the cologne, saw the bottles green, blue and purple, and then I looked at her, face all swollen from tears, so uncaring about anyone but herself. She wriggled about beneath me but I had her shoulders good and tight and I shook her.

'Bitch. Fucking bitch,' I said, over and over. 'Sending me into that. Sending your friend to a fucking rapist. A fucking rapist!'

Her mouth curled into a sly half-smile. 'Says the girl who left her own sister with two of the fuckers.'

I slapped her with so much force it hurt my hand. I remembered I'd only taken the bandage off today and then the thought was gone. I took a fistful of hair and banged her head off the floor. Once, twice, but it wasn't her face I saw when I looked down, it was a stranger's face, still female, but brown hair instead of pink, not Jojo but maybe Jojo. I stopped to look properly and it was Freak after all, her eyes empty, unseeing, not even feeling what I was doing. I climbed off her in disgust, with her, with myself, with everything. I spat on her stomach for good measure. She curled herself into a ball and cried.

'Duke says to tell you Mr Dee wants his money,' I said over the noise of her tears. If she heard me she didn't let on. I didn't even care.

In the morning, Freak and me were still laying there. I'd intended to listen out for Marjorie or Ade coming back through the night, but somehow I'd fallen asleep to the sound of her crying.

'Kitty cat Aggie,' said Freak. 'You still mew in your sleep.'

'Whatever.'

'I'm sorry for what I said.'

I wasn't ready to forgive and forget, which is what she was angling for. At the same time, I didn't want to dwell on her last words to me. I tried to push all thoughts of Jojo out my head by counting the cracks in the ceiling. Since I'd been there, they'd multiplied. Ninety-seven cracks, all spread out like a spiderweb, not fit for holding anything much less two fighting humans – sub or otherwise. The huge crack running down the wall now travelled along the baseboard and round the corner to the next wall.

'This place is shit,' I said.

Freak sat up and looked at me, as though an idea had just occurred to her. 'Why don't we just split?'

'What?'

This was a turn around.

'Serious. This place blows. Austin, that's the place to be.'

'Freak, every place is the same for girls like you and me. Wherever we go, we'll end up doing the same shit. Wherever we go...' I couldn't finish my sentence. For the first time, I understood that wherever we went there would always be a guy like Duke waiting to catch girls like us. Wherever we went it was a one-way trip down the same road. Whether she got my point or not, she didn't say anything more about it.

We went downstairs for breakfast. The cupboards were pretty bare. Tawanna had started hoarding food in her room on account of night-time feeding frenzies, despite the baby being barely more than a bump. She was packing on the pounds and drawing looks from Virginia.

'Jesus, is this all there is?' Freak held a box of Cheerios, which we knew belonged to Monty because he was a big Cheerios fiend. We decided, as he hadn't put a label on, that technically they belonged to everyone. We ate them dry from the box and sat in the empty kitchen looking out at the garden, all burned up yellow and blistered in the heat. Nothing stayed green at this time of year.

'So what was the problem?' I finally asked.

'What problem when?' Freak said, shoving a fistful of Cheerios in her mouth. Some fell out her hands and down the side of her chin to the floor.

'Last night. You were upset about something.'

'Yeah, Aggie. You beating the shit out of me.'

'Before that. You said something was wrong but I didn't want to know.'

'Oh, that. Nothing.' She took another handful of cereal, dropping more on the floor.

'Who's going to pick that up?' I said, but she just kept looking out the window and chewing.

'How was your date?' I figured the problem had to do with Ade. He'd been her whole world for weeks. She shrugged.

'Fine,' she said.

'What did you do?'

'Not a lot. Took me to the JFK museum. Introduced me to one of his friends. Some guy named Rand. Then they went off and talked a bit and I just... hung around.'

'Romantic,' I said. 'And the... investigation? How's that going?'

'Uh. I'm not sure. He... uh... I'm not sure.'

186

She made a deep sigh and her body kind of slumped. Her open hand rested on the counter with Cheerios still in it.

'You can tell me, you know,' I said, taking some cereal from her hand. 'I'm not going to tell him.'

She threw a quick look at me. 'I know you're not. It's not that. It's just... he... Oh fuck, I don't know.' She put the Cheerios down on the counter and laid her head on her forearms. I noticed a dark spot coming through her sleeve.

'He... he kinda flipped out a little,' she said, after a while.

'What kinda flipped out? Did he hurt you?'

She shook her head. 'No. More like... he's gone a bit weird. Like, won't talk to me now. He thinks... he thinks...'

'Jesus, Freak. What does he think?'

She rolled her eyes and laughed nervously.

'He thinks people are spying on him,' she said, at last. 'Like the FBI and stuff. Because of the investigation.'

I almost choked on my cereal. 'Be serious?'

'I am serious. It aint funny though, Aggie. It's kinda scary. He cut his dreads off.'

'That aint no bad thing. White guy with dreads? Gross. No offense.'

'He cut them off, because he thought there were microphones in his hair.'

'Oh. Fuck,' I said. 'Shit.'

'There's more,' she said, her face burning. She kicked the baseboard. 'Christ, I'm so stupid sometimes. I fucking gave him my money.'

'What? All of it?'

'Near enough a thousand bucks, Aggie.'

My eyes must have grown the size of planets. She shrugged. 'He said it was for lawyers to fight for the house.'

'That sounds like a good reason,' I said, relieved.

'But instead, he gave it to this guy in exchange for a bunch of papers and shit. Shit to do with JFK. That's the real reason we went into town yesterday.'

She looked real sheepish, and in the middle of the

awfulness, I was happy to find my sympathy for her was coming back.

'But that aint all, Aggie. Shit, no. That aint all.' The way she said it made me pay attention, though somewhere in the back of my mind I had an idea of what was coming. A sick feeling started way down deep in my stomach. If I looked at her, I'd kill her. I organized the loose Cheerios into a tidy pile and began to crush each one with my thumb. A sharp crumb slipped under my nail and pricked the skin.

'Shit,' I said, shoving my thumb in my mouth.

'Strictly speaking...' Freak continued.

'I need a band-aid.'

'... strictly speaking, the money wasn't mine to give away.'

The blood arched its way in a thin line beneath my nail, and dripped onto the tiny mountain I'd made.

'And I'm sorry I sent you there, Aggie,' she was saying. 'I should have told you how bad he was from the beginning.'

21

We planned for Ade to return the stuff and get the cash back, but when he rolled in later with Marjorie, it was clear he'd be useless. I'd always had him down as spineless but now he could barely stand upright. He kept his arms wrapped around himself and only moved when Marjorie told him to. She made him sit in the backyard while she tidied his hair up with clippers. Black clumps rolled through the empty vegetable patch. I hoped a bird would gather them for a nest, because I sure as hell I didn't want human content in my compost.

Me and Freak watched as Marjorie did her work, murmuring to Ade the whole time. When she finished with him, he almost looked normal.

'Time to lay down, Ade,' Marjorie said. 'Get some rest.'

'Hey Freak,' he said, with a goofy type of smile, as Marjorie led him out. Freak just nodded, confused as I was about what we were dealing with here. I expected Freak to be annoyed that Marjorie was playing mother instead of her, but whatever had gone down between her and Ade had left her pretty shook up. When Marjorie came back down, she found us waiting for her.

'How is he?' asked Freak.

'Take a seat,' she said. 'We're gonna talk.'

That's when Marjorie told us that she and Ade once had a thing going on. Of course, we knew that. What we didn't know was it had only finished when she noticed he couldn't handle his joint. It made him paranoid. Made him think strange thoughts. Ade had always had the JFK thing going on since Marjorie knew him, but when FBI agents started to spy on him because he was close to a big breakthrough, Marjorie had said maybe he should take a step back. He'd split up with her when she'd stopped his weed supply.

'And then you showed up,' Marjorie said to Freak. I'd seen Marjorie angry plenty of times, but not angry like this cold, quiet anger. 'I told you to keep away from him, didn't I?'

Freak's eyes widened. 'You didn't say anything about weed.'

'I shouldn't have to. Little girls should just do as they're told.'

'Hey, Marjorie,' I said, quietly. 'Doing as they're told sometimes gets little girls into trouble.'

She looked at me kind of surprised I had a tongue, but she didn't argue.

'Come on,' I said. 'She didn't know.'

'I would never hurt him, Marjorie,' Freak said. 'I care about Ade.'

'I care about him, too,' Marjorie growled. 'And I know him best.'

'Yeah, I think you do,' Freak said, her voice little more than a whisper. Her eyes filled with tears. She dipped her head to hide but she wasn't fooling anyone. Marjorie looked embarrassed for her.

'We've got a problem, Marjorie,' I said. 'A different problem.' And I explained about Mr Dee and the money.

'Aint anything to do with me.' Marjorie shrugged when I'd finished.

'You think these guys are going to let Ade walk away when they learn what he's done with their money?' I asked.

'Way I see it, it's Freak who's let them down. Not Ade,' Marjorie said, though she didn't sound too convinced.

I shook my head. 'They don't care. They want their money is all. Ade's in it now. We need to get that money back before they come looking.'

'Do they know anything about Ade?' Marjorie looked at Freak, just daring her to say yes.

'Course not,' said Freak, offended. 'They don't even know where I live.'

'Yet,' I said, frowning at her. 'And once they find out Ade's in charge here…'

'Huh, yeah sure he is,' Marjorie half laughed. She shrugged. 'Like I said, not my problem. They don't know where you live, no problem so far as I can see. Now look, missy,' she said to Freak. 'You and him can play hook up, okay? Let him fuck your tiny mind out for all I care. But if I hear you've let him come near so much as a sniff of weed, I will turn you over to this Mr fucking Dee myself. Do you hear me?'

Freak broke down at that point. She dipped her head, her shoulders shaking.

'Please don't, Marjorie. I swear I won't. I didn't even know weed could do that. Don't turn me over to him, please.'

Marjorie raised her eyebrows at me in surprise. Freak never rolled over like that for anyone. She was suspicious, but I thought it was genuine. Whether it was Ade's breakdown, or if it really was the idea of getting caught by Mr Dee – Freak was far from her usual self. I began to feel guilty for adding to her woes the previous night, but then I remembered Duke's hands on me and my fire came back. I tried to push away any sympathy I might feel. Most likely, she was just trying to get us onside.

Marjorie turned to me. 'I'm moving some things over to Ma's later. You got anything you want me to take?'

We had to raise our voices to hear each other over the noise of Freak's sniffling.

'You know what, Marj – I aint got it together yet. But thanks.'

She nodded. 'You just let me know, okay? We'll be ready to leave in a couple of days or so. Just got to collect some cash from a couple of places.'

Freak's head shot up at the mention of cash. Somehow through her broken-hearted routine she'd been keeping tabs on the conversation.

'Not for you, Freak-face. Me and Aggie are making a business trip.'

Marjorie went to her room, leaving me and Freak alone together, more pathetic than the two last stalks in a hay field.

'What business trip, Aggie? Can't I come?'

'Jeez, Freak. Aint no flies on you, huh?'

'I aint got no one, Aggie,' she said, her head hanging. 'I'm up against it and I aint got a single soul.'

'Sure you do, Freak.'

'Who?'

I searched for anyone but the obvious and came up with nothing. It was grudged, but at least I said it.

'You got me. And you got Ade, when he's playing with more than half a deck.'

She laughed at that and sniffed, exposing a railway track of white scars as she wiped her face with her forearm.

'About Duke, Aggie – he aint all he seems.'

'How so?'

'He's got a mean streak to him.'

'I don't need telling.'

She looked like she wanted to say more, but the last thing I wanted was to get caught in a heart-to-heart.

'Come on,' I said.

'Come on where?'

'That money aint coming back here on its own now, is it?' I said. 'Besides, I took in some cash yesterday. Even if that guy's spent some of it by now it might still be okay.'

I'd counted it up. I'd earned a hundred and thirty-five bucks when I'd swiped those wallets.

She pulled herself up like she had weights stitched into all those scars.

'It's a lost cause, Aggie,' she sighed. 'We aint seeing that money again.'

'Well, if that's the case, there's plenty more where that came from. Come on.'

Rand was a black guy who dressed like a teenage basketball player, even though he had to be on the far side of forty. The crotch of his pants dangled between his knees, chains slung around his neck like lassos. He wore three tank tops that I could see, all layered over each other. The top one was black and had the number thirty-three written on it in red. He wore a back-to-front baseball cap, which was pretty dumb because it meant he had to squint into the sun. When he squinted, his lips pulled back to show off huge front teeth just like Bugs Bunny, only not as cute.

Rand spent his days in front of the JFK museum on Dealey, trying to sell tourists all manner of shit to do with the assassination. He laid all his magazines and newspapers out along a wall and then stood back, invisible under a tree, waiting like a spider for a fly to land on his web. When a tourist made the mistake of stopping to check out the spread of stuff, he'd pounce. Surprising to me how many people shook him off. I'd always found most people easy enough to get along with, or con, I guess, if you're being specific. There were definite advantages to being young, white and female. After a while, it came clear poor old Rand worked hard for a living.

'Go now,' I said to Freak. We'd been watching from the grassy knoll. She wasn't sure he'd remember who she was.

She was nervous, a whole new Freak. 'Come with me,' she said, and I did.

As we approached, Rand managed to get a woman to stop. Out of politeness, we hung back, waiting for him to finish his schtick. Unfortunately for us, the woman was interested in what Rand had to say.

'That window up there, that's where the shots are supposed to have come from. Now down here...' He led the way and the woman followed him down the hill into the middle of the road. His voice carried back. 'The car was right here when the first bullet hit…'

'Just our luck,' I sighed, and lay back in the grass.

'Let's go,' she replied. 'He aint gonna give the money back.'

'You don't know if you don't try. Jesus, Freak. Would you rather Mr Dee came after you?'

She squirmed and shrugged. 'Maybe it would just be Duke,' she said, unconvincingly. 'I've handled Duke before.'

'Maybe you've not seen him the way I saw him yesterday.' And like that, the tension was back between us.

Rand and his tourist lady were getting on well. He gave her one of his newspapers, and she gave him a handful of ten dollar bills before moving on into the museum. We seized our chance.

'Nice work if you can get it,' I called out. He turned round and looked at us, blank.

'Huh?' he said. 'Can I help you?'

'Hey, Rand,' said Freak.

'Do I know you?' he said.

'Sure. The other day, remember? I was down here with Ade?'

'Oh, sure. I remember you. S'up?'

'Uh…' Freak looked at me for help.

'The money he gave you, mister. Wasn't his to give,' I said.

The transformation was something to see. His face shut down completely. 'Don't know nothing about no money.' He turned away from us and made to cross the road.

'Not leaving all your business stuff here, are you, mister?'

I was closer to his belongings than he was. He turned back to face us, his eyes drawn to his newspapers all lined up in a row along the wall and held down by big stones, the corners fluttering in a hot breeze.

'Anything happen to my merchandise, all it means is you'll be looking for more money than you need right now. Now why don't y'all run along before you land yourselves with a debt too big to pay. Or maybe you've done that already. Either way it aint no concern of mine.'

He ambled over to the shade of a tree where another guy was waiting. His back-up, I guessed. Rand kept his back turned but the other guy watched us the whole time. I thought about just lifting all the magazines and newspapers to sell myself, but this was the only spot in town I could hope to shift them. Here, they were a piece of history and worth something. Take them away from Dealey Plaza and all you'd be left with was tea-stained bullshit.

'Told you there was no point.' That was Freak, smug in victory, even if it meant she was screwed. She spun on her heel and walked away.

'You can't just quit,' I said, chasing after her. 'There must be something we can do.'

She shook me off and walked on, casting nervous glances about her, as though Duke might appear from any direction.

'Let's go shopping,' I suggested. 'We'll sell it on.'

'Who we gonna sell it on to? Duke?'

'There must be someone else,' I said, half running alongside her.

She stopped and turned to face me. 'If there was someone else, don't you think I might have mentioned it already? Duke knows too many people. Shit, I shouldn't even be out here.'

She darted down an alley and stood with her back flat against the red brick wall, as though a dozen sniper rifles might be trained on her.

'Shit, Freak. Come on out,' I called from the street. 'Aint nobody here. Aint nothing no one can do in broad daylight, is there?'

She shook her head, her body rigid. I sighed and walked down to stand on the other side of her.

'You can't stay here all day, can you? Won't solve nothing.'

She was looking at something beyond me, towards the end of the alley. When I turned to see what was so interesting, she pushed past me.

'No frikkin way,' she said, walking further down to where it opened up into a square. 'Remember this place?'

I followed her and slowly it dawned on me. This was where we first met. The rain and scaffolding was gone but the yellow dumpster remained. 'It's a sign!' she said, suddenly happy. Freak liked to take messages from the universe and this one, whatever it was, was a good one.

I laughed as Freak danced up and down just like she had on the night we met. It seemed so long ago. Freak scaled the dumpster for old time's sake. Perhaps she thought the universe had left her some gold bullion in there, I don't know. I'd only seen this place in the dark before. I looked up at the offices surrounding the yard, seeing them properly for the first time. Offices meant people, people meant money. I scanned ground level, looking for a way in. Every single door was a fire exit that only opened from the inside. Naturally they were all closed.

'Jack shit in here,' Freak called from inside the dumpster. She popped her head up and there behind her, six feet above, was the fire escape. I was in the dumpster in a flash. Freak made a basket with her hands and I stepped into it. She hoisted me up high as she could. I grabbed the ladder and pulled it down.

'I should do it,' said Freak as I climbed the steps.

'No offense,' I replied, 'but you aint firing on all cylinders these days. Reckon you better just keep watch. You think you can do that?'

'Sure, Aggie. Thanks. Be careful.'

The door on the first level was locked so I kept going. On the fourth floor I got an open door. I looked down and gave Freak a thumbs up, though I didn't think it looked too promising. It was a small corridor, six doors in total, with a doorway at the end that must have led in to the rest of the building. I set my hopes on the six doors I could see.

Shadows moved through the opaque glass on the first couple of doors. I ducked down and crept by. A phone rang out in the next room, and the room after that was locked. Only two doors left. I tried the handle and it swung open to reveal a kitchen. I slipped in, closing the door behind me. At the end of the room beside a cracked window was a small table with three chairs. On the back of one chair was a ladies suit jacket. I ran through the pockets but only turned out a crumpled tissue. Damn it. I thought of Freak waiting for me outside, the fear I'd seen in her. I sure didn't want to return empty handed. I went through the pockets again and again, and I'd probably still be there today if a toilet hadn't flushed.

I snapped my head round trying to figure where the noise came from, when a door at the side opened and a woman tottered out, looking down as she straightened her skirt with one hand. Looped over her other arm was a little blue purse that I just knew would have a wallet in it, if only I could will my legs to move. She took a few steps before she realized I was there. She stopped, her mouth in a perfect little O of surprise.

Before she could yell I dived round the table to give her an almighty shove. She flew backwards. 'Oh, m'am. I'm sorry. I'm so sorry,' I said. I snatched her bag and I ran. I made it back to the fire escape and had clambered halfway back down the ladder before the screaming had even started.

We ran for a block before turning the corner and forcing ourselves to walk, heads down, bag tight under my arm. We ducked into McDonald's, ordered a Happy Meal to share, only opening the bag once we were sitting down. My hands were shaking but my breathing was getting steadier.

Inside was a set of car keys. Freak wanted to go back to find the car, but I told her she was crazy and she dropped the subject. A book: *Confidence at Work: Get It, Feel It, Keep It.* I put it to one side, feeling guilty I'd sabotaged the author's efforts. I rummaged through the rest of the contents: tissues, make-up, notebook, tampons. No fucking wallet.

'I don't frikkin believe it,' I said, double-checking everything.

'Give me that,' said Freak. She ran her hand all round

the inside. 'Here it is,' she said. She'd found a small zip and pulled it back. Inside was a card with a piece of paper wrapped around it. It couldn't be, could it? I pushed my rising excitement back down. She unfolded the paper and turned it over. There, on lined paper, written in blue ink, were the beautiful magic numbers. Freak looked at me, eyes bright as stars. 'How long does it take to cancel a bank card?'

We found an ATM inside of a minute. The card glided in and Freak punched the numbers. It worked. We walked away with the daily limit. Five hundred dollars and a hellish urge to squeal.

On a different day we would have celebrated by tossing the money at nickel slots or going to a movie, but this money had to count. Freak was electric with the buzz. She wanted to hit another place but I was jangled. There's a big difference between quietly picking someone's pocket and pushing them head-on so you can take their bag. 'No one ever thinks of the thief,' I said. She thought it was funny, but I was done for the day so we took the bus home.

'Aggie,' Freak said, and from the way she said it, I knew my answer was no even before I knew what the question was. The driver watched us in his mirror and I wished we'd chosen a different seat. I kept an eye on the traffic outside, half expecting a police car to pull alongside us, siren blaring, red and blue lights flashing.

'What say we cut town and head to Austin?' she said.

'What the fuck, Freak? I already told you no.'

'I know, but I got a cousin there can set us up.'

I shook my head in disbelief. There was always something more with her. She took my silence as encouragement.

'Think about it,' she said. 'We just aint gonna get this money together. It was a good today, sure – but we need another four or five days like that before I can go see Mr Dee. Duke'll find me before then. I just know it.'

My head was beginning to ache. I squeezed the bridge of my nose.

'Austin kicks this city's butt, Aggie. People like us? We'd fit straight in. They got all types of folk there. You'd love it.'

'I can't do it, Freak. I promised Marjorie I'd help sell her stuff. She needs me. I'd feel mean running out on her now.'

Truth was I liked the selling and I was good at it, too. Marj said I could most likely sell socks to a snake, if I put my mind to it.

Freak pouted. 'Can't believe you're putting Beast Woman ahead of me.'

'That's a good one coming from you. Screwed anyone else lately?' It was cruel but it flew out my mouth before I knew it was coming. I waited for her to flip but she just got quiet. She turned away, leaned her forehead on the window and gazed out. When I thought about how she was when I first met her, I wished I hadn't said it. She used to be dynamite.

22.

The first thing Marjorie said when we told her about the ATM was, 'Did you cover your faces?'

'And look like a couple of bandits?' said Freak. 'Shit, no. That's the dumbest thing I've heard in a long while, Marjorie. Reckon we'd be arrested for sure if we did that.'

Marjorie smiled one of those smiles that don't reach the eyes. 'Dumb or not, it's just that most ATM places got cameras. Security, you know.'

'I didn't see a camera,' I said.

'Were you looking for one?' Marjorie asked, one bushy eyebrow raised. I shook my head no, even though she already knew the answer full well.

'And you knocked a lady over to get the bag?

I nodded, feeling sick.

'So that's your physical assault right there. Makes it serious. Reckon they're gonna come looking for y'all.'

'So?' said Freak. 'Just because they're looking don't mean they're gonna find us, does it? Jesus, in a city this size we're the least of anyone's concerns. We just need to lay low a few days.'

'Sure you do,' Marjorie said. 'Good luck getting your money together while you do that, by the way. This Mr Dee guy… understanding type, is he?'

'I aint ever met him,' I said, and looked at Freak. She fell silent and shook her head, face blazing.

'Seems you got a bit of trouble on your hands, Freak,'

Marjorie said. She was enjoying this.

'Why me?' wailed Freak. 'She's the one who assaulted somebody!'

'I was trying to help you out!' I yelled, jumping down from the kitchen counter. 'I wouldn't be in this frikkin mess if you hadn't been such a dumb bitch in the first place, would I?'

Freak jumped down too and squared up to me. Marjorie got in between us and pushed Freak back.

'What I mean is,' said Marjorie, 'it aint gonna be Aggie's problem, because she's coming out of town with me. Which means you're gonna be here all on your lonesome, alright?'

This was news to me. 'You got your deposit?' I said.

Marjorie turned to me with a smile so full of satisfaction, a dozen kitties swimming in cream couldn't have been much smugger.

'I sure did,' she said. 'And you and me head off in the morning.'

Freak looked at me with her jaw hanging open. 'You're dumping me for her?'

I understood where she was coming from. The timing was pretty shit, from her point of view at least. Marjorie left us to it. 'Let me just take this coke up for Ade,' was her parting shot.

'I aint dumping you, Freak,' I said. 'Me and Marj, we got some business down on the coast, that's all. It's been planned a while. I'll be back in a few days.'

Now we were alone, the last of her bravado disappeared. Her head fell forward and her shoulders slumped. 'You don't understand,' she said. 'You don't understand at all.'

She took a seat at the table and cried. 'Me and Duke, we used to have a thing.'

'A thing?' I said, totally confused. 'What thing?'

'Jesus, Aggie. Do I have to spell it out? A *thing* thing, a sex thing, alright?'

'You and Duke? But he's, like, fifty.' And wears ladies clothes and paints his nails, but I didn't say that.

'I'd just got here. I didn't know anyone. He was kind. He used to bring me food when I was on the street. I didn't know no one else. What can I say? I was grateful. I didn't plan for it to happen but one night he invited me down to his work.'

'The Sad Place?'

'Yeah, except the letters still worked. I wanted to serve behind the bar but he said he'd get fired. He just wanted me to sit there while he worked. Keep him company. Girls were coming and going through the back door. I guessed what was going on. He saw me looking and asked if I was interested in that line of work.'

'So what, you were too young for bar work but okay for being a hooker? Jeez.'

'He said I'd make real good money. Said people would pay extra, you know?'

'People make me sick.'

'Me too. I said no, no way. He was real hurt. Said he didn't mean to offend me. Thing is, Aggie, he got real upset. Like tears and everything. I just wanted to make him feel better, you know? Plus, he'd been real kind to me and everything so… I let him do it. I thought it would just be the one time but he kept coming back. Called me his little lady. I guess I didn't mind too much either.' She looked down, ashamed.

'Reckon everyone's got the right to feel special sometimes,' I said.

'But then he started saying about me working for him again. His boss, Mr Dee, was real keen to get a girl like me. I kept saying no. He'd get angry but he didn't hit me, not really, even though I could tell he wanted to. Then one day finally I said I'd do it, but I wanted the money up front. Duke said Mr Dee wouldn't go for it. I said okay, forget it. That's when Duke said he'd give me the money himself. And he did. He gave me two hundred bucks, and told me to come back later that night. He trusted me.'

'Sweet guy. What did you do next?'

'I had money so I decided to treat myself. I went into this

diner and that's where I saw Ade. I figured he'd be an easy rip-off. I got him talking while we ate and it was weird. Like, he wasn't interested in me the way most guys are. Not at all. We just talked about stuff and after a while he just offered me a room here. No strings, nothing. I didn't show for my appointment with Mr Dee. It was my new life. A new start.'

'So what happened?'

'I got stupid. One day I lifted a bunch of stuff from the Galleria. Like, I had a really, really good day. So much stuff I didn't know what to do with it. I figured it would be okay to push it through Duke.'

'Shit, Freak.'

'I know, I know. Like I said, it was stupid. Well, he acted all pleased to see me and all. Took the stuff from me, gave me good money for it as well. Didn't mention the two hundred I owed him. Begged me to take him back but I just didn't want to, you know? I mean, who would, right? But he was happy just to see me. I even started hanging out there sometimes. The girls still came and went but he never once mentioned me going to work for him again. Plus, by that time I'd met you and you were pushing stuff through him as well. More money for him. I thought he was happy with that and everything was cool.'

She shook her head and went to the sink to pour some water. I waited in silence as she gulped it back. This was the most I'd heard her speak in one go and I didn't want to put her off.

'Then,' she continued. 'Then he found out what happened, you know? About when you did my back, remember?' I wasn't likely to forget. 'He said I was a slut and a fool for letting it happen. For letting it happen for free when he… he would have made them pay.'

Her face was wet with tears. She didn't look worth a shit.

'I don't understand where the money comes in,' I said.

'Well, after he said all that, I did it.'

'Did what?'

'For his friends. You know.'

'Mr Dee?'

She looked at me kind of odd, and then shook her head.

'No, I never met him. I did it for six of his friends in a room through the back. It wasn't as bad as you'd think. Not saying it's something you'd want to do all the time, but just I got on with it. When I went to get my wages from him, he said all he'd had were complaints. Said my skin was too fucked up. It put people off. Nobody had paid, or so he said.'

'Bastard.'

'Then he said there was only one person he knew who would pay for me. Mr Dee. He was into all kinds of kinky shit. Duke said if I was willing to let myself be tied up and shit like that, I'd make good money that way.'

'You didn't, did you?'

'Fuck, no. I told him no way was I getting up close with a sick fuck like that, but then he went totally weird on me. Took hold of my arm, real tight. I told him he was hurting me and he got this look in his eye. Freaked me the fuck out. Started running his fingers across my scars and said I had to meet Mr Dee. Said I had to because I owed him. I told him if anyone owed anybody it was him owing me on account of my screwing six of his friends. I was feeling sparky because we were in the bar and it was pretty busy. I don't know what would have happened otherwise. Anyway, he had customers to serve. I wasn't thinking straight. All I knew was the till was lying open and I'm sitting there, red raw in my panties without a dime in my pocket, and this weird fuck is trying to make me do shit. So when his back was turned I cleaned him out and took his wallet, too. It only came to six hundred bucks but I hear he's bumped it up to two thousand. Hell, it might even be three by now.'

I didn't know what to say to her. She twirled a piece of hair around her finger and began to chew on it. My stomach churned like sour butter.

'You shouldn't have gone back after you met Ade,' was all

I could think of to say.

'No shit, genius.'

There was more I should have said but I couldn't find it. I wanted to wrap it all up and make it go away for her, but whatever she was feeling inside, I was feeling too. I was still mad with her for sending me to this dickball knowing everything she knew about him. Was she really so dumb to think he saved the nasties just for her? A giant knot of ugly was tangled up in the middle of me and I couldn't unwind it.

'Thing is, Aggie. If he finds me, I don't know what he'll do. I heard he gets real nasty, you know? Like, people disappear around Mr Dee. Seriously, Duke told me that, and a couple of girls at the club, too. I guess what I'm saying is… I don't want to be alone, that's all. You can see why, can't you?'

'Sure, sure, I can. But – '

'And I know you gotta take this trip with Marj, and all – '

'Yeah, I do – '

'So you reckon I could just hitch a ride with you guys for a few days?'

There it was – the sucker punch. She'd wrapped her hair around half her face by this point. Her eyes blue and hopeful shone from between puffy lids. Her lips chomped rhythmically on a blanket of pink hair. 'Please?'

'No way Marj would go for it.' I rubbed my forehead hard like I could rub out the stress I was feeling.

'You could at least say you'll ask, fuck sake.' Eyes trained on me like a sniper's gun. I wished she'd look somewhere else.

'It's only a few days, Freak.' I didn't know if I was telling the truth. Part of me was beginning to think I might just stay down there.

'Lot can happen in a few days, Aggie. What if he finds me?'

'He aint gonna find you. How long you owed him this money anyway? Why the panic now?'

'Because of how he was with you. That was a message for me. He's mad, Aggie. Plus, he's been calling and texting me all the time. He wasn't looking for me before but he is now. I don't know what he'll do when he finds me, Aggie. You gotta help me. Please. Tell Marjorie I'll do whatever she wants. I can sell shit too, you know. I can make her money.'

'We don't need another seller. We got me. I'm doing it good.'

'Okay then, I'll just lay low in the back of the car. You won't hear a word out of me. I just need some place to be.'

'What about Ade?' I said. She looked like she didn't know who I meant. 'Ade,' I said again. 'Your boyfriend? Currently flipping out upstairs? Who's gonna take care of him?'

'He's okay. All he needs to do is stay straight. Come on, sis.' I raised my eyebrows at that but she carried on regardless. 'It's not like I'd just leave him to rot, is it?'

That's exactly what you'd do, I thought. 'I don't know, Freak. Marj just won't buy it, you know? Plus, I plan on hooking up with some family while I'm there, so it would just be you and her. You'd hate it.'

Good to learn my talent for swift lies was intact. She was stumped for a second and I thought I'd won, but then she dropped her head to the side, smiled a strange little smile and frowned.

'Is it your momma, Aggie? You meet your momma there?'

Her gift for instant recall was a curse to me. We hadn't talked about my family in weeks. She was calling me out and we both knew it.

'Yeah…' I struggled for the words. 'I haven't seen her for years and…'

She gave me the sweet smile of a smug-fuck champion. 'Oh my, that's so exciting! Do you think she'll have the same candle Jojo used to give you? I bet she does. Oh, girl, you're gonna need all the moral support you can get! Okay then, that settles it. Beast Woman can't object to your best friend being there when you're going through such a tough time now, can she?'

Nothing came to me. No words, no feelings, just nothing.

She patted the inside of her denim jacket pockets where the ATM cash had found its way. 'Great work today, by the way. I owe you.' And she skipped out the room and up the stairs.

I don't know how long I stared at the wall, but I thought about it until I was the surest I'd ever been in my life. She'd taken something private and used it against me. I didn't want any harm to come to her, but as long as she laid low, Duke would never find her. If she laid low, she'd be safe. Somehow we'd get the money together and pay him off. I'd have extra cash once Marjorie sold enough to pay me. She could have that. I was going to the ocean and I didn't want to listen to Freak and Marj bitching at each other the whole way. No way was she crashing this road trip.

I went up to my room to gather the few bits and pieces I'd need for the trip. Jeans, underwear, toothbrush. Marj had said there wouldn't be much room in the car so to keep it to bare essentials. That was pretty much all I had anyway. I thought of what the ocean would be like, all blue and silver in the sun, sand between my toes, warmth seeping up through my feet. I imagined it to be wild, but for me the wildness would be calming. *I will sprinkle clean water on you, and you shall be clean from all your uncleannesses.*

I stood on tiptoe and looked out my window to the street below. There were kids squirting each other with water guns. I turned away and sank to the floor. I was running away again.

Jojo's voice was singsonging its way closer. I'd run up the track, fast through shoulder-high grass, ducking and weaving my way to the shelter of Momma's upturned boat. Its base was rotten now, bleached brittle by the sting of summer sun, but that was no deterrent. The broken trunk of an old cedar tree propped it up a little, and I climbed into its cool darkness and waited.

Aaggeee... Aaggeee...

This game bored me now, but still she made me play it. I pushed myself deeper in, like I could steer the wood, drive the boat and escape all the way to the ocean.

Aaggeee…

She was so close now. It would all be over soon.

Now where is she?

She was right outside. She drummed her fingers against the wood, and I couldn't help but squeal.

I wonder where in the world could that Aggie be? she said, in a cartoon voice. And then: *Found you!*

She peeked inside, blocking out what little daylight seeped through, and I laughed and tried to sound genuine.

I climbed from my hiding place, all the time squirming and wriggling to avoid Jojo's tickling fingers, until eventually, she let me past. We settled against the boat and fell into an expectant silence, ripping out blades of grass to keep our fingers busy. I breathed in deep and said my lines.

I'm gonna fix up this old boat and take us to the ocean, Jojo. What you reckon to that?

This is what the conversation had become. She seemed to need it. I'd discovered it was easier to go along with it than try anything else.

But how will we get there? she asked, like it was the first time she'd thought about it. *You gonna put wheels on her?*

Yeah, Jojo. Reckon I am.

Gonna do it soon?

I sure am, Jojo. I sure am.

And then some new words. *Please do it soon, Aggie.*

I was horrified to see tears spring in her eyes. Struck with fear I hadn't played my part well enough, I placed my young hand over hers, trying to find some magic words of comfort.

I'll use the wheels on my bike, Jojo. I don't care.

She forced a laugh and smiled then, pushing the hair back from my face. *Oh, Aggie, you're sweet. I'm alright really. Sometimes I just miss Momma so damn much, you know?*

For reasons I didn't know, I said, *Sorry, Jojo.*

She just picked another blade of grass and pulled it to death.

23

I woke up next day to a commotion. Through the noise the only sound I recognized was Ade and he was yelling his head off. I pulled on jeans and a top and made my way downstairs where Marjorie was trying to calm him down. Behind them, Monty was waving his empty Cheerios box and raving about nothing being safe.

'What the fuck?' I asked Freak, who was sitting on the bottom step pulling split ends out of her hair.

'Look outside,' she replied.

I opened the door and stuck my head out. It took me a moment to recognize what I was looking at. Directly opposite the house was a camera crew and a news van. I slammed the door shut.

'What the fuck?' I said again.

A hammering started up. Lloyd was pulling the plywood down in the understairs closet.

'They aint taking my secrets,' Tawanna said, a bundle of splintered wood in her arms. 'This shit's for burning.' She walked to the garden and dumped the wood in a smoking metal bin.

'It's the house,' Marjorie shouted over the hammering, her arms wrapped tight around Ade, who was sitting on the floor with his back against the wall. 'They've found out about Ade buying this place for thirty dollars. Weird, huh? The bank goes to court and all of a sudden we're national news.'

'They sent them,' Ade said. 'They're closing in.'

There was a *bump, bump, bump* down the stairs. I turned to see Virginia pulling a huge suitcase on wheels down behind her.

'Sorry, guys, I'm out of here,' she said. 'Nothing good comes when they start pointing cameras at you. There'll be more coming, mark my words.'

Monty appeared at her side and they disappeared through the door without even saying goodbye. The reporter followed them down the street, firing questions until they turned the corner.

None of us had a clue what to do. Ade was a wreck and Marjorie looked grim. Lloyd stacked the white boards in the hallway. I could still make out my handwriting beneath the paint. Tawanna came back from the garden and I helped her carry the boards out. I wanted them burned as much as she did. The flames licked around the bottom edges, sending furls of smoke to engulf us. Through the haze, Tawanna looked straight at me. In that moment, I realized her dreams had been the biggest of all of us. I wouldn't want to be in her shoes now.

'I'm sorry, Tawanna.'

'Don't be,' she said. 'I got my baby now. And no matter where I end up, aint nobody taking it away from me. My baby gonna know who I am. My baby gonna know its momma's love. Don't you go being sorry for me now, y'hear?'

Whether it was her strength or her sternness that made me blush, or maybe even something else I couldn't put words to, I hoped she'd think my red face was caused by the heat of the fire.

Back in the hallway, only Freak seemed totally relaxed about the whole thing. Marj looked at Ade with such worry and I thought I knew the reason why. She'd have trouble leaving him behind now. The trip was off.

'Hell, no. Are you crazy?' Marjorie said when I asked her about it. 'I just put seven hundred bucks down on my own place. I gotta make next month's rent, and the month after that, too. Now, I got a business appointment in Port Aransas and I'll be damned if I miss it. You getting faint-hearted on me?'

'Lord, no. I just… Ade, you know?' I replied.

He was pacing up and down the hallway, running his fingers through his new cut hair. All he said was *Shit, shit, shit*, over and over.

'Hey, Ade,' Marj called. 'What happened to those lawyer dudes you were going to see?'

Freak outright laughed. 'He's gonna sell his book first, aint you, Ade? Gonna make a fortune to bring the superfly lawyers. Aint that right?'

'I thought I'd have more time,' he replied. 'They came too soon.'

'Yeah,' sneered Freak. 'Damn shame they won't work to your schedule, aint it.'

'We need a TV,' said Marjorie. 'To see what's going on.'

'Larry at number twelve,' Ade said.

Larry was one of the few neighbors who'd welcomed Ade to the neighborhood. He was an old guy who would rather see a house being used instead of being left to rot. *Asshat bankers,* he'd said. Apparently he'd been stung by them some time in the eighties. Ade had explained it but I was hazy on the details.

'Come on,' Marjorie said, and took my arm. I followed her out to the street, trying to move faster than the reporter. Behind us, our door slammed again. 'Hold up. I'm coming too,' called Freak. I heard Marjorie swear under her breath but she just kept focus on reaching number twelve so I did the same.

Larry had seen us coming and was waiting with the door open. We didn't have to explain ourselves. He already had the TV switched to the news channel.

'It's already been on,' he said, rubbing his hands together anxiously. 'I saw it. I couldn't believe it. Our street on the news. Of course that old coot next one along from you – she's

211

already been on. Wouldn't you just know it? She couldn't wait to start bitching. If they ask me I'll only say nice things about you, you can bet on that.'

I wondered what the old coot had said, but Marjorie just said thank you and turned up the volume to drown him out. The anchor woman was saying, 'And live from the house on Oakfield Avenue…' The penny dropped at the same time for both of us, too late to do anything about it now, because suddenly there she was, Freak, in forty-eight-inch plasma, being beamed right into Larry's living room, and countless living rooms up and down the state.

'Jesus Christ,' breathed Marjorie. 'She looks like a fucking flamingo.'

As soon as the interview ended, Marjorie was out of Larry's and storming back up the street to meet Freak as she headed towards us.

'Laying low?' she yelled. 'You call that laying low?'

Freak stopped in her tracks and, as Marjorie got closer, appeared to be rooted to the spot. The reporter looked up from his phone and signaled the camera guy to switch on, but he already had the camera trained on us.

'Marjorie, shut up!' I hissed. She picked up more speed and I had to run to keep up with her. Freak turned around and hurried back to the house.

'Ade! Ade, let me in,' she called. The door opened and I managed to push both of them through just as the reporter was approaching the steps. I slammed the door in his face. I turned round to see Freak had positioned herself behind a confused-looking Ade. 'I didn't mean to talk to them,' she said. 'You didn't wait for me. I was only trying to catch y'all up before you disappeared into Larry's place. I asked you to wait but you went right ahead.' So it was our fault now. I wouldn't have thought it possible but Ade was even more agitated.

'It's endgame,' he said. I'd no idea what he meant, but he said it over and over. *Endgame, endgame.*

'Give it up, Ade,' snapped Marjorie, impatient with him at last. 'And you,' she said, turning to Freak. 'What were you thinking running out like that? Aint you got the sense you were born with?'

'I don't see what y'all are getting your panties in a bunch for.' Freak shrugged.

'My panties aint bunched, you stupid child. Who was it stuck up an ATM yesterday without hiding their face? Uh-huh. You, that's who. And how many people walk about with bright pink hair? Way to lay low, Freak. Good job.'

'Shit, Mr Dee...' Freak's eyes widened and she clapped a hand over her mouth.

Marjorie stood back, satisfied Freak finally understood how dumb she was. Leaning against the wall for support, Freak staggered backwards and collapsed onto the bottom step of the stairs. She didn't fool me. After all our talk last night about Duke chasing her down, and how much she wanted to come on the trip with us, I knew no way was she stupid enough to make a mistake like that. She had Marjorie by the balls, only Marjorie didn't know it yet.

Someone else came down the stairs and it was Ricardo, the Mexican, owner of the baseball bat I'd once found so useful.

'I cannot stay, my friends. For me, it's no good here no more.'

We understood. Of all of us, Ricardo had the most to lose by being in the spotlight. Marjorie stepped forward and hugged him.

'You take care now, y'hear?'

He nodded, embarrassed.

Ade stepped forward. 'I'm sorry, man. So sorry it's come to this.'

'No worries, Ade. Thank you for everything. And you take care of yourself, okay? This camera outside... it's not good news.' Ricardo kissed Ade on the cheek. If he noticed me and Freak he didn't say anything. He slipped out the door and was gone.

'That's it then,' said Ade. 'Lloyd and Tawanna are leaving, too. It's just us left.'

'Just you two, Ade,' said Marjorie. 'Me and Aggie's got business out of town.'

Freak was just casually braiding her hair, but Ade's eyes widened in horror. 'They're doing it. Divide and rule. Divide and rule,' he began pacing the hallway, then suddenly grabbed on to Marjorie's sleeve. 'Don't go, Marj. This is how they want it to play. They want to get me alone and then they'll take me. It's been coming. Oh, it's been coming.' And then he started to cry.

Marjorie looked down at the floor and shook her head. 'I don't believe this,' she said.

I thought I saw a quick smile on Freak's face, but it was hidden behind her hair before I could be sure.

Marjorie's revenge was to make Freak shave her hair off. Now she and Ade sat in the back of Oprah looking like a couple of refugees from some prison camp. 'We're like twins,' Freak said to Ade, and took his hand, all settled in for the journey. In the front, me and Marj were fizzing. I had a box of Marj's trinkets stuck between my legs on account of the lost space in the back. We were late setting off too, because once it was clear that Ade and Freak were along for the ride and the house would be empty, Marjorie had to make a few trips to her ma's place. The banks might have padlocked the doors by the time we got back and she didn't want to lose her stuff. Larry had come racing down to see what was going on when he saw Marj's furniture being moved out.

'Have they beat you, those ass hats?' he wanted to know.

Ade's eyes watered as he muttered something about losing the battle but not the war.

'Scum buckets, that's what they are, Ade. This country's gone to the dogs. We didn't fight to be held ransom by the banks, goddammit. Crockett's spinning in his grave, I tell you.'

In a show of solidarity he walked in front of us as we pulled away from the house, waving the state flag while the neighbors and a couple extra camera crews caught the whole thing. Marjorie drove slow out of respect for Larry but inside we were dying. I kept my head down and my hand over my face the whole way. Ade and Freak hid beneath a blanket in the back. Freak's loud giggles didn't help the general atmosphere at all.

We had to take the long way round, because Marjorie wouldn't go through Waco.

'Creepy assed shit,' was all she'd say when I asked her to tell me more about it. Freak wasn't happy about the route. 'You mean, we aint hitting Austin?'

'Aint hitting Austin,' Marjorie replied.

'Shitballs, I thought you were going through Austin,' Freak said, as though Marjorie might change her mind.

'Freak's got a cousin there,' I explained.

'Cousin, huh?' Marj pretended to think about it for a moment, and I could feel the hope rising behind me. 'That's nice. But I never said nothing about Austin.'

Balloon, popped.

Ade held Freak's hand and didn't notice the disappointment on her face. I guess she'd planned to jump out when we got there. Ade just stared out the passenger window, unless he was checking behind us to see if we'd been followed.

'We aint been followed, Ade,' Marjorie said for the sixth time. We were just hitting the edge of town by this point and already it felt we'd been going for hours.

When we stopped for gas, I went inside to pay with Marjorie. It was one of those big truck stops that sells fancy foods and gifts and films and toys and shit. We were fourth in line to pay. Marjorie told me to keep an eye on the car. She'd taken the keys with her so I don't know what she thought Freak and Ade might do, but I did as she asked.

I heard the guy at the front of the queue ask for fifty dollars on pump six. He paid and we all moved down the line. Marjorie elbowed me in the ribs. 'Come on,' she said. I followed her back out.

'What about the gas?' I asked.

'Jump in,' she instructed me. I did as I was told but before I'd even shut the door the car was moving. She turned it around and pulled up real close behind a silver Toyota, which was parked in a different filling slot. We were all quiet with confusion as she nipped out and slid down between the Toyota and the pump.

'Oh shit,' screamed Freak. 'She's stealing somebody's gas!'

And so she was. I looked around expecting some angry dude to be headed straight for us. The numbers on the pump's display board couldn't have gone round any slower. Freak was jumping up and down in her seat with excitement, while Ade hid back beneath the blanket, which, to my knowledge, hadn't been washed since that little armadillo critter had been wrapped up in it. Then Marj was hanging the pump back and we were driving off, fifty bucks of fuel heavier.

'I saw the guy pay.' She shrugged, once we were back on the Interstate. 'And then he went to the restroom. His own fault. What did he expect to happen? That's a lesson he needed to learn.'

'What about cameras though, Marjorie. Did you cover your face?' Freak snarked.

'Aint no cameras at that place. Don't tell me my business, child.' Marjorie laughed and bumped the horn. Honky-tonk crackled from the radio and the old car wheels spun round.

The roads got quieter and the sky came bigger the further out we got, but it was still nothing compared to home. Every mile south we went the more I began to wonder if I'd ever see the high plains again. I was daydreaming when the car skidded to a stop. Freak lurched forward and her head bounced into my back through the seat.

'Should have wore your seatbelt,' said Marjorie before Freak could complain.

There was nothing in front of us. I'd no clue why she'd stopped. She got out and went behind the car. All three of us craned our necks to see what she was doing. She opened the trunk, pulled something out, and walked back around to the front. I knew what she was doing before Ade and Freak.

It's going to be hell of a long journey, I thought, as she wrapped up the dead armadillo and put it in the trunk.

'Oh my actual fucking God.' Freak twisted her face in disgust. 'I can actually smell it.'

Inside Oprah it was feeling hot and small. Marjorie had got a guy to fix the air con but it still only worked when it felt like it. The heat had sent Ade to sleep. With his head tipped back and his mouth hanging loose, he looked about twelve years old. A beeping noise came from beside him and Marjorie did a double-take in the driver's mirror.

'What the fuck you doing with that?' she hissed.

I turned round to see what she was talking about. Freak was playing some game on her cell.

'What? He's asleep.' She shrugged.

'He'll flip out if he sees you with that,' Marj said. 'Put it away.' I backed Marj up and said she should put it away too, but she acted like she hadn't heard.

'Put it the fuck away, dickwipe!' Marjorie yelled. I reckon she'd been holding on to that yell for months. Of course it woke up Ade and, as Marjorie predicted, he flipped. He grabbed the phone straight out of Freak's hands and threw it out the window. Freak sat staring at the space her phone used to be. Marjorie turned back to face the front. 'Problem solved,' she said with a smirk.

'What the fuck you have to do that for?' Freak asked Ade. 'I paid for that phone.'

Ade was on his knees looking out the back window. 'They're following us,' he said.

'We aint being followed, Ade,' said Marjorie, sounding like a broken record. 'Look, aint nobody behind us at all.'

'That's what they want you to think, but now their tracking device has gone, they'll need to catch us up. You have to go faster while we've got the advantage. You should probably change route as well.'

'I thought you said he'd be better once he was off the weed?' I said to Marjorie. With one look, she told me to can it.

'I aint changing route, Ade,' Marjorie called over her shoulder. 'We're late enough as it is.'

Thirty minutes later we were holed up in a diner just off the Interstate. When Ade finally accepted Marj wasn't changing routes, he'd persuaded her to pull off the road. He was dead set on his theory that whoever was tailing us would zoom to catch us up. All we had to do was let twenty or so cars go past and by that point it would be safe to go again. It seemed a random number to pick but I wasn't sorry to stop. My legs needed to stretch. We parked behind the diner and took a window booth so we could count cars. Judging by the amount of traffic we hadn't seen, I figured we'd be there a while.

The place was called the Fantastic Fifties, but it was low on fantastic. Old seven-inch vinyls dangled from the ceiling on white-and-red ribbons. The walls were red-and-white candy stripes and covered in pictures of Marilyn and Elvis, because they were the only two famous people the fifties produced, I guess. Where it wasn't Marilyn and Elvis, newspaper scraps of local people were pinned up – the football team, cheerleaders, scholarship winners – anyone who'd found their five minutes in the spotlight was famous forever in the Fantastic Fifties. There was even a signed photo of George Bush Junior. Guess those president guys get around. Photographs of dancing troupes, Citizen of the Year 1984 through '98. So much pride, so much to celebrate about being human. Not just human – plastic replicas of all the Disney characters were all lined up along the counter: Sylvester, Tweetie-Pie, Mickey and Minnie, Winnie the Pooh, all fat and cheerful and creepy as hell. I half expected Ade to turn them upside down to inspect them for cameras, but he was locked on to the nothing happening outside.

'No sign yet,' he said to nobody in particular.

The waitress came for our order. She was seventy if she was a day, but was made up like a hooker, all black-lined eyes and purple blush. Her thin hair was dyed red and fluffy as cotton. She'd backcombed it so it resembled the ghost of a beehive. It sat so stiff, I bet she woke up looking like that. We ordered drinks and waited for Ade to give us the all clear. Freak was still pissed about the phone and not getting to Austin, while Marjorie looked resigned to whatever life was going to throw at her. As for me, I scoured the walls going from photo to photo to photo; a patchwork of black-and-white and not one thing familiar.

Everybody knows life don't give a shit who you are. Life throws you a curve ball any old time it feels like it, no matter your size, color or creed, but when Oprah got a flat, Marjorie couldn't have been more shocked if she'd just given birth to herself. She sat there, frozen, disbelieving her bad luck, while we held our breath and waited for the explosion.

'Hot damn, Oprah. How could you let a sister down like this?' she said, and then she turned to me and said, 'If anyone can get themselves back in the game, it's Oprah.' And the rest of us all breathed again.

Freak refused to get out the car on account of snakes and bears, and Ade refused to get out on account of snipers. When I asked him where he thought a sniper might be hiding amid the dry, flat land around us, he decided satellite photography would keep him inside instead. Me and Marj had just about had it with them both. We emptied the trunk of all the boxes and jacked the car with them still inside, Freak squealing with every half turn of the jack. I was impressed by Marjorie. She was strong and that tire was changed in under ten minutes.

When she finished, Marj wiped her hands on a rag, and took a look around. 'This is as good a spot as any,' she said, hands on hips. 'Since we've emptied the trunk anyway.' She took up a spade that had been in the back with all the boxes, and walked off a few feet. I knew without being asked that my job was to carry over our extra passengers, which numbered four by this point. She dug a hole while I cradled the last one like a baby, grateful for Marjorie's fondness for blankets.

We laid them side by side in the hole and Marjorie offered up a short prayer. Then she nodded at me. I took up the shovel and was about to cover them with dirt when I thought I saw one of the blankets twitch. I looked at Marj to see if she'd noticed, but she was bent over doing something with the buckle on her boot. I looked at the blanket again. It was definitely moving. With the edge of the shovel, I loosened the blanket a little, and a long, snuffling nose wormed its way out.

'Holy shit!' I must have jumped about three feet into the air. Dust rose and fell between the folds of the blanket. Marj gave me a real sharp look, pissed off with me for breaking the mood.

'It's alive, Marjorie. It's fucking alive.'

'What?' She was over in two steps. She fell to her knees and lifted the wriggling bundle out of the hole and placed it to the side, her hands hovering in the air above as though to catch a fast ball. Two feet with three sharp claws apiece joined the snuffling nose in its quest for freedom. If it occurred to me or Marj to help, we didn't do anything about it. He fought and scrabbled with the blanket until eventually it opened, and the resurrected armadillo was revealed.

'Sweet Jesus,' Marj whispered.

'You think?' I asked, honestly.

The armadillo rooted around on the blanket, oblivious to us, and seemingly none the worse for the hiccup in its day.

Marjorie ran to the car but I kept my eyes trained on that guy the whole time, in case he disappeared and we'd think we imagined the whole thing. I heard Freak whining about how hot she was and how long we were taking, but then the car door slammed and Marjorie was back with a plastic container of water. She put it down in front of the little guy and he dived straight into it, his tiny tongue lapping it right up. We watched in awe, both of us with jaws trailing the ground, neither of us doubting we were witness to a miracle. He began to wiggle away from us, his long nose on the hunt for food, when Marjorie grabbed my shoulder.

'Should we let him go?' she said, staring at me fierce. 'He's a long way from home. He might get confused, you know. This aint his natural habitat.'

The idea of driving the rest of the journey with a live armadillo in the car was too much for me. I dared to put my arm around her. 'You kidding me, Marj? Look at the little guy. He's a born survivor.'

She chewed her cheek and nodded. She hadn't shaken my arm away. 'I reckon some creatures do better away from their natural habitat,' she said.

'Aint that the truth.'

We stood together like that, each of us nodding wisely, until the armadillo disappeared into a scrubby bush. Then she stepped away from me so fast, my arm slapped against my body like a dead fish.

Marj was all for putting the remaining armadillos back in the car in case they came back to life, too. I told her if we didn't bury them soon, they'd be so alive we'd have a million flies in the car with us. Finally, she accepted they were still dead and I got to cover them over. When we went back to the car, Freak was fired up. She'd seen the whole thing.

'How do you explain that?' she wanted to know.

'I guess the little guy must have been concussed or something when we found him. Or maybe he was scared and played dead. He sure seemed dead to me.' A red-faced Marjorie shrugged.

'Or maybe he did die and that was his ghost. Maybe he's come back to haunt the fucker who ran him over,' Freak suggested. While we'd been conducting the world's weirdest funeral, she'd been looking at the map and worked out we weren't far from some shitty little place calling itself a ghost town. She wanted to pay it a visit. As lead-ins to conversations go, I thought it was a good one.

'This place, it aint a ghost town with tumbleweed and shit,' she continued. 'It's a straight-up ghost town with actual real ghosts. Haunted.'

She bounced up and down so that the car bounced too, and I thought if she burst that new tire she'd be keeping those armadillos company.

'There's no such thing as ghosts,' said Ade. It was the first sensible thing he'd said in days.

'I aint going to no place haunted,' said Marjorie. 'What I want to seek trouble for when I already got plenty?'

'Oh, come on.' Freak slapped the atlas onto her thighs. 'You guys gotta learn how to live! Aggie, come on, speak up for me, sis.'

She leaned forward and punched my shoulder.

'Ow! Quit it!'

'No point asking you, is there?' she laughed, scornfully. 'You wanna get to the ocean so you can find your *mommy*. Did you know that, Marj? She aint coming to help you out. No, no, no, that aint it at all, is it, Aggie? Why don't you tell us why you're really going? Is it because you think you're going to find your *mommy*?'

I twisted in my seat and battered my fist into her stomach, or would have done if the seat belt hadn't held me in. Instead, I caught the edge of her knee and hurt my fucking wrist.

'Alright, just calm it down,' Marjorie said. 'We aint going to no ghost town and that's the end of it. That's bad shit. Look at you two friends already squabbling like the devil's in you.'

I fumed in the front seat. It wasn't the devil inside me. It was Freak. She'd just given words to something I'd always known, but never understood. If I could just meet her, maybe I'd love her. I was ashamed by my stupidity. My heart raced fast enough to outrun Oprah, if only it could figure its way out of my body and into the world.

The best of the day was gone by the time we hit a long line of traffic, but Marjorie wasn't worried. She switched the engine off and we sat for twenty minutes. She seemed to enjoy our confusion. I was beginning to think we were there for the night when the cars in front began to move. As we edged slowly down the road, I could see ahead more clearly.

'Holy shitballs, Marjorie,' I said. 'Are we going on a boat?'

I sensed Freak sitting bolt upright in the back, bursting to ask questions but pride not letting her. Marjorie nodded like it's an every day occurrence to take a car onto a boat.

'Uh-huh.'

'Holy shitballs,' I said again, and leaned forward to get a good view. A guy in a yellow vest was directing traffic into rows. Onto a boat. A fucking boat. Cars and trucks inched their way on board, lining up to park wherever he told them.

'Marjorie,' I said, panic bubbling up inside. 'I can't fucking swim.'

Well, I didn't see what was so damn funny but everybody burst out laughing. Even Ade, who hadn't laughed in forever. 'We're not swimming across, silly Aggie,' he said.

Freak rolled down her window and waved to a guy who was standing at the side holding a clipboard. He was bare beneath his yellow vest, skin brown as raisins. 'Hey,' she called. She shouted and waved her arm some more until he looked in her direction. 'Excuse me!' The guy looked around him, as though to make sure it really was him she was calling, then he came over.

'Can I help you, miss?' He pushed back his shades and leaned down to talk. His muscles flexed in the side mirror.

'I was just wondering... Do you work out?' Freak asked. Marjorie's knuckles went white on the wheel. I turned round in amazement.

'Excuse me, miss?' the guy said.

'I said do you work out? I figured you did.' She touched his arm and slid her fingers down to his wrist. Ade turned redder than the whole of Texas. The guy took it well and laughed. 'Yeah, I guess I might work out a little.'

'Thank you,' said Ade, abruptly, as he leaned over Freak and rolled the window back up.

'Jesus, Ade,' said Freak. 'We were just talking.' The guy shrugged and walked back to his workmates. Freak blew him a kiss. Ade took her hand.

'That's how you wind up in trouble, Freak,' he said gently.

'I know, baby. I love you taking care of me,' she said, and snuggled in beside him. She shot Marjorie a look in the mirror. Every victory had to count.

It was our turn to board the ferry. A middle-aged fat guy with a face burned as boiled lobster guided us on. 'Aint he heard of sunblock?' Freak asked.

Lobster-man flapped his arms faster and faster to speed us up, but it didn't inspire Marjorie. She inched us forward, tongue poking between her lips the way it always did when she concentrated. I'd first noticed it when she was putting her little rubber armadillos together. Freak called her the Frog, and at the time, I thought she was being funny. I knew Marjorie better now and was starting to find her quirks kind of cute, but Freak wasn't catching my vibe. From behind me, a small voice croaked, 'Ribbit, ribbit.'

'Marjorie,' I said, once she'd switched the engine off and relaxed a little. 'Would you mind telling us where the actual fuck we're going?'

'Just across the water. Won't take more than ten minutes.'

'I aint never been on a boat before. Not an actual floating one.' I rolled down the window and stuck my head out. Exhaust fumes.

'I love boats,' said Ade. 'I used to go on ferries all the time when I was a boy.' He looked kind of wistful out the window at the cars all around us. 'My grandmother lived on an island,' he said. None of us replied. Truth be told, we didn't know what to do with him these days. We were so nervous of whatever crazy thing he'd come out with next. Still, grandmothers seemed a safe enough subject and Marjorie obviously wanted to encourage him. 'Oh, yeah?' she said. 'What island, Ade?' But he just stared back out at the cars. I don't think he even saw the gray sea beyond.

'I thought it would be more blue,' I said.

Freak wanted to know if we were allowed to get out of the car but none of us could tell her. We decided if others got out we would, too. We bobbed our way in silence, boat tilting from side to side.

It was dark and all the motels were full. We found the last two rooms on the island in a run-down place at the end of a dead-end street. Marjorie took the first room and left the three of us to share.

The room was big enough for two double beds. I claimed one, Ade the other, and Freak stood between us with her finger tapping her chin, pretending to wonder who she'd rather share with. Ade unplugged the TV and turned it round so the screen was facing the wall. Then he picked up the phone and ordered a pizza. He pulled the socket from the wall, wrapped the phone in a pillow case and put it in a drawer. I stifled the desire to ask was he positive there'd be no tracking devices hidden in the cheese.

'Don't you want to go out?' Freak asked.

Ade shook his head. 'Not while that car's still in the lot.'

Freak went to the window, while I flicked the pages of a magazine so hard I ripped it.

'The lot's full,' she said. 'Which car?'

'Dark blue station wagon. See it?'

Freak scanned the cars. 'The ghetto sled? Yeah, I see it.'

'It's been with us since before the ferry,' Ade said. Freak and I exchanged glances. I shook my head. Best not get him started again.

24

Next morning, Marjorie was real shook up and trying to conceal it behind a bad mood. She'd been to see her contact before we'd even woke up, and he hadn't bought anything from her.

'But he told you to come down,' I said. 'Thought he'd already seen your stuff and liked it.'

'Yeah, he likes it alright. But that little worm aint in a position to be buying stuff. He aint the frikkin boss man.'

I followed her out to the balcony.

'Damn it, Aggie,' she said to me in a low voice. 'If I'd known he wasn't the boss, I would never have put that deposit down.' She lit up a smoke with trembling hands and inhaled deeply. I was stuck for any words of comfort to offer. Started to think I was the only one that wasn't loose with my money.

Sensing the drama, Freak came over to help. 'You mean, you dragged us all the way here for nothing?' Fake outrage barely disguising the glee.

'I don't remember inviting you along, Freak-face.' Marjorie got right in her space and butted Freak's head with her own. Freak backed down straight away. Marjorie paced the floor in small circles. She looked like a lion in a cat box.

'What you always gotta push it for, Freak?' I asked. 'How far you gonna take it? Aint there a limit in Freak World?'

'Sorry,' said Freak, looking anything but. 'I just figured she'd have checked it out for real before driving us five hundred miles for nothing.'

Marjorie was fit to kill.

'It aint for nothing, Marj,' I said. 'The guy's got a boss, right? When's he back?'

'Some time tomorrow.' She flicked her cigarette over the side and fixed us with a death stare. 'I guess we wait.'

'Okay,' said Freak, brightly. 'Who's for a trip to the beach?' It was a question mainly for Ade.

'Is that car still there?' he wanted to know. 'I'm not leaving if it is.'

'Yeah, it's there,' Marjorie said, bored.

'I'll come,' I said. Blue sea, salty waves; mermaids and sea creatures.

'Marjorie?' Freak asked.

Marjorie looked from Freak to me to Ade, and bared her teeth in a smile. 'Nah,' she said, 'I'm good.'

Freak looked uncertain. 'You can't just stay in all day,' she said.

'Who can't?' growled Marj, settling onto my bed.

'Ade?' I could hear the pleading in her voice.

'Not while that car's there,' he said.

I could see her thought process. Looking at Ade and then Marjorie.

'Actually, now that I think about it, I'm feeling kind of sick,' she said, and lay down on the other bed. Ade was sitting in the only chair and had his nose stuck in some tourist leaflets. The room was small and getting smaller.

'Have a nice day, y'all,' I said, with relief. Better to be alone than in bad company.

It felt good to move after being cooped up in the car the day before. And it felt good to be alone. I walked through the parking lot and headed back up the street to the main road, butterflies fluttering away in the pit of my stomach. The sea.

Something about having space around you leaves room for thoughts of the future to creep in. I'd no home in the city now. Maybe I could stay with Marjorie in her new place for a while. Maybe we'd become business partners. Hell, how likely was that? Maybe I'd just stay here. Pitch a tent on the beach. Maybe Momma would float back to the shore and find me one day. Maybe we'd go back for Jojo, together. Something about having space around you leaves room for childish dreams.

I reached the end of the street and looked for the beach. Nothing but a bunch of low rises far as I could see. Guess it was stupid to think I'd just fall upon it. I tried to remember which way we'd come in the night before, but we'd made so many stops looking for some place to stay, I'd lost my bearings. I made my best guess and took a left.

I passed a cafe with a few people eating outside. I thought about asking, but I was Little Miss Independent and I decided I'd find it on my own. Forty minutes later I was regretting that decision. I wandered up and down quiet residential streets and couldn't see so much as a sign to point the way.

A little old lady was asleep on a lounger in her yard. As I stood at her gate with my hand on the latch, wondering if it would be too rude to wake her up, a navy blue station wagon pulled up a hundred yards down the street. It looked out of place in the bright morning light. An amused half-thought floated across my mind, something about the three of them back at the motel being free to go out now. I took my hand off the latch and began to walk down to ask the driver, when a nasally voice said, 'I'm not asleep, sweetheart.'

I turned back round and she was sitting up, skin tanned as leather, hair white and fluffy as a dandelion clock. I waited as she struggled her way to standing and made her way over. The skin around her knees sagged and quivered with every step.

'I'm sorry to disturb you, m'am,' I said, as she reached the gate.

'Disturb me?' she wheezed. 'Oh, you're not disturbing me, baby doll. I haven't seen a soul… oh, must be going on a week now. I'm thinking of making some mail orders just so I can talk to the mailman. What you think about that?'

'Uh, that's a plan, I guess.'

She lifted up her sunglasses and blinked away the glare. Her face had more cracks than dried mud.

'What do you want anyway? I take it you're not here because you want to listen to me shooting off all day.'

'Oh, m'am. I'm just trying to make my way to the beach. I guess I took a wrong turn somewhere.'

'Bless your heart, honey. Would you like to come in for some iced tea? I guess not. Okay, let me think...'

It took us an hour to have a five-minute conversation, the upshot of which was I had to carry on down that road, taking the second turn on the left. I walked along the empty street, and when I saw a little golf cart carrying a family of five, I knew I was close. A kid waved a large inflatable dolphin as they passed. I ran after them until they turned on to a busy four-lane road.

I was stumped. I knew the water couldn't be too far away. Even thought I could smell it. At last, between gaps in the traffic, there it was, on the other side of the road. I looked up and down for a decent place to cross and saw a walkover a few hundred yards away. My heart leaped and I moved towards it.

Beside me was a row of garages. As I walked past, one of them sprang open. Like an idiot, I yelled and jumped with fright. I laughed it off and turned to apologize, but before I even saw his face, an arm reached out and took a hold of me. It dragged me inside.

Could have fought harder. Yelled louder. Could have not frozen like some chicken-shit retard from the back woods. Could have not played deader than a fake-dead armadillo.

His arms wrapped around me and I collapsed in on myself. He carried my limp body to the open truck of the waiting car. It was a navy blue station wagon.

A strange smell enfolded me, and the darkness fell down.

25

At first it's just dark. You think the lights are out. You sit up.
Blink. Breathe. Your eyes will adjust so you wait. And wait.

Then it starts to crawl out.

The Wondering.

And the Fear.

Knocking at your senses.

You snap them away but soon,

soon there's nothing you can do about it

and the realization slams into you.

It's a body shock.

It's not *dark* in here.

This is a wall of black like you've never experienced.

Not a blackness seen through your eyes.

It's something you feel with your soul.

A blackness that coils and stretches and wraps itself round
you.

It constricts.

Black that heaves your stomach and crushes your bones.

It fills you, snaking its way through your hair, your ears,
behind your eyes, curling down through your nostrils, your
mouth, and as your throat tightens, it fills up your lungs and
steals your air.

Black that eats your blood.

Black that twists and tangles you.

It's a blackness where the only color that can be is whatever
you find in your head, so you invite them in, all the old faces

you've pushed away so long, you scream for them to come and fill the void. And boy, don't they come, whistling like the wildest wind, rushing in like they're storming a fortress, like they've just been stood outside your head waiting, waiting a lifetime for the invitation to enter. Jojo laughing, her head thrown so far back I can see her dangly bit at the back of her throat wiggling like a worm, her eyes wider than a panicked bull, and then she's crying and knocked away and now here comes Pop, his face looming all sweaty and shaking, his voice grunting, and Cy shouting and Jojo again except this time she's snarling, foaming like a rabid mutt spitting and hissing *Found you, Aggie.* And the blood; bright, bright flowers of blood, and all the alarms are going off, high and piercing like the world's gone nuclear until I realize it's me, I'm shrieking and I'm alone in the black and thank God for the black, the black is welcome now, the faces are gone and I'm glad to be in the black.

I didn't dare lie down. I sat pressed up tight in a corner, feeling the walls behind my back. Behind them was an outside world. The walls reminded me that black wasn't the whole universe. Somewhere out there, a sun was shining. A little girl was running through grass, laughing with her sister.

Seemed I stayed awake the whole time. Hard to tell. I had unwelcome visitors for sure, visitors that only came in my dreams, but it seemed to me I was living an eternity, asleep or not.

I went the whole way around that room, exploring with my hands. The walls bumped up and down. No other way of describing it. I banged against it and the dull noise it made told me it was metal. Someone had put me in a metal box. If I'd found a weak or rusted spot maybe I could have picked a hole in it, made myself some light, but if there was, I couldn't find it. Endless smooth, bumpy walls and corners and walls and corners and walls.

The floor was dirty. Grit and dust and what I took to be splinters of wood lay at the bottom of the walls, but I never did summon the courage to explore the middle. The walls anchored me. If I stepped away from them I'd be free-falling, spinning through a black hole of galactic proportions right here on earth.

The squeak and clang of the outside bolt told me he was back. The door opened a fraction and his shadow was thrown down in the moonlight. A padlock dangled from his finger.

'You in here?'

That one question told me all I needed to know about the size of this guy's intellect. He came in further. I shrank back and pushed against the steel wall. He closed the door and the little bit of light was lost.

'Aggie, I'm gonna give us some light now, you hear? I don't want no funny business, little lady, you got that?'

A flashlight brought his face into the dark, scarier than all the others. When he caught sight of me tucked away in the top right corner, he smiled and removed his hat. A long white braid slipped over his shoulder. He was in the same suit as before.

'D-D-Duke,' I stammered.

His face became dead serious. He shook his head over and over. 'No, no, no. Not today. Today I'm introducing you to someone else.'

I looked behind him to see who else he'd brought. He laughed at my confusion. A real tight, high snickering type of laugh. 'You'll learn. Now, we need some light in here.' He set about lighting four candles, two on each side of the long walls. The flickering sent orange shapes dancing along the floor.

He took off his shoes and socks, folding each one carefully before placing them neatly to one side. He slipped out of his jacket and from the inside pocket pulled out a tie. He flicked up his collar. Placed the tie around his neck. Slid his fingers down the length of the material. Did it up with long pale fingers, all the while checking to make sure I was watching. Sapphire nails. That laugh again. Dread filled my throat.

When his tie was tight, he made a show of rolling down the sleeves of his shirt and buttoning the cuffs. Then he slipped his jacket back on and held his arms out in welcome.

'Wait, wait. Almost forgot.' He bent his head and lifted his hands. It took me a moment to realize he was removing his contacts. He shut them in a little box and laid them down.

'Meet Mr Dee, Aggie.' Duke fastened the buttons, pulled the jacket tight down and twisted his body from side to side, as though he were looking in a mirror.

'Don't he look good? I tell you what, he feels fucking great.'

He flexed his arms and grinned.

My heart was yammering so hard I thought it would burst. Mr Dee sat cross-legged on the floor at the far end of the room. He brought his thumbs and middle fingers together, closed his eyes, took a deep breath and exhaled, looking for all the world like some corporate Buddha. When his eyes snapped open, they found me immediately. I couldn't tell the real color.

'Your friend Freak owes me rather a lot of money, Aggie.' His voice sounded mellow in the closed container. 'Normally I'd find a way for silly girls to pay me back, but Freak… uh… Freak's past normal usage, you know?' He shrugged. 'It's regrettable.'

He lifted a soft square package from his lap, laid it before him and unwrapped it. Rows of sharp steel flashed in the dim light. He grinned at me, goblin-like. He liked showing off his teeth, I realized.

'Mr Dee likes it special, Aggie. Poor Freak's got nothing left to offer Mr Dee. You're a good friend to her, aren't you? A good girl? Say you're a good girl and we'll be fine'

My teeth rattled as I nodded: yes, I was a good friend, yes, I was a good girl, yes, yes, yes to whatever he said, holding on to the thin hope that this time, this one time, no one would hurt me.

'That's a good girl. Come on now. Come and lie down here for me.'

I looked at the space he'd created between the candles. An altar space. A sacrifice space. I opened my mouth to speak but the words stuck in my throat. My jaw hung open and I moved my head back and forward to dislodge the sound.

'D-D-D-Duke,' I spat the word out, finally. 'I can g-g-get your money.'

He frowned. 'You're not understanding me, Aggie. It's not about the money. Not anymore.'

'Please, Duke...'

'Mr Dee, Aggie.' He gave a wide, tight-lipped smile. I was testing his patience. 'Now come here.'

I staggered to my feet, trying to locate the closed door behind him. My only chance was to rush him, maybe knock him over, but he'd overpowered me once already. Besides, I was just discovering I could barely stand.

'Come here,' he said again, a little firmer. My feet were welded to the floor. He clicked his tongue impatiently. 'Dammit, Aggie, Mr Dee hates to use force.'

He left his position at the head of the altar and went back into his bag, which was lying against the side wall. When he turned round I thought one of his hands had turned black, and then I realized he was pointing a gun at me.

'Now get down here,' he said.

Hardest thing to do is walk toward a gun that's pointed at you. I peeled myself away from the wall and forced my feet a step closer to him.

'Jesus Christ, what's taking you so long?' He swung the flashlight straight in my face. I twisted my head to escape the glare.

'Oh, you little bitch. You've pissed yourself.'

Shielding my eyes, I looked down, and when I looked back up at him I apologized, because not only had I pissed my pants but I'd shit them, too. The evidence was staining its way right down my legs. He dropped the gun, marched over to me and hauled me into the center of the room.

'Take them off. Clean yourself up.'

I stood, frozen. I tried to read his lips to make sense of what he was saying. I held my hands out in front of me to keep them clean, and I remember thinking I was holding my arms like a dancer, like the ballerina in Momma's jewelry box that Jojo kept safe at home.

'The pants!' he screamed. 'Take off the pants! Jesus Christ, it stinks in here.'

He threw his hands up in the air as he took giant steps to the door. He pushed it open and stuck his head outside, making a big show of taking in fresh air. I stood there waiting, maybe crying, maybe not, I don't remember. What I do remember is the look on his face when he turned back round and realized that he was at one end of the room, his gun at the other, and I was standing between he and it. He looked past me, his thin, moth-like eyebrows raised to heaven, his mouth open like his jaw's about to hit the floor. I turned to see what he was looking at. In a dark corner, I saw the gun. Over my shoulder I became aware of his movement and I didn't need telling that this is my moment. We dived for it, me reaching it a split second before he did. I'm flat on my back, pointing the gun right at him, holding it level as I can given the shit-storm shakes I'm experiencing. He's three, maybe four feet away from me. I get the smallest satisfaction when I see his face flood with fear. He holds his hands out, palms toward me like they might somehow protect him from the volley of bullets I'm ready to unleash on his sick fuck ass.

'Now, little one,' he said, and his fingers start waggling, like he's playing some stupid game with a damn toddler. 'You know I don't mean you no harm, don't you? We was just fooling around. Why don't you put that down now, honey, huh?' He put out his hand to take the gun from me, and I scrabbled backwards, keeping it trained on him best I could.

'I know how to shoot this, mister. I aint afraid to use it.'

He cocked his head to the side and actually fucking smiled as he leeched towards me.

'Oh, sweetpea,' he said, taking another step, 'don't you know not to point a gun at something unless you're willing to destroy it?'

He reached out, his hand almost touching the muzzle, the charm bracelet dancing beneath his sleeve.

'Oh hell, Duke. Mr Dee. Whoever the fuck you are. You pointed at me first.'

His body spasmed and jerked like a puppet in some horror circus until somebody cut his strings and he crumpled to the floor. The noise of the shots echoed and faded as the blood crept out of his body and pooled around the candles. White wax dripped into it. Ice cream and jelly. The room shook until the sound died away.

Me and the shitty pants that had just saved my life stepped over him. His eyes were open, staring into forever. His tongue lolled to one side. He didn't seem as creepy now.

There was a sound stuck in his throat. A rasp, a gurgle. I gave him a gentle kick and the sound escaped. It all felt strangely peaceful. And then the darkness came back but this time it was in his groin area. The fucker was dead but he could still pee his pants. I picked up the padlock and shut him in.

The night was electric quiet. Beneath my skin, the shock of the gunshots still crackled. An oddness made me look down. Somehow the pistol was still in my hand, like it was welded to me. I turned and above me was sky, around me fresh air. I lifted the gun, pointed it straight to heaven and laughed. I was so alive. I took a long, deep breath and felt my lungs inflate, filling my whole chest, lifting me up. All around me were towers of shipping containers. I moved silently through the stacked-up maze, knowing there was a way out for me somewhere. Like a hound, I sniffed the air and caught the salty scent of water. I headed towards it, all the time just one thought turning over and over in my mind. It struck me as bizarre, and even a little funny, and I tried to chase it away. I was a big girl. I was a killer now. Yet all I really wanted was my momma.

The jetty was a mile long and made out of concrete blocks all stacked in, one on top of the other. I ran along it, stumbling on the uneven surface as I went. The sea ran inland both sides of it, but at the end of the jetty it went out forever.

The moon barely made it through the heavy clouds. Water whipped up and splashed me. The path was foamy with waves. I was wet up to my waist. Salt in my mouth. Jojo's voice caught on the wind: *You can't swim, Aggie.*

The wind pushed against me, knocking me sideways. I slipped and fell, my knee slicing open on a jagged rock.

I made it to the end of the jetty. Just me and the sea and the dull moon in the sky and a few inches of cement beneath to keep me from disappearing forever. Freedom. Or as far as I could go. The end and the beginning.

26

I woke up on the beach next morning, my jeans lying beside me, cleaner than they'd been. They were still damp but I pulled them on, wincing as they dragged on my cut knee. I slipped Duke's gun into my waistband. By the time I limped my way back to the motel, the sun was almost at its highest point.

Marj's car was gone. I guessed she'd set off to meet her contact again. As I walked towards my room, Freak's raised voice carried down the corridor, and what sounded like the banging of drawers, which was weird, because Marj had forbidden us from bringing more than one change of clothes on account of her rubber trinkets taking up all the space.

I slipped the keycard into the slot and the door opened. I thought they'd be freaking out that I'd been gone all night, but it seem they hadn't even noticed. Ade was sitting on the balcony, scribbling madly into a notebook. Freak, wearing only a bra and panties, was standing on one of the beds, which were now both stripped of their covers. A blood-stained bandage wrapped around her upper arm. She gave me such a look of misery, I almost turned straight back round again.

'Tell him, Aggie,' she wailed.

'I told you,' said Ade, not bothering to look up from his notes, like he'd been listening to her for hours. 'Everything's going to be okay.'

I kicked my jeans off and fell onto the vacant bed, wrestling a sheet from the tangle on the floor to wrap myself up in. I pulled a pillow over my face to block the light and rolled on to my side.

'Aggie.' I felt Freak's weight on the bed beside me. She pulled the pillow away and shook me.

I sat up. No fight left. 'What is it?'

'He's leaving. He's going back to England.'

'Scotland,' Ade said. I'm guessing he still didn't look up from his writing.

'England, Scotland, what does it matter?' Freak pouted. 'Tell him, Aggie.'

'Tell him what?'

'That he can't leave.'

'But he can,' I said. 'He can go where he likes. Wherever the fuck he likes.'

'Oh, Aggie, no!' Freak punched the pillow that seconds before had been lying across my face. The bandage on her arm began to unravel. 'That aint it. Tell him something to make him stay.'

I looked at her and then him. I tried to think of something, any reason why he should stay.

'Sorry.' I shrugged.

Ade came in from the balcony and took a seat on my bed beside Freak.

'Aint you got some sightseeing to do?' I asked, desperate for them to be gone.

'It's here, Aggie. Look.' He held out what looked like a tourist guide and pointed. 'Isn't she beautiful? She's called *Elissa*.'

'Ade, it's just a boat.' Freak exploded with tears. 'How can it have a fucking name?'

Ade stroked the photograph like a love-struck loon. 'She was built in Scotland,' he sighed.

I cast my eye over the page. 'That's a day's drive from here, Ade,' I said. 'Marjorie won't like it. Now let me sleep.'

When I woke up everything was quiet. I rolled over to see

Marjorie on the balcony, blowing smoke rings into the sunset. My head felt like it was being crushed by the devil. I tried to swallow and it was like drinking broken glass.

The room hadn't got any tidier. In fact, the other bed had been pulled away from the wall. The pizza boxes from last night were lying open on the floor by the wastepaper basket, and coke was splashed down one wall. Classy. I reached for the almost empty bottle and swigged the remains back, wincing as it washed over my raw throat. I joined Marjorie on the balcony and noticed my jeans were drying over the back of a chair. Someone had washed them for me.

'Wild night?' she asked, but I knew she didn't expect an answer. We sat in silence for a minute or two, and then she said, 'Well, Aggie, I sure hope you don't mind, but it looks like it's just you and me for the rest of the trip. Far as I'm concerned, it's good news. You lay down with dogs, you get up with fleas.'

'Where'd they go?'

She blew one huge smoke ring. We watched as it floated up. Then she stabbed it through with her smoke.

'They've gone to steal a boat and sail to Scotland,' she said, and she flicked the butt over the edge. 'Crazy fucking fuckers.'

I had nothing to say to this. I nodded like stealing a boat and sailing to some shitty butt-fuck country from nowhere was a rite of passage for every Texas teen.

'Marj,' I said.

'Uh-huh,' she replied, dancing her fingers across her lap now they needed something to do.

'I feel like shit.'

'Baby, you look like shit, too.'

'Go to the store and get me some Advil?'

'Sure thing, Aggie. Reckon you could use some strawberry milk, too.'

When she was gone, I checked in my bag. I wasn't surprised to discover Freak had cleared me out. She'd left a note scribbled on motel notepaper: *Thanks, Aggie! Love you for this!* She'd drawn a heart around the words and signed it: *Sis*. I screwed it up and tossed it in the waste basket. I lay back down on the bed to think.

They say killing is wrong. They send you to the chair for that. But there's something about killing a man that frees a person.

I'd been at one end of the room, he at the other, but already I could feel him. Pointed fingers, stabby tongue. And Jojo there, like she always was.

It's funny how your head plays tricks until your body feels it as real. I'd come as far as I could and still she was there.

Guess there's some things you can't run away from. Some things sit inside and all the time you're trying to run away, you're carrying them yourself. You're hiding them that bit deeper inside yourself. Your head plays tricks. Your body plays tricks. People had been slowly killing me for a long time and getting away with it. Maybe it was time I got away with it, too.

Marj was in a good mood when she came back. I swallowed two Advil and drank her strawberry milk and tried to listen as she prattled on about the future. She'd paint her new apartment lilac, and have a workstation set up so she could see the street below while she worked. Her bed would go opposite the window, and her bookcase in the living room. (*The fucking living room, Aggie – did you hear that?*) She'd need to find a sofa but Hank knew someone could get it for free – about time that old bastard came in useful for something. None of it was fancy, but fancy didn't suit her anyway. She cracked open a beer and leaned back in her deckchair. I'd never seen a person look more content. There wouldn't be a better time to ask.

'Marj, I been thinking.'

'I wouldn't do that, kid,' she chuckled.

There's an old saying that everybody seems normal until you get to know them, but with Marj it was the other way around. She'd gone from Beast Woman to the closest thing I had to family. Except she wasn't.

'Yeah, guess thinking leads to trouble, don't it,' I forced myself to laugh with her.

'What you been thinking, child?'

She looked at me and I don't know what she saw, but her face landed dead serious. She pinned a stare on me and waited for my reply.

I was caught in the space between here and there. The words wouldn't come. I had to drag them out. It was the obvious thing, the only thing to do. It was the right thing.

'I think I gotta go home, Marj.'

We set off early next morning. Marjorie reckoned it would be a twelve-hour drive. I reckoned if Marj thought twelve, it would be more like sixteen. But the car was light and Marj was happy and we licked along at a good pace for a few hours until she pulled off the road and wheeled into the car park of a Waffle House.

'Lunchtime,' she said. 'This do you?'

We sat at the counter to eat. You don't get much talking done that way. We made the effort but there was so much shouting between the staff we soon gave up and just watched how they ran things there.

One guy operated the waffle machine. This seemed like the best job to have. He just got on with his business, ignoring the mayhem around him. Every order that came in from a waitress was handed over to the floor manager and got shouted out so everyone knew what to do. Someone's sole job was to pour coffee and tea, and through the hatch, the kitchen was manic with sausage and grits.

'One and a half sausage and two eggs sunny-side up!'

'Short stack cinnamon pancake, bacon and syrup, table number four!'

And out front with every new customer: 'Welcome to the Waffle House, sir!'

All through the chaos, everything hung together. It worked. I found it strangely relaxing.

Marjorie was in the restroom when a guy took her seat.

'Uh, I'm sorry, sir. That there's my friend's seat.'

He smiled at me. 'Don't remember me, do you?'

The guy took off his baseball hat and scratched his beard. 'Do I know you?'

'I'd say so. Your name's Aggie, right? I'll never forget a little lady hitching a ride in my truck a year or so back. Threatened me with some nasty stuff too, I recall.'

I flicked through all the faces in my head and located him. Jesus, it was old Grizzly. My very first customer, so to speak.

'Sorry, sir. Think you got the wrong person.' I looked around in a panic for Marjorie.

He gave a little laugh. 'No, I don't think so,' he said. 'I thought about you a lot, you know. I hoped you landed up okay. You seem okay, I guess. You ever make it back to where you were running from?'

'Sir, I'm sorry, sir. I already said you have the wrong person.'

'Hey, Aggie,' called Marjorie from the door. 'You set?'

Grizzly popped his hat back on. 'Well, I just wanted to say hi. I'll take some coffee,' he said, as the server passed. 'Take it easy, Aggie.'

My eyes burned with tears as I slipped down off the stool.

'Thanks, mister,' I whispered. 'You too.'

I checked the side mirror for miles and miles, but that was the last time I ever saw Grizzly. I wondered why he'd shown up then. It was a sign, but I didn't know if it was good or bad.

'What you so agitated for? You sure this is a good idea? We can turn round right now if you want. You don't have to do nothing, you know that, don't you?'

I didn't know that. Felt like I was doing the only thing possible.

'I gotta see Jojo, Marj.'

'If you say so. What's that short for anyway?' she asked.

243

'Huh?'

'Well, nobody christens a baby Jojo, do they? What is she – a Joanne, Joanna, or what?'

She used to just be Josephine, Ash said. *Don't you remember?*

I thought hard. *Nope,* I replied. I was keeping him company while he tinkered with the engine of *Jack King.* Cy said it was a waste of time and that she was only good for firewood, but Ash loved fixing things up almost as much as Cy loved cattle. He was sure in time he'd make her seaworthy, but for now he just looked at me in disbelief.

She used to talk real funny. A stammer. You must remember that? Pass me that rag.

I threw it over and gazed back at the house as though I could make the memory come alive just by looking. This was the first I'd heard anything about a stammer.

Nope, I said again, leaning on the wheel to steer her through imaginary seas. *Don't remember.* The rag reappeared on the ground beside me.

Well, she did. She spoke as normal as you or me until one day she didn't. Just woke up and couldn't say a word without she tripped over it. I guess you were only little. Pass me the wrench, will you?

I passed it over.

Anyway, Pop hated it. Thought she was putting it on. He lined us up along the wall, made us be the audience while he set about curing her.

But she don't talk like that now, I'd said. *She got better.*

Yeah, she did. She got better. But she was Jojo by then.

'Well, your pop sounds sweet as sugar,' Marj said, when I'd done talking. Seemed I was in the mood for it.

'My pop's got a whole lot to answer for. My brother, too. I aint carrying no olive branch. And I got my sister to think about.'

I could see Marj was impressed with me. Could feel it

without even looking at her. Felt like the whole world was impressed with me. I was on the righteous path. And Duke's gun was in my pocket.

27

The world had changed from yellow to red. We were back in the land of endless skies and shanty towns. We were getting closer. The sun was sitting low. Soon it would be dark. I didn't want to go back in the dark. I wanted the sun to shine its full light on what I was about to do. Marjorie offered to stop for the night, but we were so close now. I shook my head and she went faster.

The land was carved in rust and dust. Jojo had said it took millions of years to get it looking like that. Millions of years of rain and wind and desert storms to make something that could take a person's breath away in an instant. A tourist sign said *Erosion: Sculptor of Landscapes*. It occurred to me that if the planet we live on gets worn down, it's no wonder that people do, too.

'How long since we seen a town?' Marjorie asked, tapping the fuel gauge.

'There's a gas station ahead,' I replied. We couldn't see it yet. I just knew.

Marjorie said town was too fancy a word for it. She filled up while I lay low in the front seat, spying on the street I'd spent long summers cycling up and down in. Still no one to play with and only old men with their one-stop shops to talk to.

And then we were at the gates that marked the way in to the farm. Marjorie switched off the engine and lit up a smoke.

'You aint leaving, are you, Marj?' I had one foot on the ground and my hand on the roof of the car, ready to spring back in if she looked like taking off.

She leaned her seat back and stuck her crossed legs out the window. She shrugged and sniffed and took a little look around. 'I plan on finishing my smoke and laying right back to have a little think here. You go on now. I'll be waiting.'

I looked up the track to the brow of the hill that led back to Jojo. My little sub family.

It was real quiet on the walk back up. The grass had been hacked and was too short to move with the wind. No sheep cried. No engine noise either. They must be on the far side of the farm, I reckoned. I came upon what was left of old Jack King. Someone had finally broken him down for firewood. I felt the weight of Duke's gun. I wrapped my hand around it for comfort.

The house made me stop. Even though I knew it would be there, the sight of it surprised me. It stood exactly as it always had. White walls, burnt orange shutters. I waited for Jojo to appear at the upstairs window. I half thought she might never have left it, just waited at the same spot day after day wishing for me to come back. But she didn't come. It was down to me.

I listened for the groan of a bull. I expected one of the cats to come running, trying to trip me up with friendliness. I thought I'd hear pots clang on the stove, or the radio, or Pop and Cy shouting across a field. But nothing.

Through the door there was only her. Tucked up on the blue armchair with the golden fringe, she stared into nothing, a cigarette burning down between her fingers. Her nails needed cut.

I stood unnoticed in the doorway. Nothing had changed. The sofa in front of the portable. The empty fire. But for some reason, the wooden table had just two rickety chairs tucked beneath it. The stain beneath the table stood out more than ever. Dishes piled up in the sink, crumbs spread all over the worktops, clothes and overalls lay where they'd been dropped. I'd never seen it like that before.

The whisper of a wind drifted in from the porch. The whole world was lying open behind me. Jojo lifted the smoke to her lips. She still didn't know I was there.

Dark circles framed eyes that were so much darker than I remembered. Dead pools reflecting nothing until she focused on my face. Then I thought I saw something of the old Jojo in there. I wanted to reach out and touch her but I couldn't do it. It felt like I was invading some private moment, some private moment that had lasted maybe since the day I left.

'Aggie?' Her voice crackled like an old radio. 'Aggie, that you?'

And then like rain washing away mud, her tears rushed out and cleared the dark from her eyes. She opened her arms and leaned forward to catch me as I tumbled into her arms. I didn't want ever to let go.

Eventually she pushed me back and turned me around so she could look at me. She was scrawnier than before but her grip was still strong. She held me by my shoulders and asked where I'd been.

I opened my mouth to speak but nothing came. I pushed through the darkness and reached for the first memory beyond it.

'I been on a boat,' I said, and for some reason it made me laugh.

'A boat? Oh, sweet Jesus.'

'Yeah, Jojo. I been in a car on a boat. An actual floating one. It was wild.'

'No way, an actual floating one, huh? Yeah, I guess that is pretty wild.'

We looked away from each other, like the formalities had been dealt with and now all we had left was the nitty-gritty.

'You been okay?' I said.

'Yeah, guess I been okay.' She shrugged and looked at the floor around her feet, as though down there she'd find some proof about how okay she'd been. 'I missed you, little Aggie,' she said, as she reached for a fresh smoke.

'You should have come with me.'

She tapped the cigarette on the packet. Raised her shoulders to her ears. When they realized they'd nowhere else to go, they collapsed back down again. Most defeated shrug I ever saw. Made my heart ache.

'This here is my place, Aggie.'

All the times Pop slapped her, prodded her, pulled her hair. All the time pretending to me like it was a game. Yet this was her place.

She sat quiet, like she was a little hunted mouse and I the big bad cat. I felt guilt, but looking at her made me feel huge too. Over her shoulder, down the side of the chair, was the bookcase Pop had made for Momma, and there on the top shelf, sitting all on its own, was the Bible we'd read from so many times.

'Pop keeps the Bible real nice, huh?'

Her eyes flew to the big brown book and her face flashed scarlet.

'You done any reading from it lately?' I asked. For some fucked up reason my face was smiling enough to make my jaw ache, or maybe it was just the way I gritted my teeth.

'You hungry? Want a sandwich?' She was out of the chair and cleaning the counter before I'd hardly finished speaking.

'I aint hungry and don't you walk away from me anymore. Don't you do it.'

She banged the bread knife on the counter, the exact same way she'd done it with Cy all those times he harrassed her, and turned around. Light didn't sparkle in her eyes the way it used to but the fighter was still there.

'I did my best for you, girl. You best believe it.'

I did believe it then. The faked maxi pads, her flirting with Pop to keep him distracted, picking fights with Cy to get him sent away from us. But none of that changed the fact she let it all happen.

'Where is Pop anyway?' I spat. 'He miss me? On any day apart from Friday, I mean.'

'Pop aint here no more.'

Of all the things I'd thought of, this was the one thing I wasn't ready for.

'What? Where is he?'

Her face took on a sly kind of grin as she said, 'Old bastard's slam dunk in jail where he belongs.'

I felt a sickening kind of disappointment. Bastard man, bastard father. She misread the look on my face.

'Don't you go feeling sorry for him, Aggie.'

'I aint sorry for him, Jojo. I'm sorry for me. I had something to say to him.'

I took the gun out and put it on the table. Her eyes locked on to it.

'I'd do it, too,' I said.

She looked at me like I was a question needing answered. Then she shrugged and turned away.

'What's he in for?' I asked.

'You want this sandwich or not?' she replied.

'Fuck your sandwich, Jojo. I didn't come all this way for a frikkin sandwich.'

She sat down at the table and picked up the gun. She flicked the safety on. 'You gotta keep the safety on, Aggie. Aint I taught you nothing? It loaded?' She opened the magazine and found the last two bullets. She put the gun back on the table. 'You still a good shot?'

'Hell, yes,' I replied. 'Good enough to drill a man. If I had to.'

'Guess all that tin-can shooting paid off then, didn't it?' She put her finger in the trigger hole and spun the gun around on the table.

'And the hog shooting, and the cat shooting, and the lamb shooting, Jojo. Guess it all paid off in the end.'

She nodded. 'Yeah. Maybe it did, Aggie.'

'So you gonna tell me what he's in for?'

She slid the gun towards me and I put it back in my pocket. 'He shouldn't be in there,' she said. 'Didn't do nothing. Not this time, leastways. It was Cy's doing. Remember the ranch we went to that time I shot the pig? Cy took some work on the side with them. Shady work. Smuggled some whitetail deer over the state line just so more rich folks could go hunting. Stupid. He was making money to start his own ranch. You know what he's like, Aggie. He wanted out of here real bad. Almost as much as you, I bet.'

For some reason I thought she was making a dig at me but I couldn't figure it out.

'Pop took the rap for it,' she continued. 'Don't think he was expecting jail time, mind you.'

'Pop took heat for Cy?' All the fighting and bitching between them all those years, I couldn't believe it.

Jojo frowned at me. 'Aint that what family's for, Aggie?'

I was staring at the dark patch on the floor by the table. Something about it nagged me, but Jojo's voice pulled me back.

'Loyalty, Aggie. That's what family's for.'

'Bullshit.'

'Watch your language, young lady.'

And with that one sentence I was eight years old again. I dropped my head, unable to face her.

'Sorry,' I said.

'I aint putting nothing on you, Aggie. If you're feeling bad then maybe you want to ask yourself why. What you come back for anyway?' That made me look up. I was hurt she didn't understand. With the one hand she pulled me in, with the other she pushed away.

'I came back to kill him, Jojo.' Always the honest child. She laughed at me. 'I came back to kill him and kill Cy and to take you away from here. You don't have to be here no more, Jojo. You don't have to do it. Momma aint coming back, you know she aint. There's a whole world out there. A world with malls and everything. People playing guitars for the hell of it. Folks who make investigations and rubber ornaments and watch each other's backs. We could do that for each other,

251

you and me.' I was running out of reasons for her to come, even though in the car on the way up I'd counted up over a hundred. 'Jesus, Jojo. There's cars on frikkin boats out there. And I think you should come with me. You should come with me because – '

'Shut up about it. I aint coming with you.'

'Please, Jojo! You've got to.'

'Why?'

Because now he's in jail, I can't kill him.

Because now he's in jail, I can't end it.

Because if you don't, I got no reason to leave.

'Because she said she aint. Didn't you hear her?'

I remembered that voice like I'd heard it only yesterday. He stood against the doorframe: yellow-tasseled blue-jean shirt, ten-dollar hat. He hung the hat on a hook in the wall, and stepped into the room.

'Cy,' said Jojo. 'Boots.'

He put the toes of one foot behind the heel of the other and, one by one, pushed off his boots. Jojo took them and placed them by the back door.

'You want some iced tea?' she asked.

'Sure,' he replied.

I'd forgotten about the dimple in his chin.

'So,' he smiled. 'We caught ourselves a little Aggie, huh?'

His fingers slid down the side of his collar. He pulled it away from his neck, and I caught a glimpse of purple birthmark. I'd forgotten that, too.

'I aint staying.' I moved round the table as he approached. 'You stay right where you are, do you hear me?'

He held his hands up. 'I'm just taking a seat, Aggie. Tell you what, why don't you sit down and tell us where you been this past year? We were worried about you.'

He nodded his thanks as Jojo put a glass of tea in front of him and sat down. His Adam's apple moved up and down in his throat as he drank. I felt my blush coming on and I looked away.

'You were worried, huh?' I asked when he'd finished. 'You ever call the cops? You ever ask in town if anyone had seen me? You ever advertise for me? Or did you just make out like I never existed, like you did with Momma and Ash?' Jojo stared at her hands, while Cy looked at me blankly. 'Yeah, I thought so,' I said. 'You were worried? Only worry you had was whether or not I'd blow the whistle on what was going on here.'

Cy frowned. 'Going on here? What do you mean, Aggie?'

I looked to Jojo. Her head hung low so I couldn't see her face. She used her hair like a pair of curtains to hide behind; it was an old trick. 'You know what I mean, Cy. Don't make like you don't.'

'I got no idea what you mean, little Aggie. You know what she means?' he asked Jojo. She shook her head, and he looked back at me and shrugged. 'We don't know what you mean, Aggie.'

Every Friday, week in, week out.

'Can you be a little clearer?' He clasped his hands together and leaned forward on the table.

'Jojo, let's go.' I tugged on her shirt, but she sat there, weighed down by invisible stones.

His spiteful eyes never left my face as he slid his arm across the table and took hold of Jojo's hand.

'Jojo aint going anywhere with you,' he said.

'Wanna bet?' I took the gun out of my pocket and pointed it at him.

He dropped her hand and sprang to his feet. It only made him an easier target. His chair tipped over and Jojo's head snapped up.

'Put the gun away, Aggie. Put it down,' she said.

'You touch her one more time, Cy, I swear to God I'll scatter you around this farm in tiny fucking pieces.'

Jojo stood up and moved in front of him, her arms spread wide to protect him.

'Out of my way, Jojo. I'm ending this right now.'

'No, Aggie. Please, you can't. You can't kill him.'

Tucked safe behind her, he was all but laughing at me. That smile: the white, uneven teeth. He flicked his tongue out at me like a lizard. I pulled the safety off.

'Jojo, move out the way or so help me I will shoot you down. I swear to God, I came here for this and I aint leaving until it's done.'

'You aint shooting nobody, Aggie,' he sneered. 'Not when you learn what I got to tell you.'

Jojo turned and fell against him. 'Cy, don't. I'm begging you. Please.'

His hands were on her shoulders, pushing her away. She pressed forward, punched his chest with feeble fists, begged him to keep quiet. He lifted his head higher, eyes wider than a mad bull, and jutted his chin forward. His lips moved slowly as his tongue gave shape to words that sounded like they were coming from inside my own head, an echo of something I'd heard before: *You aint gonna shoot your own momma now, are you?*

Everything fell away. The wallpaper peeled itself. All the walls of that little house crumbled away to dust. Me and Jojo were standing in the desert with nothing but sky walls.

You aint gonna shoot your own momma now, are you?

Jojo whipped back round to me, her voice barely more than a breath. 'He's lying, Aggie. Don't you believe him. He's a liar.'

My hands squeezed the grip of the gun, one tightly curled finger tempting the trigger.

'Aggie, he's lying.'

'Shut up!' I yelled.

The way she doted on me when we were little, the way she got me reading when Pop and Cy laughed at us, how she never went anywhere, never left me alone when the men were around. Not until she absolutely had to. The way she tucked me into bed at night, the way she sang sweet songs and baked pies and made secret birthday cards only for me, even though we didn't do that shit in our house. The way she taught me to climb, even though she said it scared her to see me do it. The way she was only twenty-eight but looked twenty years older. The way she was and the way she did, all of that told me what Cy said was true.

The way she stood in front of him now. That didn't make sense.

The gun was shaking in my hand. I struggled to keep my voice steady. 'Get out of my way, Jojo.'

'You can't kill him, Aggie. You can't. Please don't.' And she broke down in tears, shielding him, protecting him with her body. 'Don't kill him, Aggie. Please, please, please.'

Her face folded as she turned round so her body was once more against his, but there was no punching this time. With one hand she clung to his neck, the other she slipped into his. Their fingers entwined. Her head burrowed into his chest, and when he put his arm around her he held her so sweet, but when he lifted his eyes to mine all I saw was deep burning shame.

No one spoke for a long time. I stood with my back to the fire place, gun in hand, seeing their sorry situation, and the door behind them which led back to the real world.

'Momma? Huh.' I hated the crack in my voice as I broke the silence. Breaking silence with brokenness.

Jojo's sobs came fresh again. She took a seat at the table, laid her head on her arms and let the grief take over. Her whole body rippled as the tears surged forward. The dam was busted. Cy rested his hand on Jojo's back. He looked around him, as though an answer to the situation might present itself, ripe for plucking, straight from the very air. He puckered his lips in a tuneless whistle.

'Who are you then?' I asked him, hatred making me brave. 'You my daddy?'

Jojo lifted her head. 'Hell, no, Aggie. Don't be sick,' she moaned. I laughed and they looked at me like I was crazy. I opened my mouth to speak, but the words couldn't get out. I stayed on my feet and rocked myself back and forth.

The door remained open and night came down. The only sounds were Jojo's sobs and the occasional creak of her chair, played along to the backtrack of the crickets outside.

I sat down in the armchair, sinking into it the way I always had, though now you could feel the springs beneath forcing their way up. I reached down and ripped the loose brocade. The fringe came loose in my hand. Maybe I'd have my crown after all. The question formed itself and was out before I recognized it.

'Who was Marilyn if she aint my momma?'

It took her a mighty effort to sit up straight and look at me. 'She was my momma, baby. And Cy's. And Ash's,' she said in a hoarse, strangled whisper.

'Who was she to me?' I dangled the gold fringe in front of my eyes and looked at the stain on the floor. My voice was coming from far off.

'She was your grandmother, baby.'

'What happened to her?' Through the fringe the dark patch in the wood seemed to change shape.

'She loved you so much, baby…'

'I said, what happened to her?' I dropped the fringe in my lap. I couldn't take my eyes off the stain.

Jojo reached for her pack of cigarettes. She shook her head and tapped one on the box, flipping it over and over, before leaning in to catch a light from Cy's waiting Bic. He put his hand on her arm but she shrugged him off. Satisfaction sparked and died in me. She glanced up through the thin cloud of smoke and said, 'I always wondered what you could remember.'

'Josephine…' A heavy warning note in his tone.

'What?' she snapped back. 'Don't she deserve to know?'

And then she smoked her cigarette and told me all about it, though in truth, some part of me had always known.

It was a Friday winter's night. The snow had come and

everything was locked up and shut down on the farm. Pop had cleared the track and put the chains on the truck for Momma, who had a meeting at the church in town. Jojo stayed behind with me because I had a fever. Pop fabricated some slight Cy and Ash had caused him and they were sent to their room. I was asleep on the armchair so Pop and Jojo could keep an eye on me, dead to the world.

Momma got to the church to find the meeting had been cancelled due to illness, and she turned right around and came home. New snow was falling. The night was pretty.

She inched the truck back up the track, stopping a little further back than normal. Through the curtains in the upstairs window she saw the silhouettes of Cy and Ash brawling. She put the truck into park, switched off the lights and picked up her bag and the ring binder of paperwork that she'd brought for the meeting.

Her footsteps fell soft in the fresh whiteness. She hurried to the house as best she could, keeping her eyes on her fighting boys upstairs, keen to separate them. As she opened the door, the ring binder slipped and paper flew across the floor. She bent down to pick it up and that's when she heard it, the familiar grunt, the heavy breathing. And then something else, a lighter voice.

Father, I am Your child. I am filled with Your Spirit. I believe that I am healed now, in the Name of Jesus. Father, I am Your child, I am filled with Your Spirit. I believe I am healed now.

She crawled the two feet along the floor and pushed open the door to the kitchen. She saw her husband leaning over the kitchen table, his work pants hanging loose on his backside; she saw the urgent back and forth of his hips, and there, between the rumpled denim of his legs, she saw the thin white ankles of her only daughter. She didn't see the sleeping toddler.

The sound that came from her was like an animal in a trap. When he heard it, he jumped back like the trap's spring.

Jojo remained where she was: legs spread, belly down, hands wrapped around the Holy Bible he made us read from while he did his filth. She couldn't even turn her face to look into her mother's eyes, just in case her mother looked there and saw that Jojo had heard the truck, had heard her mother approach, had wanted her mother to find them.

It was a skillet. It was a cast-iron skillet that had been passed down through the years. It was too heavy for her to use effectively. He disarmed her easily, and with one blow she was dead on the floor. Jojo's screaming woke the baby.

'It was an accident,' said Cy.

I remembered. The only time I saw Pop doing woman's work. He was trying to scrub away the blood. I looked at the dark patch. The stain. All he'd done was push it in deeper. I tore my eyes from it to Jojo. For some weird reason she was smiling at me.

'But the good thing,' she said. 'The one good thing that came out of it was I reclaimed you.'

A moth landed on my cheek. I shook my head and it flew away. The ceiling was crawling with dozens of insects that had been drawn to the kitchen lights through the open door. I'd been here for hours, I realized. Marjorie was probably long gone.

'You reclaimed me?'

She got up and walked round to my side of the table, motivated, I suppose, by her new-found maternal role.

'I told Momma your daddy was a boy passing through town and she took you for hers, Aggie. We told everybody you were hers. At first, she didn't take to you. She was mad with me. If it ever got out it would have brought so much shame on the house. But you won her over, sweetheart.'

Every time she called me sweetheart, or baby, I wanted to explode.

'I used to get so jealous, Aggie. You were mine. You were the only thing I wanted. I earned you. I birthed you. And I couldn't get near you. I couldn't get near and now...' Her voice trailed off and her eyes drifted to Cy, who was looking anywhere but us.

'Is that why you didn't stop it when you heard the truck coming back?' I knew that wasn't the reason but I wanted to stick the knife in. I wanted to twist it, too. Her pained face told me I'd struck home. Her eyes filled with fresh tears. Seemed they'd never stop coming.

'I didn't stop him when I heard the truck, Aggie,' she said, her voice strangled, 'because I thought she would.'

None of us dared to close the open door. It remained wide all night long and the insects continued to pour in. Cy moved to the sofa. Next time I looked at him he was fast asleep. I wasn't sorry to lose his contributions to the conversation.

'And him,' I said. 'What about him?'

She wouldn't look me in the eye. I leveled the gun at him for a second and then dropped it. We were both exhausted. She didn't even react.

'What about him?' I said again, drunk on tiredness. 'You got a twisted little thing going on with him, haven't you? A twisted little *sub* thing.'

I tried to guess what she'd come out with. *He's the only one who understands, I was lonely without you, I didn't mean for it to happen.*

At last, she raised her eyes.

'Yes,' she said, simply.

I saw it then, what I'd seen in him earlier. The shame, the loathing, the desire, the need. I understood, because I hated her as much as I loved her.

'Come with me,' I said. 'Just you. Leave this. Leave it all behind. Just walk away. We can make it work. I want to make it work.'

She smiled and I had her. She locked onto me and the future was real: building a home, knocking on doors to sell rubber armadillos, making money. Making a life. Becoming a person.

259

We stared at each other for the longest time. And then she looked at him, asleep on the sofa, new growth all over his face. At last she turned back to me with drowned eyes and said, 'It aint that easy, you know, Aggie.'

The sun was rising when I fell out the front door and stumbled my way down the track. This time I didn't stop to look back. When I reached the brow of the hill and saw Oprah still sitting there, tears poured out of me in gratitude.

Marj was snoozing but she jumped awake when I pulled the door open. She took one look at me, turned the key and we were away. After about forty miles of crying, I said, 'I should have killed them, Marj. I should have killed them both. Turn the car round. Turn it round.'

'Hell, no, child. I aint taking you back there.'

And the tears kept coming. Seemed I'd had the ocean in me that whole damn time.

Marj put her foot down and we went fast and faster, trying to outrun the old world.

28

So now I'm thinking how I still got those two bullets. Sharp, golden, little straight-through-the-brain fuck-you-ups. I rattle them together in my palm sometimes. Click, click. The reality, of course, is I need three of them. Four, even, if I count my own sorry soul. I could get them. Maybe one day I will. Maybe one day I'll go back there and shake them up. Blow the roof off their warped existence. Their twisted little sub world.

Maybe.

Ha.

Let God be my guide.

We're breathing in the rust and the dust. We walk above the bones of the dead; they hold us up; they're sharp enough to keep us moving. And this land; this land with all its unexploded secrets is such a beautiful place. The sun sinks lower, the leaves come down, the snow lays thick over everything. Way down deep, little buds fight to grow.

ACKNOWLEDGEMENTS

As I sit down to write the acknowledgements for *Armadillos*, it seems to me that this is the literary equivalent of an Oscar speech. So thank you, God. Thank you, parents.

Other strong supporting characters are, in order of appearance:

Mary Gladstone, for providing the writing exercise that gave birth to *Armadillos*. The sentence I created in her class is no longer in the book, but its spirit survives.

My MLitt classmates at the University of Glasgow, and Elizabeth Reeder, an amazing tutor whose encouragement and support was invaluable.

Sceptre, for providing me with the opportunity to visit Texas, without which I would not have completed *Armadillos*.

John Murphy, for being an excellent host in Texas, and teaching me that shooting ranges and hangovers don't mix.

Thank you to my early readers, Xenia Schiller and James Carson, and to my writing girlfriends: Tania Cheston, Fiona Gibson, Hilary Hiram, Vicki Fever, Amanda McLean and Samantha McShane. A more supportive writing group there never was.

I owe a great deal to my talented agent, Donald Winchester. I'm very fortunate he found me. Thanks also to my eagle-eyed editor, Lauren Parsons, and all at Legend Press.

Thanks also to Al at Canongate Studios, Edinburgh, and the fine voices of Robin Laing, Helen McAlpine, and James MacKenzie.

And lastly, to my family. My eternal gratitude for your love, patience, and unwavering belief.

How It All Started...

I don't remember a time when I didn't tell stories, even if they were only to myself. One of my earliest memories is walking into a room and seeing a giant hole in the floor into which I would disappear if someone didn't rescue me straight away. My screams brought my parents running. They weren't impressed. It must have been a happy day for everyone when I learned how to write.

Unsurprisingly, I grew up to be an actor. And so began a long journey, telling many stories, living many lives, some of them lasting perhaps only a single day on a TV set, or months and months of finding a twist on the same yarn told on a nightly basis in a theatre somewhere. It's a wonderful life, but not one that's particularly conducive to having a family. After the birth of my first son, I picked up my pen and wrote again. For me, writing is acting, except in a chair.

Prior to *Armadillos*, I focussed on writing drama, but after the birth of my second son I wanted to explore other genres and so I undertook a variety of classes. There came a point when the only one left to try was 'Get Ready to Write Your First Novel'. The idea of writing a novel was so laughable, I almost didn't sign up. And yet, much as I adored life at home with my new baby, I knew I had to keep being creative or I would return to my toddler habit of imagining huge black holes in my living room.

'Write what you know' is standard advice for writers, but if you don't think you're going to get past 500 words, there's no real motivation to follow that advice. One week, my tutor produced a lengthy list of half-sentences. We had to pick one and carry on. The sentence I chose is no longer in *Armadillos* but it was this: I am still a long way from home, but I am beginning to believe it will never be far enough. From the very beginning I knew this was a young girl and that she was American. I also knew what her story was. I just had to figure out how she wanted to tell it. I was used to writing biographies for characters I played on stage, so writing from Aggie's point of view was a natural choice. I was also used to playing Americans so it wasn't a huge leap to step inside and write down her thoughts. Creating a believable outside world for her was a different matter.

Thankfully, we have the Internet and can find out pretty much anything at the touch of a button. I soon discovered the real task lay in deciphering what to research. As *Armadillos* is written in a first-person narrative, it was necessary to write in American English. Not only do the Americans have different spellings for certain words, but they have different words too. I developed an instinct at knowing what to check. Tyre became tire, skirting board became base board, and soon I found myself googling the ins and outs of import and property laws, or whether yellow flowers would be in season; everything, in fact, right down to the interior of public transport in Dallas. The idea of making a mistake terrified me so I double- and triple-checked everything. I found myself contacting animal-welfare organisations and truck companies. I even joined a forum for people in the legal profession. It was extremely time-consuming and surprisingly energetic work. Occasionally I'd walk away from the computer breathless with the effort of navigating various encounters with people who clearly thought I was wasting their time. However, I never doubted the necessity of these exchanges and I remain grateful to everyone who responded to me.

Marvellous as the Internet is, we all know it doesn't beat

the real thing, so when I was awarded the Sceptre Prize for Fiction at the University of Glasgow, I used the money to fund a trip to Texas. This was a massive step forward for me, both professionally and personally. I'd been a stay-at-home mum for a few years by this point, and suddenly I was on a different continent all by myself, driving on the wrong side of the road, not knowing where I was going to sleep that night. It was a remarkable and exhilarating adventure.

At university, I'd been advised to relocate the book from Texas to the Highlands. Sensible advice, I agree, but my character already had a Texan accent! By that point, I'd also read Larry McMurtry's epic *Lonesome Dove* – where a group of cowboys drive a herd of cattle from South to North Texas – and it had left a strong impression on me. I needed Aggie to be in a place where anything could happen, and I wanted her surrounding landscape to be capable of reflecting her internal world. Magnificent as the Highlands undoubtedly are, I just didn't see them in that light. There was also the question over how a teenager could disappear so completely in an area so small, and so there was no doubt in my mind that Aggie belonged to Texas. My view was confirmed within hours of touching down in Dallas.

My plan was as follows:

1. Pick up rental car.
2. Resist all up-selling because I was on a tight budget.
3. Find my motel, sleep.
4. Drive to the nearest Walmart to buy a satnav because this was cheaper than hiring one.

Simple enough, right?

Wrong.

The very reason for me choosing Texas, i.e. its vastness, was my undoing. At home in Scotland I'd printed out a few pages from Google Maps to help me stateside, but I hadn't banked on driving unfamiliar roads, on the wrong side, having been awake for almost twenty-four hours. Neither had I banked on the massive construction works that surrounded the area by the airport. My maps were redundant. The cheap motel I'd booked was only an eight-minute drive away, but this was no comfort when I was still searching for it five hours later. By this point I no longer gave a damn about my extremely tight budget. I spied a Holiday Inn and headed there. It's still a source of pride to me that I didn't cry when they told me they were full. They printed out more Google Maps and pointed me in the right direction. En route, I was overtaken by two young men driving too fast, pursued by a police car with its lights flashing and sirens wailing. Despite my tiredness, I felt a flutter of excitement, as though I were watching an episode of *Starsky and Hutch*.

I awoke the next morning refreshed and optimistic. I took a free coffee in a polystyrene cup from the motel lobby, rechecked my Walmart's location, and headed out. It took approximately ninety seconds for me to be redirected. I swore and banged the wheel like a crazy woman. I left the Interstate at the first available opportunity and made a U-turn into a pothole. My tyre (tire) blew out. I didn't need a Google map to tell me I was stranded.

Desperately holding on to the last remnants of that morning's positivity, I recalled I'd changed a tyre before. Okay, it had been almost twenty years, but I could do it again. I checked the car manual and opened the boot. Nothing in the boot correlated with the manual. Plus, I'd just noticed the actual wheel was dented. I would have to call someone official. My skin prickled as it began to cook in the rising heat and I proceeded to have a very American panic attack. I thought of all the extras I'd turned down at the airport and began to doubt I was insured to drive at all. I pulled out my mobile phone (budget be damned) and called my partner at home, feeling small and utterly ashamed. What on earth had made me think I was capable of doing this? If I could have pressed a button to instantly transport myself back to the safety of my little town, I wouldn't have hesitated. Thankfully Robin said all the right things. I called a number on my key fob, somehow explained where I was, and a man came to put on the replacement tyre. I felt marginally better when he assured me there was no way I could have replaced it on my own because the tools weren't there. With hindsight, it was probably a good thing. The way I was going, I'd only have messed it up.

My next task was to find my way back to the airport. By this point it was almost noon, it was 38 degrees, and I was sweating in a most ungainly fashion. When I finally made it, no one batted an eyelid. Seemingly, potholes are par for the course around those parts. Needless to say, I hired that bloody satnav, and from that point everything began to look up.

I'd worried that perhaps the trip would reveal my writing to be shallow and one-dimensional, that I'd created a world that bore little resemblance to the real thing, but the more I drove the better I felt about what I had so far. Whenever I spotted things I'd described in the book I was elated, even if it was only a blue car outside a liquor store. American culture really permeates our society and I'd obviously reaped the benefit of that. However, I had only around a third of the story. There was a lot of work still to be done.

The most important thing I took from the trip was the certain knowledge that Texas is so massive; everything and anyone can exist there, which is incredibly liberating for a writer. It also became apparent that unless I wanted to spend the entire time in the car, I'd better drop some destinations from my itinerary. Sadly, I never made it to Big Bend country, photographs of which had influenced so much of my writing, but I did experience things I hadn't anticipated. Bats emerging from a bridge in Austin, black rubber on the highways, certain diners and bars, even Hank's walk is based on someone I saw. The petrol scam Marjorie pulls is based on a real incident, and the reason everyone ends up on the coast, is because I accidentally found myself in a queue to board a ferry and decided to roll with it. And of course, there is no way in this world I could ever have come up with something as bizarre and wonderful as chicken shit bingo had I not seen it with my own eyes.

As invaluable as all these experiences were, the area I was most anxious about getting right was the abuse. I think we've all become more aware of this in recent years, and because more brave people are coming forward to share their experiences, there's more to be read on this subject than ever before. I spent a long time reading their stories, wondering whether I should get in touch. Ultimately though, I decided against this. Although the forums are open to anyone, it is clear they are a safe space for survivors to talk. It would have been wrong of me to interrupt that. To those few people who shared with me their experience in real life, my thanks for your trust.

My biggest wish for *Armadillos* is for survivors of abuse to feel I've been sensitive and truthful. I learned that survivors of sexual abuse rarely, if ever, achieve closure. That's why Pop had to be in prison when Aggie returns to shoot him. Jojo's decision to stay with Cy, rather than take up a new life with her daughter, signifies the damage that's been done to them all. Ultimately, there could be no winners in this book, but Aggie is her own light at the end of the tunnel, which is what I think we should all aspire to be.

We hope you enjoyed *Armadillos*, a striking debut from a promising new author. At Legend Press, we pride ourselves on publishing original, thought-provoking fiction, and so if you'd like to find more compelling reads…

Come visit us at
www.legendpress.co.uk

Follow us
@legend_press